OTHER BOOKS BY
COLUMBUS CREATIVE COOPERATIVE

The Ides of March
An Anthology of Ohio Poets

Triskaidekan
13 Stories for 2013

Columbus
Past, Present and Future

While You Were Out
Short Stories of Resurrection

Across Town
Stories of Columbus

Overgrown
Tales of the Unexpected

Origins
An Anthology

BEST OF OHIO SHORT STORIES

VOLUME ONE

Edited By
Brad Pauquette

Proudly Presented By

COLUMBUS CREATIVE COOPERATIVE

WWW.COLUMBUSCOOP.ORG

Pauquette ltd
dba Columbus Creative Cooperative
2997 Indianola Ave.
Columbus, OH 43202
www.ColumbusCoop.org

Cover by Michelle Berki
Design by Brad Pauquette Design

Print ISBN 978-0-9890645-2-1
Ebook ISBN 978-0-9890645-3-8

Printed in the United States of America
1 3 5 7 9 10 8 6 4 2

Contents

Introduction	**1**
Besançon • Mark D. Baumgartner	**3**
Open House • Maria Hummer	**14**
Cinderbox Road • Scott Geisel	**19**
A Day in the Sun • Joseph Downing	**30**
Late Date • Brenda Layman	**37**
Monsters • Sara Ross Witt	**45**
Saint Vinny and the Devil's Brother • Kevin Duffy	**57**
Chrysalis • Heather Sinclair Shaw	**72**
Fallen Timbers • S.E. White	**80**
Off the Record • Lin Rice	**96**
Faster Than I Could Follow • Anna Scotti	**123**
On Wilson • Brad Pauquette	**134**
Resetting • Kelsey Lynne	**144**
Let Me Know • David Armstrong	**158**
Harvest • Ann Brimacombe Elliot	**168**
Twilight of the Revolution • Justin Hanson	**172**
Blood Off Rusted Steel • Brooks Rexroat	**202**
A Test of Faith • Alice G. Otto	**212**
Acknowledgments	**240**
Author Biographies	**241**
Editor Biography	**246**

Introduction

I recently saw an internet meme "The United States of Shame" that listed Ohio as the "nerdiest" state based on the National Center for Education Statistics record of library visits. Apparently the citizens of Ohio go to the library more than the citizens of any other state. I'm not sure what to make of that—based on the meme's title, I was expecting some kind of criticism.

When Columbus Creative Cooperative opened its call for the writers of Ohio to submit stories for our next anthology, we found that not only can Ohioans read, we can also write great fiction. The quality and quantity of submissions that we received were truly impressive.

In a blind process (no names), we narrowed a pool of hundreds of submissions down to a list of about sixty candidates that our Cooperative members agreed were great stories. From there, the editorial team further pared down the list.

Ultimately, I made the final decision to print the stories that stuck with me. A week later, which stories was I thinking about while I was driving my car or doing the dishes? Those are the stories we featured in this anthology.

They're not all life-changing tales. As with all of Columbus Creative Cooperative's anthologies, variety was a priority in our selection process—we want to produce books that not only engage all kinds of readers but also provide opportunities for all kinds of writers. You will find more so-called "literary" fiction in this anthology than in our past titles, but you'll also find plenty of popular fiction as well—science fiction, humor, adventure, historical fiction and romance.

This book features many light, quirky, fun reads. But it also contains a couple of heavy stories—the abrupt candor with which these stories address relevant social issues will stick to your gut and prompt hard questions.

There is a profound but elusive difference between a story that is *provocative* and one that is *evocative*, I'm only interested in printing the latter.

As you read this anthology, I hope that three things are true. I hope that you're entertained—we've worked hard to select stories that can carry a beat from beginning to end. I hope that you're informed—I hope that this anthology exposes you to new worlds and ideas. And finally, I hope that you're moved—I hope that at least one story in this book causes you to pause and consider things differently.

Thank you to all of the members of Columbus Creative Cooperative who participate in our community of artists and insist that we produce great books. And thank you to all of the writers who submitted work for consideration.

Thank you, reader, for supporting our endeavor to produce great books. Without you, our cause is lost.

Enjoy the *Best of Ohio Short Stories*!

-Brad Pauquette
www.ColumbusCoop.org

2

Besançon

Mark D. Baumgartner

Chad's father is long dead by this point. Mugged and shot twice, arm and chest, in a far suburb of Cleveland. We have no way of knowing this yet; the murder occurred late at night Eastern Standard Time, early morning in France, and we wouldn't hear anything for some time. It's the heart of winter, and around the university all anyone can talk about is politics and American foreign policy. The French are obsessed by a war gathering in someone else's desert. The wind is unseasonably cold, ice everywhere. Chad thinks we brought it with us from the Midwest, the war, the foul weather, but I'm certain I know better—these are not things that can be carried by men.

At seven on this particular morning Chad and I stand in the foyer of our host family's house, up in the hills surrounding Besançon. We've been in France for two weeks now, out of contact with friends and family save for the odd postcard now and again. We look and smell awful, hung-over to the point of imminent disintegration. Chad has on this ridiculous t-shirt, red with black lettering, which depicts Victor Hugo in the style of a porn star from the late seventies. It was a gift from his homely, bookish girlfriend and he wears it everywhere—to class, to the pub, to bed. I keep pleading

3

with him to take off the shirt, but he is unrelenting. Chad is studying to be an EMT, he is a distinctly American blend of confidence and blithe indifference. He fancies himself an emissary of sorts; he loves to talk politics and has a few carefully prepared phrases he likes to try out on the locals. His French is mangled and incomprehensible, as is mine, but this doesn't keep him from trying. We care nothing for war, Chad insists to all who'll listen, we are Americans trying to escape the wayward drift of our own history. There are many ways to call someone an idiot in French, and with the aid of my journal and a pocket dictionary I have deciphered at least six. Even Chad seems to have picked up on the sense that we are not wanted here.

Our hostess is firing off a series of complex, interrelated questions at Chad and I. I'm not certain, but I believe she's asking where her husband has gone. She's worried because she hasn't seen him since he went out for his morning walk. Chad does not catch this, thinks he hears something about breakfast.

"*Dos huevos, si vous plait*," answers Chad.

Our hostess looks at him, then at me.

I don't know enough French to field the question about her husband, so instead I correct Chad. "It's an *oeuf*," I say. *A fucking oeuf.* I am tired of being asked questions for which I have no answer; I am tired of Chad. I am a little bit in love with the wife, and France as a whole, and Chad has become a stone around my neck.

She looks at me for a long moment, then walks into the kitchen to start the stove. I apologize and move to intercept her—I can make the eggs myself. There's a note in French tacked to the icebox which reads, essentially: *CHAD CALL HOME.* He doesn't.

At eight, Chad and I step out onto the front porch to smoke a cigarette.

4

It's cold—balls cold, as Chad likes to say—and smoke pours from our lips and nostrils each time we exhale. There's a half-inch of freshly fallen snow over everything. Beneath the snow the ground is covered in a continuous, unremitting sheet of ice. The drive swoops steeply down the hill towards the house, and at the end of the declivity lays the missing husband, wedged up against a post. From the broad track in the snow it appears he fell high up the hill and slid all the way down the icy asphalt to the house.

Frost is beginning to form on his whiskers, but he smiles and gives a thumbs up when we ask if he's alright. Chad looks him over. The husband's complexion is darker than usual; I figure he's of Middle Eastern descent, although I'm uncertain if he speaks French with any particular accent. I knock on a window, call for his wife by name. She appears out on the drive—still in her nightgown—a flurry of movement, hands and lips. She fires off a series of questions and commands at her husband, at Chad, at me.

In English, Chad explains in a calm, officious voice that her husband has a badly sprained knee, possibly a torn ACL.

The wife looks to me for a translation.

The only word that comes to mind is *strain*, which I conjugate for her a few different ways.

When nothing else happens, Chad heads inside to call for help.

Minutes pass. The wife says something sharp and angular to her husband, looks at me. I notice through the opening in her slippers that her toes are starting to turn pink. When Chad comes back, he's holding a blanket from one of the beds, which he wraps gently, professionally even, around the husband.

"*Merci,*" says the husband, again with a thumbs up.

Chad stands slowly, deliberately. He leans in close to my ear, his breath hot and wet and panicked, whispers: "How do you do 911 in French?"

I stare at him for some time; Chad squats down and administers to the leg, tries to look busy, important. Eventually the wife turns and goes inside, makes the call herself.

Around eleven o'clock Chad disappears. No explanation, no words at all, nothing—just poof and he's gone. Our hostess rode with the medics and her husband to the hospital, and I'm alone in the house. I walk through each room, marvel at the differences and similarities, mostly similarities, between home here and home in Ohio. I wash the breakfast dishes and put them back in their appointed place. The phone rings twice, but I don't answer; it's not my phone.

Chad returns shortly. Only half an hour has passed, although it seems longer. His hair is wind-blown and his nose and eyes are red. In his left hand he holds a brand new snow shovel, price tag still affixed, and slung over his shoulder is a giant sack of road salt. When I ask him how he found these things so quickly, he shrugs. "Shopping is the same everywhere," he says. This is witty and pointed and distinctly out of character. I don't know what's gotten into him.

We spend the next hour shoveling the drive. Rather, Chad shovels the drive. I crack the ice with a metal spade and smoke cigarettes, lighting each one from the last. Chad is a tank; he blows steam high into the air, sweats through his wool coat, clears wide swaths of snow from the pavement without pause or complaint. He is slow but inexorable, set now in a fixed direction. Once, I step too close to his path and he shoves me out of the way with the flattened blade of the shovel. "Move," he says, and I do. Together we spread handfuls of salt the breadth and length of the steep drive.

On the 12:15 train to the university, Chad and I are quiet. The car is mostly empty, save for a lone family. They are dressed nice, like they are going to visit relatives, a funeral maybe. There are two children, boy and

6

girl, and they are fascinated by us. They move to the seat in front of us, glance at us over the seat backs. "Where are you from?" the girl asks in near-perfect English.

"Chicago," Chad lies. In truth we are from Ohio, a tiny town some distance south of Cleveland—a highway rest stop and little else. Chicago is a convenient invention; like Jerry Lewis and fast food, Chicago seems to catch these French folks' fancy.

The children whisper to each other in French. Then the boy asks a few questions, all in French, all in rapid succession. I can't be certain, but I believe he is asking whether Chad and I are, of all things, gangsters. I relay this to Chad, who sticks his hand in his coat pocket in the shape of a gun. He points at the children, makes a gun sound with his mouth. Brother and sister giggle, scatter back toward their parents.

From the front of the car I can hear them; they make gun sounds with their mouths, airplane noises, explosions. Their parents tell them to shush and they comply. They are, like most French children, explicitly, congenitally well-behaved.

What I can't figure out is how they knew we were Americans before we even opened our mouths.

Chad must be thinking the same thing because he begins to tell a story. In the second World War, he explains, the Nazis could pick out the American spies, la résistance, with a glance, quick and easy. "*Un*," he says holding up his thumb, "the French count on their hands backwards, thumb to pinky. *Deux*," he says extending thumb and pointer, "the French cross their legs at the knee, not at the ankle. *Trois…*" he says, but I am no longer listening.

Brother and sister are quiet up in the front of the car; they watch us continuously over the seat backs, their eyes gray and impossibly wide.

It's one o'clock when we arrive at the university and nothing is doing.

7

Class of course, but really—nothing. Instead we head to the bar.

The establishment we choose is our favorite place in Besançon. They speak English here, and gladly so. Locals come here for the sole purpose of trying out their English on American students. They taunt us over politics and war, hard and soft diplomacy, missing WMDs. They ask us questions we have no answers to. Always I nod in vague agreement and buy another round. I have the good sense to keep quiet, but Chad is easily baited. He has no love of war, but he likes being talked down to even less. I keep telling myself this is a time-honored tradition—a quiet American traveling with a stupid one. Certainly good times and high hilarity must ensue.

We order two shots of bourbon, two beers, then two more shots from a Frenchman wearing a Ted Nugent t-shirt. We shoot some pool, challenge two locals to a game of foosball. We lose twenty euros on a friendly wager, twenty more on a not-so-friendly one. On the television over the bar there is a news report—a muted clip of an American tank rolling through a sandstorm, buildings aflame. The patrons boo and hiss and Chad and I join in, feeling thrilled and slightly seditious. "*See*," I tell the nearest Frenchman, "*the fires of empire burn.*" Something must get lost in the translation however, and he moves to another table.

We order bread and cheese that has the peculiar smell and texture of a human foot. We devour this, order two more shots. Everything is running smoothly, all systems normal.

Time passes. It's dark outside, but seems darker inside the bar. It's snowing again, and the sky outside the narrow window is a bright, pinkish gray. Hip-hop thuds out of the sound system; it sounds like American hip-hop, but the lyrics are utterly foreign. People enter the bar, people we know in the same program as us from back home. Vague acquaintances at best—a girl from Boston and a guy everyone calls East Texas. They

8

stomp the snow from their boots, in French they greet the entire bar as a collective, organic whole. Chad is on fire, in flames. He drains his beer and shouts at them over the music. His words are a strange hodgepodge of slurred English and mangled French; it's no language I've heard before, it's no language ever spoken on the face of the Earth.

I ignore them all, order another beer. I have no desire to speak French with snooty Americans. I'd rather talk English with fake French people. The group I'm with slides onto the dance floor and sucks me with them. Americans are always a hit on the dance floor, regardless of ability or effort. One of the guys reaches over and undoes the top three buttons on my shirt. "*Pour les femmes,*" he says. The blonde to my left fairly reeks of perfume and something earthy, rank. A slight breeze comes off the speakers and the air is alive with a humming electric sibilance. Bodies move. I can feel a hand in my shirt, I'm not certain whose. "Stop touching my nipple," I say to no one in particular. I don't care about the nipple, not really, it's just something to say—*Please stop touching my nipple.*

When I look up again, a familiar face is coming towards me, a girl I recognize from college back home—Boston girl. She's dead ahead, bearing down through the throng on the floor. There's a look of grim excitement on her face and she holds a glowing, euro-style cell phone high over her head. She's Lady Liberty herself, a giant copper and iron statue looming on the horizon. I'm thinking: *There is no place in this great wide world you can't be found.* I'm thinking: *There are invisible wires buried deep in the ground and in the sky pulling us all off to parts unknown.*

I turn to move off through the crowd but there's nowhere to go. She catches me, finally, and over the dull pulse of the music she says: "Chad's mother called the Dean of Students who called customs in Paris who called Agnés and said Chad's father was shot dead once in the arm and once in the chest just for good measure and Chad needs to go home *now.*" She says it

all run together just like that, except for the "just for good measure part"—
I add that in myself, mentally, as she's speaking. She's towering with the
news, glowing, lit from behind or below. When she's done, she hands me
the cell phone and when I tell her to get the hell out, she does.

I take the cell phone over to the bar, order two more beers. I don't
see Chad anywhere. I rest my face against the cool naugahyde trim of the
bar top.

Later. The beer is warm. When I look around, I see Chad standing
back in a corner not more than ten feet away. I have no idea what to say. I
take a sip of beer and watch him for a while. He's standing with some guys
I don't recognize; there's no one I know at all in the bar anymore except
Chad and the bartender and East Texas. Chad is listing heavily to port and
his eyes are half-closed. His French however appears vastly improved. The
talk has turned back to war, the only subject it seems either of us are con-
versant in. I light a cigarette and decide I'm not moving until I finish. His
father isn't getting any deader and Chad certainly isn't getting any more
sober. So I smoke my cigarette, aware that in a moment I'm going to take
Chad by the elbow and explain to him as calmly and evenly as I can that
his father is dead. But first:

Chad laughs raucously and chats with his newfound friends. He works
his hands wildly, sloshing beer on the floor. East Texas walks over, takes
the beer out of his hand, sips. "That's crap," says East Texas, "get yourself
a new one, something dark and I'll be back to make sure it's real dark."
Chad says something half in French and the other guys start to laugh. It's an
awful sound—mirthless and mocking. They are not laughing with him, but
at him. Chad walks over to the bar and gets another beer, something dark.
He drinks the top off immediately. He steps back into the corner, unzips his
pants, urinates, tops off the glass. This is unacceptable behavior, anywhere,

in any language, but the French guys egg him on. Then Chad stands there and holds the beer like nothing's going on. This is too much.

I stand up and pat him on the shoulder. "Let's step outside for a minute," I say.

"*En francais, s'il vous plait,*" says Chad.

"Come on," I say, "*rapidement.*" Chad just stands there, eyes half-closed, holding the beer.

When the Texan returns, he takes the beer from Chad's hand. "What's this?" he says.

"*La Fleur,*" says Chad. "It's new."

East Texas takes a long pull off the glass; his lips curl up, then his nose. He sets the beer slowly on the bar top, turns, walks straight for the restrooms. The Frenchmen laugh their mirthless laugh.

Chad looks at me, grinning. "*Now,*" he says in French, "*how can I help you?*"

I take him by the elbow and lead him back into the darker recesses of the bar. I begin to explain to him the nature of things—slowly at first, then faster.

I tell him: "Your mother called the Dean of Students who called customs in Paris who called Agnés who called Boston girl who told me your father was shot dead once in the arm and once in the chest just for good measure and you need to go home *now.*"

When I don't get any satisfactory response, I begin to repeat myself. Midway through, Chad begins to pace back and forth, his head down like a wounded, dangerous animal, knuckles white on the empty pilsner glass, and I am afraid. He takes the cell phone from my hand and strides out of the bar. I follow. When he holds up his hand to hail a cab, there is murder in his eyes—not murder reflected, but the thing itself.

The sky seems to be getting lighter, but it's difficult to say. It could be dawn, or another dusk—we could have lost an entire day. I'm standing back in the foyer of our host family's house, up in the hills around Besançon. Chad is mostly sober, partly not. He hasn't spoken since we left the bar, save for a brief, subdued phone conversation with his mother. All I could make out were five words over and over again: *I am fit to kill. I am fit to kill.*

This seems to me not only self-evident, but entirely reasonable. The phrase has a nice heft to it, like an axe handle or a brick. I try it out in my mouth and it tastes like home. *Fit to kill*, says Chad, and who am I to say otherwise?

Chad carries his bags and personal effects out to the car—one trip, then two—he doesn't even bother to pack. An unlit cigarette squirms between his clenched teeth. He balances awkward objects on his arms and shoulders, pours his things heedlessly into the back of the cab. He blows steam high into the air; he is a tank; he is unstoppable. I take the lighter from my pocket and light up his cigarette; the steam becomes smoke.

Our host family, husband and lovely wife, watches all of this. They have no idea what is going on, but they have sense enough to keep out of our way. They are dressed for bed; they blink tiredly at the lamplight. The husband's leg is in a cast and propped up on a kitchen chair. His face is slack with medication. The wife stands behind him, her hand on his chair.

Chad brushes past with his final load, and by either accident or design he knocks a lamp off the bureau in the front hall. There is a bright shatter of sound, glass everywhere, but no one says a word. Tragedy has, in some sense, enlarged him. He is in command here and I, his chief lieutenant. If he tells me to raid the larder and set the curtains afire, I will.

No orders are forthcoming, however. Chad has larger matters to attend to. He is out on the walk, on the drive. Smoke pours out of the front of his head, his cigarette glows red.

Behind me, the wife hazards a question. It's maddening, these people and their incessant questions. I respond with two words, clipped and in French. *"Father, gun."* I understand some better explanation is required, some final accounting, but the words all smolder in my throat. Outside, Chad slams the trunk, slams the passenger door—and then he's gone. The sound of the car engine disappears down the hill.

The husband makes a pistol out of his thumb and forefinger, points it at my chest. *"Bang, bang,"* he says. The wife repeats her question.

Open House

Maria Hummer

Before we view the house we get new clothes, new haircuts and new names. We decide we are Amy and Todd. We know we can't live here, not in this house, not the people we are now. The people we are now live in a tiny shared apartment with friends who don't do dishes and smoke too much pot and eat our cereal when they get hungry. The people we are now bathe in showers black with mold, shoo mice from the crumb-floored kitchen, and pinch our noses when we open the fridge to keep out the smell of rotting oranges. The people we are now stopped kissing each other goodnight, we just climb into bed and sigh. We don't want to be these tired and going-nowhere people. We want to be Amy and Todd.

Amy and Todd have clean fingernails and dressers full of fresh paired socks. Amy and Todd get up early on Sundays, and wear slippers, and vacuum floors, and organize spice racks by color. Amy and Todd bake pies.

They do not scrape cigarette butts out of crusty coffee mugs, or pick the bodies of ants from their cereal like unwanted raisins. Amy and Todd go for walks in the neighborhood, down streets lined with matching houses like a litter of new puppies sitting in a row. The cars are unscratched, the children riding past on bikes say "excuse me," and the evening air is filled with real birdsong, not the throaty complaints of crows.

We could be these people. We could be Amy and Todd and drink fruit tea and read books about European history and get excited about light fixtures, which is the first thing we comment on—the front hallway light fixture—when Joe shows us his house, his life, the life that could be ours.

"Lovely," I say. Amy and Todd say words like lovely.

There is a side table in the hallway with nothing on it. Its only purpose is to be a table and I, Amy, am charmed by this.

The house smells of clean rugs and lentil soup. Joe's wife Melanie is cooking in the kitchen. It smells beautiful, and she stirs the soup and she is beautiful. I could be her.

"Are you vegetarians?" I ask, and Melanie says no, they just like to eat healthy. I approve.

Joe shows us everything in the kitchen that could belong to Amy and Todd: clean white fridge with ice dispenser, new dishwasher, expensive coffee grinder, a set of hand-painted plates, white with blue fish. Even the half-used boxes of rice and pasta. "Everything you see," says Melanie.

Joe squeezes her shoulders. "Except for my Melanie," he says. Melanie gives Joe an adoring look. We beam.

Joe takes us to a room he calls the sitting room. In the shared apartment we call it the living room, but I like the word Joe uses and I think Amy would use it too. I'm glad there's not one designated room for living. The kitchen, the bathroom, the room where you sleep, they are all for living, for laughing and drinking wine and spilling spaghetti sauce and trying tai chi one cold winter morning in socks. Every room is a room for such living and Joe takes us through them all.

Todd—it's his name now—asks Joe the practical questions. How old is that, when should this be replaced, is it possible to move this to here. I peer out the windows of every room like it's the most important thing. It's vital to Amy that each window look out on a vision of what her life could be—something green and flowering, or maybe soft and fluttering like laundry on a line. I check every window and I don't see broken things or loose garbage. I see patience, and healthy grass, and hope. Amy would delight in these windows.

Todd and I follow Joe and we look at the things he points at and go: Mm. Right. Nice. When Joe looks away we widen our eyes at each other and make big gasping shapes with our mouths, like we're at the Grand Canyon, like we're seeing the best sunset of our lives. We touch the clean white walls and we wonder if we deserve this, this cleanliness, but then we stop caring if we deserve it, we just want it so bad.

Joe shows us his study. The chestnut desk is covered in piles of books and papers.

"I'm a creative man at heart," he says. "Been writing a novel in my spare time. It's unfinished, but you might have fun fixing it up."

Todd and I look at each other. We didn't count on this, but we suppose it makes sense, some things left unfinished, and it's fair for us to inherit that. We're young, we're fresh, we like a challenge.

"What about jobs?" asks Todd. A good question.

Joe tells us he works in a bank and Melanie stays at home. "Obviously," he says, "either of you could fill either role. We're not sexist here. But someone would have to stay home."

"Can the one who stays at home also work?" I ask. "Like freelance or something."

"I don't see why not," says Joe, "but you might find it difficult."

Todd and I look at each other. Difficult because of another unfinished project? Another novel?

"The girls want lots of attention," says Joe. "They're very sweet, but don't expect them to leave you alone for very long."

Todd and I avoid each other's eyes, trying not to panic. The ad said nothing about girls. *Seeking young, energetic couple for quiet family life in the suburbs. Newly-renovated house. Amazing space. Lots of potential. Call Joe to arrange a viewing.* My stomach churns as I remember the ad. Family. Potential. We hadn't interpreted it this way.

We follow Joe. Down the hall trickles the sound of young voices and toys being dropped. Joe opens the door to something he says is the play room. We step inside.

The girls.

"This one's Tilly," says Joe, touching the soft ponytail of a girl, about five years old, eating a cereal bar. She grins at us, oats and chocolate in her teeth. Joe picks up the other girl, smaller than Tilly and playing with a plastic penguin. He gives her a loud kiss on the cheek and she giggles, dark eyebrows twitching. "And this is Nona," he says.

"Hi," we say to the girls. They ignore us and go back to playing.

"All the toys are included," he says. "All the clothes. If you decide to take it we'll go over the details, like their likes and dislikes and fears and things that make them feel better. Nona, for example, always stops crying if you give her a little peanut butter. Always. We don't know why."

We ask Joe if we can talk it over a moment. We go into the bathroom. We close the door.

The bathroom is huge. It has a tub and separate shower and a vanity table. Todd and I blink in its whiteness like two people woken suddenly from a nap. We'd forgotten the world could be this bright. We'd been asleep.

"I think I love it," says Todd.

I twist the sink handles. Hot on, cold on, hot off, cold off. The water comes out smooth as an icicle.

17

"But the girls," I say.

"Yeah," he says.

"I didn't think we were looking for that sort of life."

"Yeah. But I think we could make it work."

I look out the window. It always helps, when making a decision, to just look out the window.

"I do like the big backyard," I say.

"And that extra freezer," says Todd.

We go back into the room with Tilly and Nona. Joe is gone and Todd leaves to find him and talk about rent and other particulars. I stay with the girls. They ask me if I want to play penguins and I say that I do. I hear Todd's voice coming from somewhere in the house. His voice is deep and filling. Good enough for a meal, I always say. I can feel it filling the house, slipping between kitchen plates and table legs and under couches and into this room, like rising bread. I'm in this room playing penguins with Tilly and Nona and Todd's voice fills me like risen bread, and I know we can do this, we can host game nights and wax floors and tie little girls' shoes in this house as Amy and Todd.

Cinderbox Road

Scott Geisel

We're driving down Cinderbox Road, bright afternoon sun bouncing off the corn that's starting to turn brown in the late summer heat, when a buck jumps in front of the pickup. It's the last curve before home, a zag to the right so sharp it's almost a turn. This one always gets you, makes you dig your nails just a little into the palms of your hands.

The road drops here, and we can see the house below, peeking through the cornstalks where they melt into the edge of town. The buck stands rigid in the center of the lane, staring straight at us, eyes locked on ours. He's a big one.

You scream, and I hit the brakes. There's no place to go; the road is a high berm between two steep ditches. The truck goes into a deep slide on the loose gravel scattered across the two-lane. The buck doesn't move, watches as the bumper tags him high on the haunches. It's a glancing blow, but a solid one. He staggers, confused, eyes big and wet.

"No. Oh, no!" you shout.

The buck takes a step, stumbles, rights himself and steps again. He tries to run, crashes awkwardly off the road and limps to a drainage run-off where the stalks are thin, and disappears inside.

He doesn't look good.

"Shit," I say, gripping the wheel. "Shit."

We've been here before. Not here, exactly, but we've had this conversation. One of your greatest fears since we moved to the farmhouse is that you'll hit something. But we both knew that when it happened it would be me behind the wheel.

"He's hurt," you say. Your hands are still clenched. I can see where your fingernails will leave imprints.

"We didn't kill him," I try. We're still in the middle of the road, mostly sideways. The engine purrs from the tune-up I gave it yesterday, out in the shade behind the barn.

"He didn't even try to move. He just stood there, like he wanted to get hit."

Your elbow twitches, and you turn away to the window. I want to touch you, break the spell, but I know it would be too much. You're breathing shallow, at the top of your lungs, keeping most of the air in and letting only the smallest amount escape. Like when you're having a bad dream and I lay beside you. I know that the air in your lungs must be getting stale, turning to carbon dioxide, blue, purple. I reach over—

"He's too hurt. He won't be able to survive."

"You don't know that."

"You don't either! You killed him."

Your hands fall into the seat now, and I know it's time to go. But Roy comes out of the field behind us on his tractor, closing at a good clip. I can see that he's shouting, but I can't hear what he's saying.

"Go," you whisper, too late. Roy is edging up beside us.

"Everything all right?" he shouts, and it comes out much too loud now.

I give him a salute, our usual greeting when he's out in the fields, but he's probably too high on the tractor seat to see it. "Fine," I say, twisting my head out the window. "Buck in the road."

Roy has lived on Cinderbox Road his whole life. Got the farm from his daddy and raised his kids here. He knows every inch of every acre for miles.

He scans the crop line, looks at the skid marks behind us. "Where?"

"Run off," I say, pointing.

Roy nods. "You missed him, then?"

I shake my head. He bends to try to see you, can't, and inches the tractor forward until he's in front of the windshield. "You all right, 'Lizbeth?" he asks, looking in through the glass.

You lean forward to let him see you better, give him a piece of a smile, and he seems satisfied.

"All right then," Roy says. He turns and looks down the line of corn, takes off his hat and holds it against the sun.

"I better get her out of the road," I say through the window.

Roy looks at me, then gives the salute and rumbles off in a hurry.

I ease the truck into gear and back it up to straighten out in the lane, hoping you won't see Roy when he bumps off the road and disappears into the wash where the deer ran.

We drive the half mile home at about five miles an hour.

You jump out as soon as the truck stops, and I call after you, "What do you think I could have done?"

You spin, mid-step. "You know I hate that road."

"That's the way home," I say, more harsh than I know I should. "You can't keep trying to avoid it." It's a mistake. This was going to be a good night. Our anniversary. Six years. Three months to the day since the miscarriage. We were just starting to move forward again.

You're in the flowerbed beside the barn. I don't have to see you to know. You're running your fingers through the ground, picking at the starts of weeds, searching for tiny new shoots that have appeared since you last checked. The garden went in after we lost him. You put in perennials, things that would come back. Cone flowers and black-eyed susans. Columbines and coreopsis. You wanted bleeding hearts, but those tender springtime shoots were long gone by then. You'll have to wait until next year to plant that memory.

I could watch you through the upstairs window, but I won't. You'll stay in the flowers a few minutes or maybe the rest of the day, and when you come in your hands will smell like mulch. Tonight while you're asleep, I'll sit over you and breathe deeply, hoping that scent is still there.

I unload the truck—lumber and screws and something special I picked up while you were buying stamps at the P.O.—and stack it all to carry back to the chicken coop. Something's been digging back there, trying to get in, and I'm going to run an extra course of planks around the bottom and tighten up every loose spot I can find to keep it out.

There's a tuft of hair stuck to the front bumper, and when I pull it off a red stain shows on the fender. I rub it away with a rag from under the seat.

I work the rest of the day without stopping, and when the sun starts to reach the tree line, Roy pulls up in his truck and circles the little turnaround in front of the house. I close the chicken coop door and go out to greet him.

"There's no supper tonight," I say apologetically. "We're running behind. Just going to grab something from the—"

"That's not it," he says, waving me off. "I just come by to see if you still need help gettin' that tractor of yours to run."

Roy is going to teach me to farm.

We've been here a year, and that's my goal—learn to work the land we live on. The house came with forty-two acres. We wanted to split it up, just buy the house and an acre or two, but the family wouldn't make a deal.

22

It was the guy's kids. He'd farmed this place alone into his seventies, selling off parcels and doling out others for lease as he worked ever smaller plots close to the house.

That's how we get by now. Roy plants fifteen acres near the house, and Orvie Campbell twenty-five more back to the fence line. The rent on those fields along with my job welding parts at the plant in Durban was just enough for us to get the loan.

Roy has this idea that once he's gone, we'll take over his fifteen acres. It won't bring in much, maybe less than we could get leasing it to Orvie. Those other guys farm three, four hundred acres to make a living, more if they can get it. And I've seen more than one of them pulling shifts at the plant when the big runs come in and they hire temporary. But Roy is as determined as I am that I at least learn what it means to live here. With his own wife and kids gone, I think his plans run bigger than that, but we never talk about anything more than just the fifteen acres.

"I haven't had time to think about the tractor," I confess. "Something getting into the chicken coop."

Roy nods, looks back between the house and the barn. "She likes those chickens, doesn't she?"

"Yep."

"Tomorrow?" he says.

"Tomorrow," I say. "The sooner the better."

We talk about the weather and when it might rain and he talks about the soy leaves and if they start to curl, and we really could use that rain. I mostly listen, and Roy seems to appreciate that.

Then he gets to the buck, says he found him down by DeCamp's Pond, pretty banged up. "Orvie's making jerky," he says.

I nod.

"He says you ought to get some, if you want. You're the one that hit him."

"No," I say, and Roy understands. I know he's only asking because he wouldn't have felt right if he didn't.

We both look at the house. "So no dinner then?" he says.

Before I can answer, the screen door squeaks and you come down the steps wiping your hands on a kitchen towel. "I've set a plate," you say to Roy. "You going to sit down with us?"

Roy at our table for dinner is nothing new, and it's been getting more regular since this time of the season there's more waiting and watching the weather. I'm silently thankful he's here. He looks at you sometimes almost like you're his own daughter, and these last couple of months the most I've seen you smile and act like yourself is when he turns his attention to you.

Tonight, he holds your chair out while you sit. "Smells wonderful, 'Lizbeth," he says, and pats your arm as he slides the chair in. You let him touch you. Small, friendly gestures. Not like me. I'm still dangerous to you.

We pass around a bowl of potatoes and another of beans. "There's no meat tonight," you say. "There's been enough killing for one day."

Roy lifts an eyebrow to me, then quickly looks away. I'm the only guy around here who doesn't hunt. The only one without a bag of jerky in my pocket on those cold winter nights when Roy invites me to the tavern to sit with the guys and talk about spring and when they can get back into the fields again. Since we lost the baby, you don't even like me killing the chickens when they're too old or sick to lay.

Roy picks up a platter of tomatoes and squash he knows are from the garden and winks. "We'll make farmers of you two yet."

You almost blush and pass him the steamed carrots and salad. "There's some to take with you, too, if you don't eat it all," you say, and he laughs. For a moment, I think I'm jealous, but then I remember how thankful I am for Roy and I try to laugh too.

24

You're wearing a white and yellow sun dress you bought at a barn sale last spring. It's always jeans or work pants around the house during the day, but lately you've been changing into something lighter, a summer dress or a skirt, in the evenings.

I look across the table at you, and with a big mouthful of carrots I say, "That dress looks great on you."

There's something in the way you look back at me that I don't understand. Roy looks down at his plate and shovels in potatoes.

When you bring out the ice cream and cookies for dessert, Roy reaches into the pocket of his overalls and pulls out a box that looks too big to have fit in there. "For you," he says, looking at both of us but setting the box at your end of the table. "Happy anniversary."

You tilt your head. "How did you know?"

"Maggie," he says. "Her anniversary was two days ago. You mentioned yours once last summer, and that's why it stuck with me."

Your eyes cut to the floor, then back to Roy. "Maggie? She's your youngest, right?"

Roy nods.

"I think we met her at Christmas." You glance at me for confirmation.

"That'd be about it," Roy says. "Don't none of them get out to the farm very much anymore. John—Maggie's husband—he got on at the mill up in Clarksville and things are going good there."

"Maybe Christmas then," you say.

Roy looks thoughtful for a moment, then taps the box at your elbow. "You gonna open it?"

You look at me, but we both know whatever Roy has brought is mostly for you. I nod, and you pull the top off. Inside there's a picture frame with a photo of you and me sitting on a bench downtown in the bright sunshine. The street is crowded with people and there are flags flying in front

25

of the stores. You're sitting so close that half of you disappears behind me, but it's a great shot of your face, your mouth thrown open with laughter.

"Fourth of July," you say, though I read your lips more than I hear the words.

"The parade last year," Roy says.

I lean over. "That was right after we moved in here."

"I was taking pictures for the Odd Fellows," he says. "You two were right there and it was such a good shot…" Roy folds his hands back like he momentarily doesn't know what to do with them. "I've been meaning to give that to you. Now seemed like a good time."

You look at the picture, then back up at me. My hand brushes yours, and you slip a finger into my palm.

Roy's hands have reoriented themselves, and he grabs the scoop and digs into the ice cream. "Get it before it melts," he says.

You and I walk with Roy out to his truck, our hands touching, not quite holding, but almost. It's nearly full dark, and he's looking at the orange glow that's just sunk below the horizon, tracing pink streaks across the sky. Thinking about the weather, I guess, and tomorrow, but then he turns to us with something different on his mind.

"I'm sorry about your deer, 'Lizbeth," he says. "It weren't your fault."

Your fingers slip away from mine, and I feel a space of air open between us. I can't figure why Roy has brought this up again, why he had to tell you. I wait for that faraway look in your eye, the clenched fists, but they don't come.

We all just stand there, and then Roy puts a hand on your shoulder and says, "I know things have been tough for you. When my Kate passed, I thought nothing would ever be the same."

You give him a hard look, something I don't think I've seen you do before with Roy, and say, "And are they?"

Roy drops his hand, looks at his boots. "No." He shuffles his feet. "'Lizbeth, you know I'd do just about anything I could for you if I was able, don't you?"

You nod your head shakily, then lean into him and the two of you hug while I watch stupidly until you turn and walk into the house.

"Sorry," Roy says.

"Don't be," I say, and hold out my hand. "You've been the best thing for her."

Instead of taking my hand, Roy gives me the salute, and I give it back to him.

"Get to that tractor tomorrow, then?" I say.

"Tomorrow," he nods, and climbs into his truck and eases out onto the road.

I squint behind the truck seat in the little light from the dome and reach in to grab the package I stashed there this afternoon. You're not in the kitchen. The dinner plates are still on the table, and the ice cream has melted in the carton. I stick it in the freezer and go looking for you.

You're upstairs on the bed, holding the photo Roy gave to us. You set it on the nightstand when I say, "I got you something," and pull the gift from behind my back.

I step closer and lay the box across your lap. You wipe your eye, and a tear rolls down your hand. There's that look from the dinner table again, but I recognize it this time. It's the first I've seen you cry since we lost him.

"I didn't get you anything," you sniff.

"It's okay," I say, and my hand goes instinctively to touch your hair. You let me, and I rub the wet spot on your cheek. "Open it," I whisper.

You sniff again and your fingers flutter on the ribbon. The box pops open and a white and blue sun dress spills out. There's a blue sash around the middle and lace at the breast that looks exactly like on your wedding dress. A loose pattern of calla lilies circles the shoulders. You stare for a second. "It looks like…"

"Our wedding," I say for you.

You hold the fabric to your face and I can hear you breathing through the cloth. "He'd be born just about now," you say. "An anniversary baby."

"Don't…"

You bury your face deeper into the fabric. "You must hate me."

"No."

"But I lost your son."

I reach for the dress, try to get you to lower it, but you won't let go. "There's nothing we could have done."

"I killed him. He could have lived. If I'd done something… Something…"

Your grip relaxes a little and I get the dress down and look at you. "He couldn't have lived. Doctor Hackett said so. There was never any chance."

"But I wanted…"

I get my arm around you now, awkwardly. "I did too."

"I wanted to give you your son."

"Our son," I say. "Your son."

We sit like that for a long time. My arm is still around you. It aches from the uncomfortable angle, but I won't move it. You've stopped crying. I didn't notice when.

You wipe your eyes again. "I was so sad."

"I know," I say.

"But that never meant I didn't want you to touch me."

Something plunks inside me and I squeeze you tighter and we sit some more.

28

Finally, you get up and hold the dress in front of you and look at yourself in the mirror while I watch, then slip it on a hanger and leave it on the outside of the closet door where we can see it.

"Okay?" you say.

"Okay," I say, and we go downstairs to clean up the kitchen.

When we're done in the kitchen, I get the flashlight and go out to check on the chickens. There's still boards and tools and my drill sitting out and a box of screws lying open. I stack the boards and put the tools back in the barn and make one last round of the place before I come in. Roy's corn is tall and silent at the edge of the yard. I walk the length and touch every stalk as I pass.

The light is still on in the bathroom, but you're already asleep. I undress and brush my teeth as quietly as I can. I want to sit with you, over you, watch you, but I'm too tired. I lie down next to you and let my hand fall onto your shoulder. It slides to your hip where it rests as I fall asleep.

Bright moonlight fills the room when a noise outside wakes me. Immediately I think *chicken coop!* and get up to look out the window. That's when I see that the dress is gone and you're not in the bed.

The chickens are quiet but there's movement in the flowerbed. I know it's you before I see the dress shining like a memory in the moonlight, and then I'm running, struggling to pull on pants and shoes as I clamber down the stairs. I've never been in your flower garden before, and I know you're waiting, wanting. I can feel your hand in mine even before I race across the lawn to touch you.

A Day in the Sun

Joseph Downing

The Pacific stretched wide, vast and dark, the blue-green waves rolling softly and teasingly until, seemingly from nowhere, a breaker would slam into the beach, driving the tourists floating and bobbing in the shallows violently to the sandy floor. Still, they rose up coughing and snorting and, somehow, laughing. My father and I sat in the hotel's plastic beach chairs, watching all this. I sprawled in the late afternoon sun, feeding on the warmth like a last meal before our return to winter, but my father stayed in the shade of the umbrella. The bucket of beers sat in the sand between us, linking our private worlds together. It was our third day in Puerto Vallarta, and it was already starting to feel like a mistake to have come.

"This was your mom's favorite spot, right here," my father said. "We would push her all the way out to the sand, and she would sit with a beach towel wrapped around her knees, still cold even in this heat. But she loved every minute of it."

I felt him looking at me, waiting. I scooped a chunk of ice from the bucket and pressed it to the back of my neck. The ice melted in seconds.

"You remember that, right?"

He wouldn't let it go. "Yeah. I remember." I also remembered the extra doses of pain medication. The calls to the front desk at 3:00 a.m. for clean sheets.

"Sometimes I even forgot she was sick, at least until—"

"Do you want another beer?" I handed him one without waiting for an answer and then pulled a lime slice from the bucket and tossed it to him. It landed in his lap and the task of stuffing it into the bottle momentarily occupied him. I took the opportunity to slip on the earphones of my iPod, leaving the power off.

All around us seagulls squawked as they dove for stray bits of food tourists had dropped in the sand. A mixture of mariachi and dated American pop music poured from the cantina behind us, only to be drowned out by the crashing waves. These sounds compensated for our silence.

A beach hawker, dressed in the required white and looking not much different, I imagined, than his Mayan ancestors, approached us, his arms draped in brightly colored scarves. We would be approached every ten minutes by someone—selling jewelry, woodcarvings, hammocks, temporary tattoos. They usually didn't annoy me, but today irritation bubbled under my skin. The man was young, flashed us a smile, and asked us the standard: *"How many?"*

I shook my head no, and he asked again. I pulled off my earphones.

"No, gracias," I replied.

"She loved to haggle with those guys," my father said when the hawker had finally given up and moved on. "They knew her after the first day and man, did they find her quick. She drove a hard bargain." He chuckled. He wasn't lying. Ninety pounds and dropping, she haggled with them as if she needed every last dime for a rainy day. Didn't she know we—I— would have paid any price for what she wanted that week? A month later the cancer would finally win, and all her bargained-for trinkets, the colorful plates and blankets, the masks, the jewelry, would be given to her sisters in a rush of grief by my father.

I reached for another beer.

"This is how we should spend Christmas every year," he said. "It's not like you or I are going to be hanging stockings and decorating trees."

I looked at his white arms, his soft belly poking out under the Hawaiian shirt he had pressed to come to the beach. He had aged significantly in the last year. His reclusiveness had grown to the point he relied on me as his only social outlet, and I both resented this and felt guilty for resenting it. The random phone calls—usually late at night, often drunken—where he would go on and on. When I cut him off he would be hurt and I might not hear from him for weeks.

An hour later, a beach hawker, this one much older, passed below us along the water's edge with a tray of jewelry, trying, with little luck, to catch the eye of one of the many women sunning. My father noticed him and sat up in his chair.

"That's him," he said. When I didn't respond, he nudged my shoulder and repeated what he said.

"Who?"

"That's the guy that she bought all the jewelry from, you know, the one she liked so much? You have to remember that."

I did remember. He was jovial, funny, courteous. Came every day. My mom watched for him. They had joked and both enjoyed the game. I removed my sunglasses and looked closer. A bit chubby. Gray hair poking out from under his straw hat.

"The guy you're thinking of had a mustache," I said. "And was taller. That's not him."

"No, that's him. I know it." He waved to the man, who saw us and hurried over, squatting down and resting his wares on his knee. Glittering fake silver and stones, rings, necklaces, earrings.

"*Hola, señor.* How many?"

"We were here last year," my father said, excitedly. "My wife bought a whole mess of jewelry from you. Do you remember?"

The desperation, the need in my father's voice made my heart ache. This guy sees thousands of tourists a week, and we're asking him about a woman he saw a few times a year ago. How and why would he remember?

"Necklace, *señor*? Very good price."

"No—my wife. From last year. You used to make her laugh and she bought—" he looked at the corkboard and pointed to a necklace, "one like that from you."

My father went on to describe my mother in detail while the man stared at him blankly.

"She was in the wheelchair, and—"

"Dad, it's not him," I said.

"Tim, I know it is. Why—"

"It doesn't matter. Don't you get it? *It doesn't matter.*" I turned to the hawker. "*Nada, por favor.*"

The man's eyes moved from me to my father and then back, following our exchange. "*Lo siento,*" he said, and then turned away and continued down the beach. My father faced the water and was silent. His disappointment hung like smoke.

The sun was fading, the sky moving from blue to yellow to red, and people were packing up and heading back to their hotels, their minds already on the thing they were going to do later, and the thing after that, the thing *tomorrow, tomorrow, tomorrow,* as if the future never ends. All I could see was myself pushing her wheelchair off the cobblestone walk and into the sand on that last day, my father back in the hotel, napping, exhausted from lack of sleep due to being awake all night while my mother heaved and wretched. It was just the two of us, she and I, watching the sun drop, just like it's dropping now, and her voice, the voice I had known since before I took my first breath, asking quietly, softly, heartbreakingly, *can we stay one more day?* And me, saying no, we had to get back—my work, my job, my responsibilities, something important needing attention back in Ohio, something that I don't even remember today and will never remember again—and still there was the longing, the longing in her voice, for just one more day.

"We shouldn't have come here," I blurted.

"What?" my father said, incredulous. "Being here is the point."

"We shouldn't have come."

"But it was your—"

I pushed off the chair and walked through the cooling sand to the water and dove in. Deep, embryonic silence. I opened my eyes but could see nothing. I stayed submerged until my lungs burned and I could hear my heart thumping in my head. I broke the surface, gulping for air. From this distance my father seemed so small in the shadow of his umbrella. Families—mom, dad, kids, grandparents—paraded by him on their way to wherever. I watched him a few more minutes and then swam back. When I sat back down, he stayed quiet.

"You want to head back?" I asked, after a moment.

"And then what, son?" he said.

I didn't have an answer. All the beer was gone and the ice had melted, leaving two shriveled slices of lime floating in the water. I watched as the tide receded, leaving a smooth swath of sand in its wake, erasing all evidence that it had ever been walked on. A child ran across the sand with a bucket and a shovel, and I wanted to make her stop, to convince her to leave the sand pristine for just a while longer. I wanted to grab her and squeeze her to my chest and tell her things she couldn't possibly understand. My father was watching her, too. I decided I would wait until after dinner to tell him that I was going to change our flight so that we could go home tomorrow.

It wasn't much later that dad's beach hawker came hustling his way through the few remaining sunbathers and beach towels toward us. *Great*, I thought. He had seen an opening, and he wasn't going to give up. We would buy something yet, he knew. And I would gladly buy something from him if he would just go away and not get my father's hopes up again. But he set his tray of jewelry on the sand behind him and squatted in front of my father, smiling excitedly.

"*Leenda*," he said.

My father was quiet for a moment. I was too. Then, "What? What did you say?"

The man pointed to my dad. "*Vuestro Mujer. Leenda.*"

"Yes! Yes! *Linda.*" My dad jumped up, laughing as he grabbed the man's hand.

"*Si, Leenda*," the man said again, now laughing also. "Francisco," he said, pointing to his chest.

"Bob," my father said, never letting go of his hand. "I knew it," my father said again and again while Francisco nodded and smiled. He turned to me, joy spread across his face. "See?"

I smiled. "Yeah. I see."

Francisco pulled a wallet from his pocket and flipped it open to show a faded photograph of a dark-haired woman, posing formally. "Angelita," he said, pointing to his heart.

"*Muy bonita*," my father enunciated carefully. He pointed to me. "This is my son. He brought her here. As a gift." Francisco shook my hand. "Hey, get a picture of us," my father said.

I picked up the camera. "Wait—you want in?" he said, glancing around for someone else to ask.

"No. It should be just the two of you."

By the end of the week we would decide this would be our memorial trip for my mom; that each year we would return, together. But we never did. It would be many years before my father's heart would do quickly for him what the cancer took agonizing months to do for my mother. To my surprise I would start a family of my own, life would become full of other things, and I still hadn't been back to Mexico. But the photo of my father and Francisco remained on his mantle year after year after year.

But maybe it doesn't really matter that we didn't go again. Some things can't be recreated. On that day, at that moment, we weren't thinking about the future. I watched as my father put his arm around Francisco, who took off his hat and held it in his hands. They both smiled for the camera, their small figures framed by the dying sunlight and endless sea.

"*Leenda*," Francisco said, proudly. I looked at my father and we both laughed.

"Leenda," my dad and I said in unison.

Late Date

Brenda Layman

Little clumps of ice crystals stuck together and collected around the edges of the windshield. The temperature had dropped steadily all afternoon until grey drizzle became heavy snow, followed by more drizzle that froze into an icy glaze, coating bare branches, power lines and the road before them. Jen tried not to show worry. Robert's hands gripped the wheel. They were old hands, gnarled and arthritic, tendons standing out beneath thin skin. His cheekbones and jawline were still strong, his nose beneath black-framed glasses prominent in his aging face.

"Don't worry. I've driven through worse," he said, and she knew her attempt to appear unconcerned had failed. "Just twenty miles or so and we'll be over the hill and the worst will be behind us."

The hill lay between them and their destination. Every mile took them higher and pushed the temperature lower. The dashboard thermometer reported the downward progression faithfully and without judgment. Thirty-three degrees. Thirty-two. The layer of ice grew steadily as the temperature dropped.

"So, you were saying…" Robert picked up the thread of dropped conversation. She knew he wanted to keep her mind off the treacherous drive, and she played along.

"Yeah, about the play," she said. "I was saying that I guess I feel sorry for Rothko. I mean, he was so fierce and so vulnerable at the same time."

"We all have our time, and then it's somebody else's time. His conflict is ours, isn't it?"

"Well, I don't think my time is over yet," Jen replied. She was sixteen years Robert's junior.

"Nor mine, but the day will come. I got used to that idea a long time ago."

Robert was a poet, really a poet with published volumes of verse and a number of prestigious literary awards under his belt. He still wrote prolifically, pages and pages of lines each day, words like living things emerging from his fingertips and making their way toward the sunlight, seeking approval and thus survival. He smiled.

"Change," he said. "Change is the future. It's everything. Shit!" He swore as the car suddenly fishtailed. "Sorry."

"It's ok. Do you think we should stop somewhere?" she asked.

"Nowhere to stop until we make it to the other side." He looked at her and grinned. "Are you saying you want to get a room? On our first date?"

Jen felt her cheeks burn and was amazed that she could still blush like a young girl. Robert was confusing, one moment a wise old man and the next a mischievous boy.

"No, I mean, it's just the weather, and the ice, and visibility is decreasing." She tried to recover some dignity with the formality of the phrase, but visibility was indeed decreasing, and steadily. Thick, white fog had dropped, or maybe they had simply plunged into it from beneath as they climbed. Taillights flickered in and out of view a few yards ahead of them.

After the play, they had walked across campus to the Faculty Club, holding on to one another to keep from falling on the slippery walkways as the snow flew. Once safe and dry inside, Robert introduced Jen to his colleagues as "my new friend and lovely date for the evening."

Jen hadn't been sure of the date, but going to see a student performance of John Logan's play, *Red*, at the local university, accompanied by a professor who had enjoyed a stellar career there, was appealing. Robert had taken her by surprise when he asked her, at a party hosted by one of her clients. She had dismissed him as attractive, but too old. Apparently he had no such qualms, and he had brought her a drink, engaged her in conversation, and then sprung the invitation with practiced ease. She was surprised to hear herself assent.

Afterward, she went online and did some research. She found mentions of his work here and there, and read the poems they quoted. She read his early writings, the poems he wrote at what was considered the height of his career, and his last published effort, released five years earlier. It was unlike the stuff of contemporary poets, less raw and more cerebral. Even his early work, written when he was still in his twenties, had a reserve about it. The passion of his youth ran crimson and hot, but it ran beneath a decorous veneer of literary device.

After Burgundy wine, cheese and conversation at the Faculty Club, they returned to the parking garage and drove carefully to the freeway exit. Jen sat quietly. Structure mattered then, she thought as she watched the windshield wipers rhythmically swiping ice aside, more than it does now. Now it's feeling creating form; then it was form supporting feeling.

As if he heard her inner voice, Robert said, "Now, take Rothko. He loved being an iconoclast—reveled in it. But the problem with being an iconoclast is, as soon as you start being anything, you set yourself up for the end."

"I wonder how such a young actor felt about the part?" Jen mused. "He did a great job with it, but it's hard to imagine he understood it." The tall, thin young man with his hair streaked silver and lines drawn onto his forehead and the corners of his eyes and mouth had given a masterful effort.

"Yeah." Robert tapped the brakes and the car slid, then they felt the tires grip. "When I was an undergrad, W.H. Auden came to our school. We all turned out to hear him read. We had to wear jackets and ties then. None of this shorts and t-shirts business. I was thrilled to be there, but I thought him terribly old. The next day our professor asked us what we thought of the lines: 'There is no such thing as The State/And no one exists alone.'"

"What did you say?"

"I hemmed and hawed and came up with some nonsense about existentialism. Dear God, I had no idea. The only thing I was thinking about was whether or not the girls found me handsome in my new sweater. By the way, do you like this one? I confess I bought it to impress you."

"It's very nice. You look good in russet."

He smiled. "I know, and at my age I try to make good use of every flattering thing I can find."

"Me too." Jen laughed.

"Ah, but you are so much less in need of flattery."

"What a line."

"But true."

Before Jen could reply, red taillights glowed through the darkness and white mist. Robert hit the brakes and the car skidded to a stop. "Looks like we're stopping," he observed.

"What—"

Jen felt rather than saw Robert's body tense as his gaze locked on the rearview mirror.

"Jesus, Jen, hold on."

She heard the collisions, metal screaming and objects colliding, sounds being hurled toward them through the dense, cold air. Impact threw them against their restraints as the airbags burst, filling the car with fine powder that seemed as if the fog from outside was pumping into the car, into Jen's face, filling her lungs even as the force of the exploding bag struck her in the chest with a blow that left her gasping for air.

Then there was stillness, and silence. She turned to Robert. He was leaning forward, hands still gripping the wheel. His glasses were gone. She slid her hand down the shoulder strap, unlatched her seatbelt, and reached for him.

"Robert!"

He lifted his head. "Are you alright?" he asked.

"I think so."

Robert unbuckled his seat belt and tried to open his door. It resisted, but he threw his weight against it and it gave. Jen's wouldn't open, so she crawled across and Robert helped her climb out the driver's side.

Icy wind whipped their hair and stole their breath as they stood there steadying each other. Robert pulled his phone out of his coat pocket and called 911.

"This could be bad," he told Jen. They ventured down the line of smashed cars behind them. Some people had already left their vehicles and were wandering in the snowy road. One teenage girl was shoeless, standing with a small group of friends who huddled together behind a crumpled Honda.

"Where are your shoes?" Jen asked her. "Let's get them."

"I don't know. I don't know what happened. I was asleep in the back seat," the girl told her. "I don't know what to do."

The rear door was open. Jen leaned inside, groping around in the dark until she located the shoes. She knelt in the snow, knees crackling in protest, and brushed each of the girl's feet off before sliding them into the shoes.

Satisfied that the teens were all right, Jen moved on to the next car, and then the next, helping people with coats and boots. The fourth car had rolled onto its side. She heard crying, heard the harsh ragged sobs of the young man before she saw him. She stood on tiptoe and looked inside. She could see two figures, one rocking back and forth, the other motionless. She pulled on the door and it moved, but she didn't have the strength to pull it upward and open.

Robert's arms reached past her. He pulled the door open a bit and said to the distraught man inside, "Push it open if you can. Help us get you out."

"Oh, God, he's dead. Evan is dead," came the reply.

"Maybe not. Let's get you out of there and see what we can do. Help is coming." Robert's voice was calm. "Come on now, push. That's it."

The young man pushed from inside and the door opened. He climbed out, tears streaming down his face. Jen thought he looked about twenty years old, and the tears made him seem even younger and more vulnerable.

"He can't be alive. There's no way. Look at him." Free of the car, the young man was shaking from cold and shock.

Robert put both hands on the car and hoisted himself up.

"Give me a push, Jen."

She grabbed his legs and shoved upward. He wriggled into the car. Jen couldn't follow him. She put one foot on a tire, clutched the edge of the window, and dragged herself up. Pebble-shaped glass bits were scattered across the fender. She lay full-length over them and looked into the wrecked car through a jagged hole in the shattered windshield. The freed young man wiped away his tears, then climbed up and lay beside her, still choking back sobs as he looked inside at his friend.

Headlights tilted at weird angles and illuminated the scene in streaks and patches. Inside the car, Robert curled at an angle behind the body of a young man of perhaps nineteen. There was grey paint in the boy, Evan's, hair. The actor was little more than a child, yet he had just played the part of an aging artist. Debris and junk of the sort college kids collect in back seats had been thrown throughout the car and then come to rest in the downhill side of the passenger compartment. A strip of light lay across Robert and the face he cradled in his hands, a face with blood trickling from the nose and mouth, with one eye dangling sightless from its socket. Robert pressed what looked like a wadded T shirt against the side of the boy's head.

"He's breathing, Jen."

The words left Robert's lips in little puffs of vapor. He bent close to the bloodied face.

"Say your lines," he commanded.

An eyelid fluttered.

"Do you hear me? We've got a show to do. Say your lines," Robert insisted.

The boy began to mutter.

"I can't hear you. Speak up. Enunciate."

The good eye opened. The young actor looked at Robert and began to speak. Jen could hardly believe what was happening. The lines came forth, mumbled in places, but coherent.

"So, now, what do you see?—Be specific. No, be exact. Be exact—but sensitive. You understand? Be kind. Be a human being, that's all I can say. Be a human being for once in your life!"

He stopped, and Robert urged him on. "Go on, go on. Keep going. What's next?" Evan mumbled something unintelligible, then he spoke clearly again.

"There is only one thing I fear in life, my friend...one day the black will swallow the red."

Line after line the actor spoke, blood bubbling between his lips. It

43

seemed to Jen they had been there for hours when she heard sirens. Seconds later they were surrounded by state patrol officers and paramedics.

"Help us. There's somebody badly hurt here," she told them. The young man beside Jen slid himself to the ground. An officer helped Jen climb down, and minutes later men lifted the student from the wreckage and placed him on a gurney. Robert crawled out behind him. Both his hands were covered in blood; blood was smeared down the front of his coat.

"Are you alright, sir?" A paramedic supported Robert until he was steady on his feet.

"Yes, thank you. It's not my blood."

"Come on, let's go back to the car and get out of this wind," Jen told Robert. She put her arm around him and felt him shivering. He pulled a handkerchief from his pocket, wet it in the snow, and wiped off his bloody hands, which were already blue from the cold. They walked together, their breath visible before them. Jen's knees had begun to ache. They climbed back into the car and Robert pulled her onto his lap, wrapping his arms around her. They snuggled together for warmth, Robert's head on Jen's shoulder. For a long time neither spoke. They simply sat there, holding one another in the car that, although damaged, still provided shelter from the freezing darkness.

"I was so afraid he would die," Robert said at last. "His blood, you know? It was so warm and red. His blood convinced me that I could keep him alive. No one with blood like that could stop living."

"None of us is ready to stop living," she told him, and she stroked his steel-grey hair.

Monsters

Sara Ross Witt

Right now, my sisters, Anne and Cass, are trying to take a picture of one of the twins naked. They know he is embarrassed and his trauma is funny to them. I think this is strange, though I am staring at them as I stare at the TV on Saturday mornings, in a cartoon coma.

I will be ten at the end of the summer. My four older half-siblings—twin brothers and two sisters—will be gone by then. They will go home, a three-hour drive south of here, to live in their big house, retreating into their large individual bedrooms. They don't have to share. Their father and stepmother will excitedly greet them. (I know because I've watched their reunion from Mom's car.)

Confused? Yeah. Me too. Let me explain: my mother married her first husband and had those four older kids I just mentioned, my half-siblings who visit us for a few weeks every summer and for certain holidays. Mom divorced their dad, married my dad, had Jonathan and I, then divorced my dad. I am the youngest of six kids. We're the poor ones.

After their visit it will just be Jonathan and me. I'll have a quiet birthday with him, my mother, Granny and Dad. Dad will be apologetic for avoiding us for the last half of summer. He doesn't like our older half-siblings, the leftovers from mother's first marriage. That's what he calls them. Jonathan and I like them, I think. They are dangerous and sometimes mean; they enjoy embarrassing each other, playing pranks on one another, and picking on our neighbors. They are without mercy. We now have a feud going with the kid living two houses down. One of the twins, I cannot remember which one, threw a mud patty at him. He cried. My siblings found this very funny, except Jonathan, who hung back from the group and forced a smile. He was doing that for show, I knew, because if he didn't they'd tease him, call him fatty.

Like me, Jonathan knows that we aren't the popular kids in our school and we have to be at the bus stop in the fall with that boy. We live in a run-down duplex, we wear hand-me-downs (do you know how traumatic it is for me, a little girl, to wear her brother's oversized old clothes?), our mother works two jobs "just to feed us," and we receive donated gifts for Christmas.

Anne and Cass have Jamie cornered in the bathroom; the other twin, Will, as always is trying to defend his brother. The girls are pushing the bathroom door in; the boys are holding it closed. Hinges groan from their abuse. Anne and Cass are cackling because Jamie is screaming high-pitched and girly.

I am sitting on my hands. Grandma told me that is what she had to do while growing up. "Children were seen and not heard," she said. I don't know how sitting on her hands made her quiet.

"Okay, Jamie. We give up," Cass calls. She shoves the camera into the waistband of her white and red shorts. Anne has a matching pair because my mother likes dressing all four of her children alike—the girls in matching outfits as well as the twins. Jonathan and I sit shabby next to them. We don't have a matching anything.

"Give me my clothes," Jamie yells. Anne throws them at the door,

46

the belt buckle smacking the hollow wood, a dull thud. Jonathan jumps at the sound.

"Come on, guys. Leave Jamie alone," he says.

"Quiet, Johnny or I'll give you another titty twister," Cass tells him. He drops the Atari controller and covers his chest with his arms.

The bathroom door opens a crack, Jamie's hand darts out feeling along the carpet for the crumpled clothes. The girls rush the door, crashing into it. There's a loud noise, the splitting of wood. We all start screaming.

Through our screams, we hear it: the sound of the garage door lifting, a car engine shutting off. It's late and dark. Our mother is home from work.

Now the six of us huddle in the bedroom Jonathan and I share. He is hiding beneath his blue E.T. covers trying to cry without notice. Anne and Cass are squished together on my twin bed. They aren't crying but I can tell Cass wants to. Her eyelids blink rapidly. Will and Jamie are stretched skinny beside each other on the floor, lips in stiff straight lines. I am standing by the door, fingering the edge of my nightgown, a faded pink lace. I have been wearing it for three years, it is too short really to be an appropriate nightgown—Lori Denson told me so when I wore it to my one and only slumber party last year. A pity invite for the poor girl.

There's no space for me. They never make space for me even though it's my room, my bed. As the youngest, I'm automatically pushed out. I'm pretty sure Cass, or maybe it was Anne, said I shouldn't own anything anyway. They don't trust me.

I open the door. "Going to tattle, Chrissy?" Anne asks.

"No," I say as I slam the door.

"Do not slam doors in this house!" Mother screams from her bedroom. Her door is also closed.

"Sorry," I mumble into it. "Can I come in?"

I press my ear against the door. I listen for movement. I tap the wood again with my tiny fist. "Please?"

My stomach knots a hundred times before she opens it. Even though her eyes are puffy, red and rubbed raw from her tears, she is beautiful. Her hair is white blonde and curled daintily against her chin. Her teeth are capped pearly-whites; she flashes them often, especially when she laughs. She has a deep belly laugh that bursts forth from her wide-open mouth and travels around her shiny perfect teeth. People recognize her laugh. It is an infectious laugh. Her eyes are lawn bright green. My eyes are brown and my hair is an even lazier shade of brown.

People tell me I look like Anne but Anne looks like Mom, and I know I am not pretty like she is. Jonathan and I are dark like our Dad; dark hair and dark eyes, with soft edges and puffy cheeks.

I sit next to her on the bed as she cries fresh tears. "My children are monsters."

She lumps me with them. I want to say that I was being good, that even Jonathan was trying to calm those four. We did not break the door. But that would be tattling, and she wouldn't believe me anyway.

"I'm going to send them home. I'll call their father in the morning."

"Please don't," I say.

"Why not?" She is furious that I contradict her, I defend them, but I know this is what she wants, what she expects. This routine happens every visit—trouble ensues, mother yells, tells them she will send them home to their father, I talk her out of it, and the next day she is all smiles for them. She cooks them breakfast, bacon and eggs with buttery toast. They will snicker at me and call me a traitor, even though I saved them, and Mother won't come to my defense because she hates me a little bit too. Jonathan and I are her mistakes.

She has told me she never loved my dad. God, that hurts. Why tell me? I was eight, I think, when she first said that. See, Mom thinks it's okay to say these things to me because, as she says, I have psychic talent. According to her, I can tell how people are feeling, what they are thinking, and what will happen to them in the future. She believes this about me because that's what her psychic friend Dolores told her. That my spirit is blue or something, and now I have to hear things that hurt.

"Because they're good. They're having fun," I say. "They love you."

"They love their father. They don't even know me."

"No. They hate him, they told me. He drinks."

Mother nods, "I know. He's an alcoholic. He's no good for them. The courts gave him custody because his parents have money." This story I have heard many times before.

"Cass's crying," I tell her.

"Really?" Mom asks. "She doesn't want me to send her home?"

I shake my head.

"That door is going to cost a lot to replace. How am I going to afford that? I can't tell the landlord, either. He'd kick us out for sure. I'm making friends here, Christine. We need this." Then, tucking herself into bed she says, "I'll think about it. I'll call Dolores in the morning." She turns off the light. "Go to bed, Chrissy."

I maneuver out of her dark room. There is nowhere for me to sleep in my room; Jonathan and the four having fallen asleep despite their fears. I walk in the dark downstairs and curl into a ball on the couch.

I wake up cold, curled in the same tight ball. The twins at the end of the couch are playing Atari. Jonathan is watching, giving commands they shrug off. I unfold from my cramped position, mumbling "ow."

"Should've used a blanket," Will says. His eyes never leave the TV.

I want to say *There weren't any extra blankets, asshole.* Mother calls us that when she's upset, "her asshole children." But I keep my mouth shut and walk past the duct taped bathroom door into the kitchen. Cass is helping with breakfast, carefully breaking the eggs over the hot skillet. Mother, her arm around Anne's shoulder, is singing along to the radio as she presses bacon into the pan.

Every morning I eat breakfast of bitter oatmeal. I hate oatmeal, always have. Mother never comes to Parent's Day at my school. She gave my snail away to that fat snob Bryan McBibb! I think all of this as I watch their happy little scene and I want to throw myself onto the ground, have a good childish tantrum, the kind I've only ever witnessed at the mall. Instead, I stick out my tongue at their cute little scene and march to my room.

It is empty. And quiet.

I'm still cold so I tug on jeans and a sweatshirt. I pick up the phone to call Dad and complain. I dial the first three digits: eight–nine–zero. By the time the dial completes the rotation from zero, I hang up. If he answered, he would tell me to have fun and not to worry. He would say I will be okay. I want to tell him it will never be "okay," even after my half-siblings have gone home. I have a fear of the future, of my whole life being lived in this cramped, noisy, moldy house, never escaping. My chest starts beating quickly. I feel my breath coming out funny. I sit down on my bed and rest my head on my knees. Nobody knows I get like this—freaked out.

My sheets smell of the sisters' perfume, bubblegummy sickly sweet. I pull my pink blankie from under my bed, shoved there when they arrived two weeks ago, and wrap it around my head. It smells of me. I feel calmer with each inhale. I pull my book from under the bed, too. *Bridge to Terabithia* feels warm in my hand, and I read until my eyelids droop, then I put it next to my blanketed face and fall asleep.

I'm hanging from a rope over a black gulf. The edge that I must have jumped from has disappeared. The other edge that I was jumping towards has also disappeared. My dream world is fading. There's a black noise that's eating it.

There it is again. I hear it more fully. It's not just a noise: it's several voices. I cannot keep pretending my dream hasn't been interrupted by the outside world. My eyelids flick open and I scan the room for Jonathan's digital clock. *8:00 p.m.* How did I sleep through the entire day?

I dangle my one arm and one leg out of bed. Moving feels like a chore. Staying in bed and finishing my book is appealing, but those aren't just loud voices, they're sharp yells. Then I hear Cassie's scream, it's really scary and animal, and I'm on my feet and hopping down the stairs cricket-quick, blinded because every light in the house is on. The sound is chaotic, I can't understand a word of the accusations, but my eye catches the shoe in Cass's hand and I feel in my stomach that this is not going to end well. Cass punches hard like a boy. She once beat the crap out of some girl in a bathroom for poking fun at Anne.

It's one of the twins she's aiming at now. "Watch out!" I yell to Jamie. He ducks as the shoe blasts out of her hand. It sounds like someone hammering a rock when it hits the wall; it goes right into the wall, it just digs in.

"Damn," Jamie wails. Of course they've all forgotten themselves, because there's Mom, fuming, her jaw clinched, her brow furrowed. I feel like I can see every bone and vein in her face. Why, or how, did she let them get so out of hand? She stalks over to the shoe buried in the wall; glares at it, like her stare will make it go away.

Jonathan walks over and pops the shoe out of the wall. I can see splintered wood and crackling drywall and cotton candy insulation. He drops the shoe in front of the hole, wipes his hands on his jeans, like touching it will mean he did it. Jamie's on the verge of tears, and of course Will is pissed; pretty soon he'll be shouting and throwing his fists. I'm still not sure why Cass wanted to hurt Jamie so bad.

I look back at Cass. She's just shaking, sort of how the tree in our front yard moves during a storm, like it might snap. I watch sort of hoping that it will snap. Cass is looking at Mom. Mom is looking at the wall. Anne has her arms crossed, her hip cocked to the side, her toe tapping. Her face is calm, like this happens all the time, and with those four I imagine that it does, and there's a tug on her mouth, she might laugh.

God. Please don't laugh. Please don't laugh.

Mom is quiet. We're waiting for the eruption, for the screaming, for the threats. For the hitting. I wasn't here. I don't know what happened but I'd better think of something quick, something that will soothe the situation.

She's still not speaking—the angry hum of the appliances filling the space. Mom grabs her car keys from the hook by the door, walks into the garage, and leaves the door to the house wide open. She never does that. She never does this; no talking, just walking away. I look at Anne, who raises her eyebrows and shrugs. She follows Mom. I go too, closing the door behind me, and get in the backseat of the car, just as Mom backs down the driveway. I hope Jonathan is okay with Cass and the twins. They were about to kill each other but this—being in the car with Mom and Anne—feels much scarier.

I close my eyes for the entire drive, which isn't very long. I don't want to see how we're getting to wherever we're going because that feels safer. Anne hasn't said anything, which is a relief because she tends to say things that piss Mom off. Everything pisses Mom off. But this quiet is killing me.

I peek out the window. It's not pitch black yet. Just a summer dark that starts gray, goes to purple, and then finally races to black. Right now we're in purple and I can see curved headstones and shadowy statues.

We're in the middle of Blendon Cemetery. Mom turns off the car, gets out and picks her way amongst the graves. Then suddenly she's on her knees near a grave in the dark.

"This is creepy," Anne says. "What the hell's she doing?"

Getting out of the car, I follow Mom's path. I don't know what she's doing, but I feel like I can't sit in the car with Anne. There's a sense of adventure, and also, separation, the need to pull away from Anne, Cass, and the twins, to take back my summer.

Sliding along the grass, careful to avoid walking over graves, I find Mom kneeling by a new plot—just a metal marker bearing a name I can't read in the darkness and a mound of soil. Her hands are in the dirt, she's looking up at the sky, waiting. I'm used to this, Mom's bizarre meditative moments: Indian dances, séances, taking a day off school to drive two states west to have her aura cleansed. Trying to trance so she can have an out-of-body experience. Writing fake checks to herself and hiding them for good fortune. This is almost a normal Saturday night for me.

"What are you doing?" Anne asks, finding us as the sky turns all black and I finally notice the moon. It seems to hang low, a pendant.

"I'm gathering dirt," Mom says.

"What the hell for?"

"For a curse."

I get on my hands and knees to help her remove dirt from the fresh grave. The soil feels like cookie dough in my hand, wet, as though it has recently rained. It hasn't rained here in weeks. If he was buried today, could the tears have soaked the ground or is it juice from the dead? I've never been to a funeral and have only visited cemeteries during daylight. Every horror movie I've ever watched is playing through my brain. I shudder.

Stop it, brain.

"Mom, this is fucked up." Anne says. She must get away with cursing at her dad's home. Mom usually never allows it but she doesn't stop shoveling handfuls of dirt into a little brown paper bag. "This is crazy," she says. I hear how frightened Anne is. There's a tremble in her voice. "Dad's right. You're nuts."

She walks toward the cemetery gate. "Where are you going?" Mom asks.

"Home!" Anne yells back. "To Dad!"

I'm guessing Anne can make the walk back to our house easily; we've ridden our bikes to the cemetery many times.

"Christine, we're going to spread this on Chuck's welcome mat," Mom says. "We're going to leave a message to all who enter his home that he is a false man."

"You mean a liar?"

"A false man."

I don't really understand what she means. I've met Chuck once; I know he is a real man. I also know he is married but he told my mother he loved her. The one time he came over to our house, he told Mom that he was going to leave his wife. She and Chuck held hands and kissed. I was upstairs in my room but I could hear their talking and their laughter and imagined how they embraced, then they called me downstairs and I saw that my imaginings were true. "Tell her, Chuck," Mom encouraged. "Tell her."

"I'm going to marry your mom. I'm going to live with you, be like your dad. 'Kay?"

"Okay," I said, though I knew no one would be like my dad. My dad is quiet and sweet and silly and teaches me new words from the dictionary. Words like *ennui* because I am always telling him I'm bored, even when I'm not. Chuck was loud and had no sense of humor. He pretended to like us. I suspected like my father he would have a hard time with "other people's children."

Chuck went home the next morning to "get his stuff." He and his wife made up so he broke it off with Mom. That was a year ago. Since then, if a car pulls into our driveway and then backs out, she goes to the window and wonders if it was Chuck thinking about coming back to her. Or if the phone rings but no one is on the line, she thinks it was Chuck checking on her.

Now we're driving the voodoo dirt to Chuck's home. My hands are definitely being sat upon. I peer at the grave dirt in the back seat. Every time I look back I expect to find the ghost sitting there, the owner of that sacred dirt, and he'll be mad because we stole something from him. We stole his peace. He just wanted to pull the dirt over him like a heavy quilt, we took it away. I worry he'll haunt us for the rest of our lives.

She turns off the headlights as we enter Chuck's cul-de-sac. We park near the entrance of the street, darting our eyes from lit window to window. There's an upstairs light on at Chuck's house, she tells me. She opens her door, I get out too. I stand there, in eighty-degree heat, the heat from the sidewalk pushing up against my legs, crawling on my skin like spiders, yet I shiver. I'm holding the bag of dirt, it's damp, and I feel cold to my bones. Mom cuts through yards to avoid the street lights and sidles up against his house. I mimic her every movement, though I am shaking and the bag feels heavy, feels a ton. I have never lifted anything so heavy. My arms ache.

She whispers in my ear, "Christine, you've got to do it. I can't walk past his house. I'll be seen through the window."

"No one's downstairs. The lights are off," I say.

"You never know."

"You could crawl."

"I don't think—"

I cut her off. This is probably a defining moment that will be recounted to her psychic friends for the next ten years, but I don't give a damn. I am not cursing Chuck. "If I do it, the curse won't take. I'm not the one he upset, it was you. You definitely have to do it. But I'll...I'll help you."

In the darkness I can't see her face but I know she's giving me the same look she gives me when I predict her future the way she wants to hear it. "You're right. You're absolutely right," she finally says.

We crawl between his bushes through mulch, our knees pierced by the wood, splinters in our hands. We shake the bag over his front porch and really push the grave dirt into the cement. The whole time I tell myself not to think a single bad thought about Chuck or anyone.

We crawl back to the side of his house, stand up and start running. The ghost is behind us. I can feel its breath on my shoulders and if I look back, he will swallow me taking me straight to Hell. I wrench open the car door and jump on the seat with my eyes closed. I don't open them again until we're out of his neighborhood.

"I'm afraid to look in my rearview mirror," Mom says.

"I was afraid to open my eyes when we were running," I say. "I didn't fall. I thought I would trip and fall."

"No, you didn't fall." She says. Then she laughs her deep belly laugh, and I turn to look at her fully, see the glint of her white teeth. "Do you think Anne walked all the way to her Dad's?"

I'm supposed to say *I'm sure she's waiting for us at the house.* I don't. She's their mother; she should want them to stay. I shouldn't have to convince her and I shouldn't have to curse her ex-boyfriends. But I did. And I would do it again. Maybe my siblings are the normal ones and I'm crazy? I don't care. I didn't have one of my "attacks" and I can run. I can run without looking back.

"I think they want to go home," Mom says. "They aren't having any fun. I never realized how different they've become. They're not like us, Chrissy."

Saint Vinny
and the Devil's Brother

Kevin Duffy

I've got seven monitors in front of me. The max. Status symbol. Information is king. Broker on my Bluetooth is bearish on the buck for '09. I don't agree. No trade. I shrug, take the guy on my landline off hold and do a deal with him. Two monitors to the right I see that the Yen has moved up three since the last time I looked. I see on the Bloomberg crawler that the Bank of Japan has scheduled a special meeting next week. They'll take another action. Will it work? No. I go long on July Yen.

The Nerf football that's always flyin' around the trading floor is headed toward Jabba the Hut at the desk next to mine. My left hand's busy doing the trade, but I reach up with my right and deflect it to the row of desks in front of us. Fat nerd with the coke bottle glasses woulda' muffed it anyway. Hell of a trader, though, always neck and neck with me for the highest PnL in our group.

Jabba and me are definitely the studs on this corner of the floor. We've got the stingiest lead trader in the whole damn company and I still pulled down six hundred K last year. I think Jabba was just a little behind me. That might sound like a lot, but it's chicken shit compared to what the partners make. I'm in my third year here, and my goal is to make partner in a year or so. Pretty quick, but it's been done.

I make a few more trades before close, then shut down my book and wait for the day's PnL. While we're waiting, I start to rag Jabba. This is our time to bullshit, 'cause we're too busy making money the rest of the day.

I'm like: "Jabba, have you ever actually *been* with a girl?"

Jabba puts on a big grin. "Saint," he says, "you'd be surprised how much a high six-figure income improves your looks."

I'm like: "Yeah, yeah. Admit it. You got to buy it."

"Don't we all?" he says without losing his grin.

I change the subject to one of our favorite games. "Jabba, who's dumber? Government regulators or ratings analysts?" We've started at the bottom of the food chain, except for *"the muppets"*—the clients.

Jabba says the analysts win, hands down. I play Devil's advocate, "I don't know. The regulators have an office right here in the building and they still don't have a clue what's going on in the company."

"The analysts are still dumber," Jabba says. "Think about it. There's this dude in my apartment building, one floor down. He's unemployed. Used to be a bus driver."

"So what," I say.

"Well, he just bought a co-op on the Lower East Side. The bank not only lent him the money, they lent him the down payment. They'll lend money to *anybody.* What do they care? They just sell the mortgage to somebody who bundles a bunch of these shaky loans up into bonds. And the analysts are saying these are safe investments. The safest—triple-A.*"

"You're right, the analysts are dumber," I concede.

Jabba gets serious and tells me the smart money is betting against these crappy bonds. "I'm putting my own jack in it. I hope you are."

"Yeah," I lie, "as much as my lifestyle permits."

All of us prop traders like to brag about how we're at the top of the pecking order.

I tell Jabba, "About a month ago I'm talkin' to this distant cousin at a family wedding. He's from Ohio or Iowa or some damn place like that, and is in B school out there. He's all impressed that I work on Wall Street. He says he's gonna get an MBA and try to come out here. I tell him prop trading is where it's at and they don't recruit from the B schools. It's mostly engineering and math majors like you and me. MBA gets you some lame ass job like analyst, agency trader or broker. But I tell him they don't take your average engineer who wants to sit in a cubicle and design rocket engines. They want somebody who can think on his feet, do complicated math problems in his head and is super aggressive and a risk taker."

Jabba's like: "So what'd he say?"

"Well, he pretended that he got it, but to be honest, I think he recognizes that he's not cut out for this. Not many are."

At about seven, I go over to Smith and Wolly's, where some of the guys in our group are at the usual table. Spiky Mikey is already there, Al Kada, and a few others. Toxic Tanya is sitting at the corner of the table sippin' on a Pickleback—Jameson's and pickle juice.

"Hey Toxic!" I yell, "Show more cleavage!"

"Not for you losers," she fires back. She's one of the few chicks on the floor, and they're all tough bitches like her. Not anyone you'd want to date. They'd cut your balls off—which is why they're good traders.

The table has already polished off a bottle of Poligny Montachets, and they're starting on another. They'll be poundin' down a whole bunch of appetizers, steak and lobster and a lot more two hundred dollar bottles of wine before the night's over—buncha young guys with more money than they know what to do with. I order a club soda and a light seafood pasta dish. I'm like: "You assholes are gonna come in hung over again tomorrow and I'll smoke your asses, as usual."

"Sure, Saint," says Mikey. "Listen to Mr. Healthy Lifestyle." He puts two fingers up to his nose and makes sniffing sounds.

"Hey." I say. "Alcohol puts you to sleep. Blow keeps my mind racing, like I want it to."

And so goes the juicer versus doper debate. Both sides are right. We're all pissin' away our money and wreckin' our health. The only smart one is Jabba. Every night he gets take-out Chinese and goes back to his apartment to play *Call of Duty*.

I cruise over to the bar area, where I see my main man's gold chain before I see him.

I call out, "Sergei! *Zdrasvatye,* Bro!"

"*Zdasvetye, Tovarisch,*" he says with a big smile.

Having exhausted my knowledge of Russian, we get down to business. We go outside, get in his Carrerra and take a little ride. I leave ten sleeves on his lap and he leaves ten grams of high-grade blow on mine. Back at the restaurant, I go in the men's room and do a line, and then I'm back at the table.

About nine o'clock I get a text from Amy: "Whr RU?"

She's this chick I've been dating about a month. Lives all the way out in Queens. I get my Beemer Z5 from the valet, head out through the Midtown Tunnel and get on the L.I.E. I'm makin' good time until I get stuck behind some blue-haired fossil in a granny wagon—maroon Crown Vic. I'm ridin' her ass and laying on the horn, but she's not speeding up. Probably can't hear me. I see a small opening on the right and cut off a soccer mom in an SUV. She flips me the bird. I flip her back.

But I'm around the old coot, and the lane ahead is wide open. I gun it.

I glance in my rear view mirror. Flashing lights about a mile back.

Nothing unusual. I glance back again. They're getting closer! My throat tightens. *Is he after me?* He moves into my lane. I lighten up on the pedal. Maybe he hasn't clocked me. No such luck. He's crowding in on me. *If he finds my stash I'm in deep shit...*

My heart is pounding like a snare drum. Easy—coolness under pressure. That's what makes me good at what I do and that's what I need now. I ease over onto the berm and crunch to a stop. I switch off the CD player, snap on my never-used seat belt, fish five crisp sleeves out of the center console and put 'em in my wallet next to where I keep my registration. I put my wallet away. I make as little movement as I can while I'm doing all this.

The cop sits in his car for what seems like forever, but he finally comes over to me. He shines his flashlight around the front seat area of my car for a few seconds.

"Take those fancy sunglasses off!" he barks.

A detail I forgot. I slide off my Louis Vuitons.

"License!"

I hand him my license and he studies it for about a minute. "You're a Wall Street trader, right?"

"Yes, sir."

"Figured as much. Twenty four year old kid with a car like this either has a rich daddy, or he's a trader or drug dealer. You're not preppy enough to be Ritchie Rich and if you were a drug dealer, you'd be wearin' sweats and sneakers instead of that designer shirt and fag-ass Italian loafers."

Good, I'm thinking. *This guy's no straight arrow. He just might go for the C-notes.*

"Registration!"

I hold my wallet up near the window and fish around for the registration. "It's in here somewhere," I say. Meanwhile, the sleeves are sticking out.

He snatches the bills and stuffs them in his shirt pocket.

"Do you know you were doing ninety in a sixty-five zone?" he asks.

"No officer, I had a lot on my mind and just lost track of my speed."

"Well, Mr. Vincent Santamaria," he says, "you better slow it down. You just might kill yourself and some innocent people."

"Yes, sir," I say in my best ass-kissing voice.

He starts to turn like he's leaving, then he says, "Just one more thing."

He leans his head forward and crooks his index finger a couple of inches in front of his mouth and wiggles it, like he wants to whisper a secret in my ear. I lean my head toward him, and in a flash he wheels around and smashes his elbow into the left side of my face. Bright lights flash in my head and I feel an explosion of pain. In spite of myself, tears are rollin' out of my eyes. I cringe, waiting for another smack, but it doesn't come. I open my eyes and in the side-view mirror I see his fat ass waddling away, radio on his left hip and gun on his right. Without turning his head, he yells, "Something to remember me by, you little prick!"

I'm shaking from shock and red with rage at the sadistic bastard. My jaw feels like it's on fire and blood is dripping from my mouth. I reach in and find one of my upper teeth loose. Another comes out in my hand. *Goddamn!* To get my head right, I get out my hand mirror, roll up a bill and do a line. After a while, I realize I better get back on the road, or I'll draw another cop. I text Amy: "B L8. Xplain L8r."

Back on the freeway, I start thinking a little more philosophically. *What made him do that? Was he dishin' out his own punishment? Is he jealous of some little prick who makes ten times his salary?* Whatever, I got off with a sock in the jaw and a five hundred dollar donation. I could be on my way to prison.

By the time I reach Amy's apartment, I'm back in a good mood. I sprint up the back stairs and knock. Through the window I see her and Raj, her roommate's boyfriend, at the dinette playing some board game.

Amy has red hair, supermodel looks and an awesome python tat that runs across her back from her left shoulder to her right butt cheek. When she opens the door she says "Omigod! Vinny! What happened to you?"

"I got smacked by a cop," I tell her. My jaw is swollen the size of a softball and a little blood is still trickling from my mouth. I hold out the missing tooth in my left hand.

She's like: "EEEW! Smacked by a cop? Why?"

"He stopped me for speeding and I guess I rubbed him the wrong way."

"You should file a complaint against him," she says. "Did you get his badge number?"

I start giggling. I can't help it. I manage to choke out, "I'm goin' to file a complaint against some crooked, sadist cop who already knows my name, address, the car I drive and license number?"

Amy furrows her brow. "Why do you say he's crooked?"

I say, "Well, because he hit me." Not that great, but she buys it.

Amy is a nurse, and has lots of meds at home, so she gets to work. She cleans the blood out of my mouth and swabs it with Novocain, then some sticky stuff to stop the bleeding. She's got some super-duper pre-scription Tylenol and I take a couple.

After everybody gets over the cop story, we're sitting around the di-nette and I take a closer look at the board game Amy and Raj were playing. It's cardboard, but looks like old weathered wood. It's got the alphabet written in old-fashioned letters, and below that the numbers zero through nine. In the upper left corner there's a full moon and the word "Yes" and in the right corner a crescent moon and star and the word "No." Under the numbers it says "Good Bye." There's a little yellow plastic thing shaped like a heart, with legs and a round clear plastic window in the middle.

"Is that a *Weegie* Board?" I ask. I've got some memories of nerds playing this at college.

"Actually, it's a *Wee-ja* Board," says Raj. He points to the top of the board where it says "OUIJA" "'*Oui*', as in French for 'yes', and '*Ja*', as in German for 'yes,'" he explains.

When Raj talks, I listen. He's Indian, second generation, and he knows *everything*. Dude should totally go on *Jeopardy*. He'd clean up. He's got his Masters in advanced math, and is as good at it as I am, but he also knows all the other stuff—languages, literature, you name it. He just got his Ph.D in Classical Studies from Queens College. He's a graduate assistant over there, but figures he'll be getting tenure soon, 'cause he's a friggin' genius.

"How do you play?" I ask. I'm not familiar with any game that isn't electronic.

Amy shows me. She puts the heart thing in the middle of the board, and puts the fingers of her right hand on it, then asks me to do the same. "Touch it very lightly," she instructs me. "Now we ask it questions."

She asks the Ouija, "Does Vinny have other girlfriends?"

The yellow heart thing kind of floats over to "No," which happens to be true at the time.

I'm like: "You were pushing it!"

"No, I wasn't. Were you?"

"No," I tell her. "I swear I wasn't."

She's like: "That's how it works. It just moves! I didn't think I believed in spirits, but now I'm not so sure."

"It's psychophysiological," says Raj, "the ideomotor effect. Body movements can be independent of conscious thoughts or emotions, you know. It's very well documented."

64

The dude knows everything.

Amy's like: "Anyway, I'm glad you don't have other girlfriends."

Now she asks it to spell out an answer. "When is Raj going to get tenure?" Yellow heart moves around from letter to letter spelling *A-U-G-U-S-T.*

Raj tells us that's when the committee votes. This impresses me, since neither Amy nor I knew that. I'm getting some respect for this Ouija, whatever it is.

She asks it a few more romance questions, like whether Raj is going to ask her roommate Suzie to marry him. Ouija says, *Yes.* Raj is like: "Don't tell her."

After a while, I say, "Let's try this. Should I go long or short on '09 Euros?" Damn thing spells out *S-H-O-R-T.*

I try again, "I went long on July Yen today. Was I right?" Ouija says, *Yes.*

I'm getting some more good intelligence from the spirit when Suzie walks in.

"Hah, guys, whatch y'all doin?" she asks. Suzie is a real trip. She's a hick from Tennessee or Georgia or some damn place, and she's a sure-enough fundamentalist Christian. No drugs, liquor, tobacco, nothin'. The only thing her religion doesn't seem to forbid is acrobatic sex with Raj and two or three other guys she's got on the line. Raj knows about the other dudes and is cool with it—a real open-minded guy.

Suzie comes over to the table and her eyes get as big as saucers. She starts flapping her hands up and down and screaming, "That's a Ouija board! It's the *Divil!* Git it out of here!"

Raj tries to calm her down, but it doesn't work. She runs into her room and slams the door.

Raj goes over and tries the door, but it's locked. "C'mon, baby!" he pleads. "It's just a toy!"

"Go away, you Godless heathen!" Suzie screams through the door, "I'm not coming out 'till you get that outta' here!"

It's true. Raj is an Atheist. His mom's a Buddhist and dad's a Hindu. How he got hooked up with Suzie is a mystery.

Amy seems a little weirded out. "Do you really think it's the Devil?" she asks.

I'm like: "Beats me. Let's ask it." So we ask Ouija straight out, "Are you the Devil?" It immediately floats over to *No*.

This seems to calm Amy down, but I'm not so sure. Would the Devil tell the truth about whether he's the Devil? We ask, "Who are you?"

It spells out *W-I-L-L-I-A-M-F-U-L-D*.

Raj is still trying to sweet talk Amy out of her room. I yell for him to come over.

"Ouija says he's William Fuld. Who the hell is that?" I ask.

Raj is like: "He's the father of the Ouija. He popularized it and marketed it in the early twentieth century. By the way, that's a common Ouija answer."

I'm like: "Never heard of him." Then, thinking out loud, I say, "We've got a Fuld on Wall Street."

"Yes," says Raj, "Richard Fuld, CEO of Lehmann Brothers." Again, I'm impressed. I couldn't tell you who the president of Queens College is.

Raj says, "I'm afraid I'm going to have to get rid of this thing if I want to see Suzie tonight." He yells that he's throwing the Ouija away.

Suzie yells, "Not innywhere around here! You maght as well leave now and dump it somewhere on your way home. I really don't feel lahk seein' you any more tonaght."

Raj rolls his eyes. He boxes up the board and tucks it under his arm. I'm sure he has no intention of dumping it. "Can I call you tomorrow?" he shouts.

A long pause. "Maybe," she calls in a pouty voice. That's good enough for Raj, and he splits.

Amy brings out a pillow and blanket and makes up a little bed for me on the couch. She sits down on the floor and starts gently brushing my hair away from my forehead and saying "Poor Vinny." So, neither Raj or me is gettin' any tonight. He's in the doghouse and I'm an invalid. I flip on the Yankees game and start watching it, but my eyes are getting heavy. Super Tylenol is working. I crash early, about midnight.

It's been a few months since the cop incident. Got the tooth fixed, and Ouija is doing wonders for my PnL, but Wall Street as a whole has gone to shit. Every day another big company whose idiot managers have loaded up on subprime bonds is going down the tubes. We got our own set of idiots. Rumors are flying around the floor that we're all gonna get canned.

Sure enough, here's the e-mail. Meeting in the convo center at ten. Juniors only. High rollers have their own. Everybody's shouting, even louder than usual. Trading stops, which is unheard of.

At ten, we all file into the convo center and take the seats up front. There's two suits up on the stage—one from Legal and one from HR. Some assistants are passing out a one-page printout.

Legal Dude talks first. "Today at eleven o'clock, the company will announce that we will no longer be in the business of proprietary trading." He's reading from the same paper we all have. "That means, unfortunately, that it will be necessary for us to terminate your employment." A loud hum comes up from the audience. He goes on reading, "The reasons for this decision are as follows..."

It's spelled out on the paper, in corporate speak. The company is "on the verge of insolvency," they're talking with "high government officials" and "other financial institutions" to "explore solutions." There's a "perception" among these officials and "others" that proprietary trading that may take actions that are "inconsistent with the core business" is a "conflict of interest." "We don't agree, but…" blah, blah, blah.

I can't take it anymore. I yell out, "Why don't you cut all the bullshit and tell it like it is. You're cavin' to a bunch of bureaucrats who can't find their asses with both hands, and you're throwin' us under the bus!"

Legal Dude is not amused. What do I care? What are they gonna do, fire me?

Dude is like: "What's your name?"

"Vincent Santamaria."

He's like: "*Floor* name!"

"Saint Vinny or just Saint."

"How long you been here?"

"Three years."

He's like: "Well, *Saint,* I was a trader for ten years before I joined the legal department, and I'm not talkin' some half-assed Junior. So let me put this in language you'll understand: The company is fucked if we don't get some help from the feds. The feds think we shouldn't do prop trading. Connect the dots. You're history, asshole!"

HR Dude looks like he's gonna' have a stroke, and all the traders start shouting at once. Toxic yells out over all the others, "What about our bonuses?"

This shuts everybody up, and Legal Dude lapses back into lawspeak. Basically, he says that if there's a bankruptcy, it'll be a long time before we see "some or all" of the money they owe us. Even if there's no bankruptcy, there still may be a problem. Something about bonuses being a "controversial political issue."

This sends the traders into a frenzy. Everybody's pissed off and yelling. Everybody, that is, except Jabba. He's sitting back smiling like he just scored a date with Gisele Bundchen.

See, Jabba used all his savings, plus every nickel he could borrow, to short the subprime mortgage bond market. He found a hedge firm that was loading up on credit default swaps, bought into it, and cashed out of them at just the right time. Then he started shorting financial stocks. Basically, he was betting that the housing bubble would burst, and sink everybody who was loaded up on that crap, which was basically everybody on Wall Street. Course, he wasn't the only one who saw the crash coming, and some of us made a few bucks on it, but nobody put as much dough into it or managed the timing like Jabba. Plus he was real careful about not using insider information. So Jabba could care less that he's being fired. He's a *very* rich man.

It's been about a month since they canned me. Haven't done much about trying to get another job. Some of the guys talked about going into business together, but it wouldn't work. We'd kill each other.

I'm laying around Megan's apartment. She's my latest squeeze. Amy caught me snortin' and gave me a bad time about it, so I dumped her.

I'm doing way too much coke and burning through what dough I have left at a record pace. But today I'm having fun. I'm watching cable news, and they're covering the Senate hearings on the Crash. It's funnier than Ron White and Louie CK rolled together.

Today Dick Fuld from Lehmann is up. This Senator is grilling him, real indignant like. I'm yelling at the TV.

"Yeah, you pompous hypocrite! How much money did *you* get from Wall Street?"

Hypocrite lowers his voice. He's like: "Since 2000, you've been paid more than five hundred million dollars by Lehmann Brothers. Is that correct?"

I'm like: "*Five…Hundred…Million…Dollars!* I get beat up by a cop 'cause I make what this moron loses in the seat cushions every night."

I've seen this kind of testimony before. Pretty soon he'll say what they always say—he didn't know what was going on in his company. Please! Obviously these guys are either lying or incredibly stupid. How's that for a defense: "I'm not a crook, I'm an idiot!"

Course, everybody thinks they're lying, because, well, they couldn't possibly be that stupid, could they? But what people don't know, and what's really scary, is *yes, they're really that stupid…* They're dumber than manatees. They're dumber than stones. You know those people on that show *American Greed* who put all their life savings into bonds, because a crooked preacher tells them they're gonna earn two hundred percent? *They're dumber than those people!*

"Hey Fuld," I yell, "buy *low*, sell *high*! Don't borrow more than you can pay back! Didja miss those classes at B school?"

I text Jabba: "Ultimate Who's Dumber - Wall Street CEOs or the boards that pay em hundreds of millions?"

Comes up: "Delivery failure."

I try his cell. "No longer in service."

Figures. Knowin' Jabba, he's on some South Sea Island playing video games nonstop with topless chicks in grass skirts bringing him root beer floats.

Now they're showing protestors outside the Lehmann building. Raggedy bunch. There's an Asian dude who's a little better dressed than the rest. He's with a tall chick in Daisy Dukes and a halter-top. Camera pans in and *damned if it isn't Raj and Suzie.*

I'm like: "*Give 'em hell, guys!*"

They interview a protester. Dude has purple hair, gauges in his ears and lightning bolt tats going up his neck. Red-rimmed eyes—he's been hittin' the reefer real hard. Dude says all the Wall Street CEOs should be in prison.

I'm thinking, *hey, right now this dude and I have the same occupation—layin' around doin' drugs all day. And he's absolutely right! Assholes should all be in jail—one, for tryin' to steal my bonus; two, for felony stupidity...oh, yeah, and for rippin' off the muppets and wreckin' the economy.*

Camera zooms out and you can see the signs they're carrying. One chick has a sign that says *RICHARD FULD IS THE DEVIL.*

I'm like: *"Naaah...*he's not the Devil. He's the Devil's brother."

Chrysalis

Heather Sinclair Shaw

I'm not a native of the city but I try to act like one. I miss the wildlife mostly. You can walk from the meatpacking district all the way to St. John the Divine and never see a sparrow. At home we mark the change of the seasons by the birds at the feeder—mockingbirds in the spring, red-winged blackbirds in summer, warblers in the fall, and juncos in winter, before the first snow. Here they use the shop windows. And they slap a giant park in the middle of it all like an eloquent apology.

Today I found a caterpillar on the 79th St. transverse through the park. I was on my way to work and the rain was picking up, so I set my bag down under the overpass to pull up my hood. The caterpillar lay fat and sluggish on the wet cement, ready to pupate, its tail-end attached to a smooth twig that had been plucked by a thoughtless child, or the wind, or who knows. Some ignoble mixture of charity and curiosity made me thrust it in my pocket and keep walking.

David got me a job a while back at a little market called The Whole Shebang. It's one of those neighborhood food co-ops that's out to save the earth, and I've been oozing with guilt since I hooked up with that place.

They have an annual 5K called the Tofu Trot to raise money for LGBTQA awareness, and they also have these local simple-living chapters to help you rid your home of plastic and chemicals of every stripe. I've come to tolerate the smell—a strange mix of exotic bulk grains, coffee grounds and nag champa, which is inexplicable because I've never seen any burning incense in the store, but I kind of suspect the cashiers of burning the stuff after-hours to cover up the smell of marijuana and sex. The place is poorly-lit, and the aisles are a little too narrow so you're always bumping into some kind of homeopathic end-cap. Or a clerk with a bull-ring and vegan shoes, like David.

I am an INTJ, a brilliant sub-group of Meyers-Briggs testers who represent only 1.5% of the population. I have a hard time believing that, because no one ever accused me of being brilliant until I took that test online. David is an ENTJ, which I think means that he would make an excellent world leader. My point: if Meyers-Briggs could recommend a grocery store for me I'm pretty sure it would be the opposite of The Whole Shebang. But, I keep working there because I am trying to save the world. That's the short answer. A slightly longer answer is that I love David, and David is trying to save the world. An even longer answer: local economies, pesticide run-off, Big Organic, the ozone layer (Do people talk about that anymore?), fair-trade, banana republics, BPA, child labor, personal responsibility. I could go on but willful ignorance is powerful. Big box stores are destroying the world because they make the world's most powerful influence, the American Consumer, believe that she is not personally responsible for her purchases other than to swipe her credit card and load up her trunk—here is your receipt please do not think about the poor orphans who picked your bananas.

I learned all this, perhaps too quickly, from David. Most people experience gradual enlightenment—they stumble upon some new truth, and they've got a little time to adjust to a lifestyle change before they discover the next thing. But David spews enlightenment like a leaky faucet; before I know it I have enlightenment pooling around my ankles like floodwater. And then it's too late—I can't pretend I don't know. With great knowledge comes great responsibility and all that.

It's helpful to know that David was raised on millet and dried figs, and he's studying entomology to become a professional beekeeper. I studied theater and I was raised on peanut butter and banana sandwiches. The kind with the deliciously creamy peanut butter that can only be achieved with the use of chemical stabilizers, on the white bread that can only be achieved with the use of bleached and bromated white flour. Neither of us could've predicted what an impediment this would be.

The day I found the caterpillar, a new girl came into The Whole Shebang in a dress that looked like it might have been made for Laura Ingalls when she was five, black tights and work boots remarkably similar to a pair that languished in the mudroom at my childhood home. She wore an unflappable expression and vintage jewelry. Her too-short dress made her arms seem unnaturally long, like a praying mantis.

"Can I help you?" I said, which was not what I was trained to say. I was trained to say "Shalom," or "Namaste," or "Blessings," or some equally mystical greeting that I can never manage with the same level of subtle irony that my coworkers—and David—find effortless.

"Is David here?" she said.

"What do you want with David?" I said.

I didn't really say that. I said, "I don't think so," like an idiot. And she looked at me like the idiot I was verifying myself to be, raising her eyebrows to the level of her blunt-cut bangs.

"He isn't," I added. "I'm meeting him at the Met later." And I answered the phone, and turned my back to her. It all felt perfect—subtly affirming my relationship to David and shunning her at the same time. Then I pulled a pencil out of my pocket to take down a number, and both I and the unflappable girl gasped in unison.

There, on the tip of my pencil that was not a pencil but the stick I had forgotten, the caterpillar was gyrating spasmodically. Its skin was peeled back away from its body and a tender, glistening chrysalis was slowly revealing itself.

Recognition, then disproportionate horror, flashed across her face. "Oh my God, why is that in your pocket?" she cried, with the emphasis on "pocket," as though mine might be full of parasitic wasps. Her arms extended forward in a lightning-quick motion as she lunged toward the pupa.

"What are you doing?" I said, jerking backward.

She sidestepped, and for a moment I thought she might try to jump over the counter. "You can't carry a pupating monarch around in your pocket!" She was leaning over the cash register. "Where did you get it? Why didn't you take it to safety?"

"I thought I had," I managed. How did she know it was a monarch?

"Please give it to me." She was very still now, with her hands folded in front of her, predatory. Then it hit me.

"Oh God. You're studying entomology with David, aren't you." I said. She tucked her hair behind one ear, and I tried in vain to read her expression. My confidence faltered, and, as is customary for me in moments of self-doubt, I started to think about bananas.

Bananas have no place in the sustainable lifestyle. They require too many transport resources, and there's too much corruption within the market. I used to dream of flying to South America for a banana vacation in which I would find banana trees growing wild on the sides of the road and I would eat them until I could no longer walk. After I met David, I didn't eat a single banana for two years. Then I had a little episode.

I passed a supermarket and saw them in the window—an exotic yellow hill in the produce section—and I was paralyzed. I forced myself to think about little children with brown faces, picking bananas in the hot sunshine, sweating and being sworn at by an invisible taskmaster. I thought about an evil Banana Republic gunning down some small plantation owner in an invisible South American village. About a giant diesel truck, spewing black smoke, driving a load of bananas from Mexico through the midwest, its grill awash with dead butterflies.

Then I thought of my childhood kitchen table. A green melamine plate bedecked by a tower of soft white sandwich bread, creamy peanut butter and glorious bananas. I thought about chocolate milk, and I snapped. At the supermarket I bought eight bananas, a jar of creamy peanut butter, a loaf of white sandwich bread, a can of powdered chocolate milk mix, a half-gallon of conventional milk from cows leading a wretched life of confinement, and a bag of Cheetos. And soft toilet paper, not the recycled kind. The cashier was so annoyed trying to stuff everything into my floppy hemp bags that she finally gave up and bagged everything else in plastic. By then I was feeling that strange mixture of elation and shame which comes to people who knowingly break the rules they have set for themselves. It feels like winning and losing at the same time.

When David came home I was halfway through my second sandwich. Plastic grocery bags were strewn over the countertop. "Cheetos?" was all he said. I licked my teeth clean behind pursed lips.

The unflappable girl was still sanding there, motionless—waiting for me to make the first move, I could tell. There was something on the tip of my tongue about the folly of ridiculing attempts at goodness that fall short of perfection, about the integrity of the small gesture. Who said that? And who was this girl? In my head, I was feeling INTJ brilliance. I was ranting against elitism, championing the cause of sincerity. It was all happening, in my head.

I said, "I'll leave the chrysalis in the park after my shift."

"Try to find a flowering bush or, if you can, one that will flower in a couple of weeks," she said. "Just don't leave it in your pocket."

Trying to do everything right is so goddamn difficult, like trying to memorize the train schedule. Just when you think you have it figured out, you don't.

I frequently meet David at the Pandora, because that's where we first met. People think it takes a lot to bond two people together, but sometimes you just need one thing. Redon's painting of Pandora is the only thing we agree on at the museum and most other places. When we first met he told me that inside her box there were governments and corporations and pesticides and guns. I don't think he makes much distinction between them. He said hope remained in the box so we could fight. I said if she wanted us to fight, why didn't she let hope out of the box so it could do us some good, and he smiled the Mona Lisa smile of someone who knows everything and gets handed an angle they hadn't considered. We've been meeting at the Pandora ever since. We stand side by side staring at the first woman looking down on her ineffable box while we catch up on the more effable moments of our week.

I kept the chrysalis in my pocket and went on to meet David. He settled into his contemplative stance, and made sure I was doing the same before he spoke. He never looks at me during this strange ritual we've created. Or, he looks at me by looking at the painting. I wonder in these moments what pulls him back to the Pandora over and over again—if it's the closed box, the evil that will escape, the hope that will remain, or me.

"Have you heard of butterfly butter?" he asked finally.

"Butterflies make butter? Wait—please tell me this isn't something we eat."

"No, no, no."

I cast a glance in his direction and followed the line of his unkempt beard, which shifted slightly when he smiled.

"Butterfly butter is what happens inside the chrysalis," he said. "People think caterpillars just hang out in there and sprout wings and a proboscis. But the truth is crazier: they dissolve. Entomologists don't have a name for it so they call it 'butterfly butter'."

I turned toward him, but he continued to stare ahead. I didn't tell him about the chrysalis, because I don't like the way he smirks at me when I make even the most subtle references to fate, synchronicity, karma, whatever.

"Its caterpillar cells break down into a stem cell ooze," he continued, "then reform into butterfly cells—wings, legs, antennae, proboscis, body. Everything is new. But its all programmed in there somehow. The cells know what they're supposed to become."

I reached into my pocket and felt the cool, toughened skin of the chrysalis. I stared ahead and tried to imagine it, translucent and green, hanging from the tree behind Pandora. I imagined it until I saw it, until I could hold it in my vision, and I considered my words. There may have been five minutes of silence between us but to me it was a fullness, an era, the Age of the Caterpillar.

"A girl came looking for you at work today," I said.

David turned to look at me, and I tried in vain to read his expression. I tried to imagine them together at a lab table, her unnaturally long arms brushing his. I thought, *they deserve each other. She'll bite his head off.*

I went back to the park and walked around until I found a large bush in bud. I pulled the twig from my pocket and squatted down in the dirt, thrusting my hands into the wet foliage. There was no good way to attach the twig to the bush, so I nestled it as best I could between two forked limbs, then I took off my coat and sat down in the wet grass. Now I stare. The chrysalis dangles precariously amid the budding branches. I stare at it like David and I stare at the Pandora. I stare until my coat and skirt are soaked through with rain. I stare until I see it, until I can hold it in my vision, and I wait.

Fallen Timbers

S.E. White

In the eighties, my father sold insurance, protection against *those rainy
days*, but it wasn't raining the night he came home from work four hours
late. That night had been clear and dry. He didn't speak for two full days.
His suit that night (the blue pinstripe his father had wanted to be buried
in but Grandma claimed had too much wear left) wasn't even wrinkled
when he seemingly strolled up the sidewalk to the back step, gingerly seat-
ed himself and pulled a baby bird from his breast pocket. He cradled the
bird, closed his hands as if to pray, and sobbed until my mother opened
the screen door and hugged his shoulders. I stayed inside the house and
watched my father through the glass window—his body distorted by a flaw
in the panes. The sight of him is as clear to me now, a woman in her late
thirties, as when I held my breath and watched my insurance salesman
father weep over a baby bird who'd fallen from its nest.

Before that night and our eventual move to Oregon, my father built
model ships in the room at the top of the stairs. He would close the door,
hunch over the bench where he sat walled in by maritime books, X-Acto
knives and long tweezers, and slip bits of wood through the narrow neck of
empty bottles of Southern Comfort. The wind chimes outside the window

played a tune I've stopped dead in traffic remembering.

"People are like ships in bottles," he said once, scolding me for touching things in his hallowed room. He pushed up his wire-rim glasses and looked me squarely in the eyes. "The most beautiful part is what you can see but can never quite touch." He held one of the bottles up to the window and whispered, "They're too fragile to be touched."

That night, after my father gave the bird to my mother as if it were as fragile as one of those model ships, he wandered up the stairs and smashed every ship in a bottle he'd ever built. Splinters of glass sprayed the walls, ships floated on glistening shards, crunched beneath his leather wing-tip shoes. He grabbed one after the other by the neck and shattered them. Hulls, masts, decks no larger than a thumbnail sprinkled onto his desk. I stood at the base of the stairs. My mother was halfway up. She ran her fingers through her short, black hair, fumbled with the buttons on her business suit. She didn't look down at me. I didn't look past her. We both stood staring at the shadows flashing on the white, white ceiling of the room at the top of the stairs.

Two months later, we packed up our lives and drove from Ohio to Oregon where my father with the pale, smooth hands got a job as a logger. The beard he spent days growing was as full and black as the bruise on his right cheek. The only words he ever offered on that crescent slice were, "You should've seen the other guy." I never cared what happened to "the other guy;" all I wanted to know is what happened to my father, the man I'd known.

I was too young at the time, ten years old, to realize what my father might've been going through, and nobody in the early eighties would have considered the idea of "rape," much less of a tryst gone bad. The official statement my mother issued on the subject was that my father had been *mugged.*

"If anyone asks," she told me at breakfast the next morning, "your father was mugged."

Nobody asked. But the people I told at school believed me, or seemed to. I could tell a good lie when I knew it wasn't the truth. The way my mother told me, stern faced, hands wrapped around a steaming mug of coffee, made me think there was more to know. We moved to Oregon two months later. My father stopped selling insurance, stopped building model ships, and simply stopped being the man he was before. My mother grew her short, black hair long, long enough to braid, long enough for my father to touch and lose his hands in. She wore more dresses, quit her job working in a bank, and spent her days at home. From time to time, she would peer out the glass windows and rub her hands against the panes.

We sit, my father and I, on a bench, staring at a piece of land protected and preserved to commemorate a battle that took place across the road. A statue of three men stares off with us. Those men, enemies in the flesh, now stand as brothers in stone. A pioneer with a straggly beard, a muscular native, General "Mad" Anthony Wayne: each looking properly grim. My father is old. Blue and violet veins are pronounced on his pale, scarred hands, each winding around cartilage and bone like the glimpse of a river we see flickering in the distance, beyond a snatch of road and a field overgrown and weedy and not the place where the Battle of Fallen Timber was fought. But this is where it is remembered.

Ten years ago, my son Dane and I moved back to Ohio, brought my father with us. His beard is gone, shaved like it was before he was *mugged.* His chin juts; neck seems unnaturally long and vulnerable. He has little to say to the question I just asked him. *Why did he want to stop here before he and Dane went fishing?*

My father rubs his chin. "Let's just fish."

Dane sits in the parking lot, barely visible beyond the distant glare of the car's windshield; the boat is attached to the back of the car, poles in the backseat. He won't come out of the car to sit with us on the bench. I know he didn't want me to come on this fishing trip. Ever since he was charged with identity theft—using a fake ID, using other people's credit cards—he keeps his distance from me. But, I knew that he would want to fish with his grandfather, so I had to come.

Slowly, I turn my head and stare at my father's crescent scar, listening to sparrows and starlings chirp to one another. Songs of warning.

"Then, let's fish," I reply. He only has a few hours before I have to take him back to the nursing home for dinner.

The muddy, undulating Maumee is close by. It is the river where Wayne's forces camped before the Battle of Fallen Timbers. Rumors claim that Tecumseh had been there. Indians and soldiers fought each other in a grove where the trees had been felled by a tornado. The bark gnarled, scarred: the spot is scenic in a weather-beaten way. Sitting here all these years later, centuries now, that bloodshed feels senseless: bravery or greed? They fought for land that only truly belongs to itself—the weaving of earthworms, tunneling of ants. These trees wait here, as if to outlast us all.

The walk to the car feels like a long one for a man as seemingly fragile as my father. We pass Turkey Foot Rock where Little Turtle stood to rally his troops. Gourds and a few shucks of corn have been placed there as an offering to their memory.

"I proposed to your mother here," my father mumbles through his cracked lips.

I look at him. "I didn't know that, Dad." That's not the story my mother told.

My father nods.

"I thought you popped the question in the middle of a dance floor on New Year's Eve."

His eyes cloud over. He grunts. We come to the parking lot, and he scratches at the crescent on his cheek.

I help my father into the car, allow my fingertips to graze his shoulder blade. I don't know when I ever touched my father—a hug, a peck on the cheek, a random brush of his arm. The last time I touched any man was ten years ago.

My ex-husband had been abusive to our son Dane. He left one night after he slapped Dane, and I finally hit him back. He whipped his belt from its loops, smacked it against the refrigerator. Dane rushed into the kitchen when he heard me tumble into the dishes and drop to the floor. The black leather tip of Danny's belt licked Dane across the face. I balled my fist until the nails bit my palm, and swung. My knuckles cracked, and his crooked front teeth ground across the bone. He blinked, staggering a step or two, then wiped the blood—both his and mine—from his lips.

"Fuck me," the words dripped from his bottom lip.

He grimaced, stared at me like I'd done more than punched him.

That night, he packed his things and left—the screen door softly bumping closed. His golden blonde hair glowed down the sidewalk until he disappeared.

Now, Dane sits with my father in that old red fishing boat. The water is shallow enough at this time of year to almost walk across. I tied my father into a lifejacket despite his grumbling. His calloused hands take hold of one of the poles, and he slips a minnow onto a hook before he drops it through the Maumee's muddy, beige surface. My son watches him, looks at his grandfather to provide a model of manhood for him. He has never said that, nor would he ever say it. But it's in his eyes, the way they follow my father's every move.

My son Dane is almost sixteen, well beyond the age of listening to his mother and well within the age of battling any man in order to prove his own strength to himself. His earring. His tattoo. All of the anger in his face. These things I see reflect what he feels inside, I'm sure. But I can't reach inside him, can't touch what he holds so deeply in those clear, blue eyes. But, with my father, he listens, sits passive, studies.

Together, they drift in a boat, while I dip a pole into the shallow water along the banks. They don't speak to one another. The rippling of the Maumee rushing downstream speaks enough to justify their silence. Dane shifts, runs the back of his hand across his mouth—his father's nervous gesture—but stares hard into the river and clenches his jaw.

Each ripple of the river flashes in the sun like bits of shattered glass. The boat continues to drift downstream. My father looks old, delicate; the sagging skin on his face resembles tissue paper. Trees overhang the boat the farther my father and son float away from me; the leaves cradle flocks of invisible birds, and with each gust of wind, I hear the soft rustling of a lore I can only witness. I realize that the silence between my father and my son is their way of communicating—this is a language I cannot speak, cannot hear.

The gnarled bark of the trees reminds me of Oregon, of my father with the tan, rough fingers, full bushy beard. I hear him. I feel the coolness of his shadow beside me, and I peer upwards into his bearded face as it blocks the sun. He takes my ten-year-old hand, and we stroll together through the Oregon woods.

"Trees are like any other crop," he tells me. "Sometimes they need to be harvested."

He touches the bark, looks down at me and winks.

"Mother Nature doesn't always have the best hygiene," he puffs his chest. "Loggers are like surgeons. You've got to amputate before the limbs get too rotten and useless."

Here in Oregon, he wears every piece of stereotypical flannel his money can buy, leather boots with a bull emblazoned on the tongues. When he comes home at night, he has chips of wood, sprinkles of the insides of these trees on his shoulders, in his beard, on his clothes. He has mud, and occasionally feathers, caked to the soles of his boots—a tree himself.

He drives the Rock Caterpillar, laughs when the other men who work with him call him "Doc," especially when they see him around town after they've spent the night drinking beers and whatever else they did after-hours. In Oregon, he comes home late, later than that night he was *mugged*. Mom waits up for him less and less. At least, she lets him know less and less about how she waits up for him.

I remember the night she sat on the couch, in the dark, wrapped in the seaweed green afghan her mother spent nights knitting years before, the moonlight drenching her shoulders and the black hair she cut that afternoon. My father wanted her to grow it long before the move, so she did. But, that afternoon, she had cut it short, shorter than his own hair.

I see her silhouette through the rungs in the stairway railing—both of us drowning in the darkness.

When the door slams, we both jump. My father has been drinking, still swigs from a bottle of Jack Daniels. His eyes are glassy.

"I don't need you waiting up for me," he says.

"I was worried," she answers.

His hand strokes his full, bushy beard. "I can take care of myself."

She sits silent, tilts her face downward in that "all-knowing" way of hers, in that way I still miss.

"I get home when I get home," he says. "I'm the man of this house."

He stumbles over the coffee table.

"I'm a goddamn logger," he slurs. "If I can handle a saw, I can handle being out after dark. I don't need my wife waiting up for me."

This man is not my father. My father, who sold insurance, with the pale, smooth fingers, never raised his voice. He wore suits, wing-tipped shoes. He built model ships, enjoyed working in his garden. He wouldn't have moved us to Oregon, or worn flannel, let alone handled a saw. This man is tan, rough, falling, falling towards something he's afraid he'll hit but can't stop himself from reaching out for.

He sits down and starts laughing, pulls out a cigarette, flicks his lighter and laughs some more.

"They hired a woman foreman today," he says.

I cling tighter to the railing. My heart throbs. I cannot breathe.

"What in the hell did you do?" he demands. "What the hell did you do to your hair? You look like a damn man. Why didn't you ask me first?"

"I got a job today, too," she answers, her words measured, voice low.

"You don't need to work."

"I need to get out."

He runs his hand over his face, pulls at his beard. He knocks his boots together in front of his outstretched legs.

"You'll quit," he says.

She looks at him and says, "No."

He twists the wedding ring on his finger, laughs.

"You'll do what I feel is best."

"I moved out here with you because I love you," she says, unwrapping herself, rising to her feet.

He stands, too, stuffs one hand into the front pocket of his tight Levis, the other he hooks onto his belt. He squares himself, leans as if he might uncoil and slap her. I feel trapped behind the rungs.

"And?" he asks.

She lets the afghan fall to the floor. The moonlight catches the white of her eyes as she glances over to where I sit. I crouch down but know it's too late.

"Go to bed," she tells me. Her voice sounds tired, firm. She walks up the stairs and closes the door to their bedroom.

My father stands alone in the living room. He heads for the front door, then stops, turns towards where I'm still crouching on the staircase. He extends his hand to me. I am in my nightgown. My feet feel cold but I go with him—outside the door, outside into the crisp night air, outside the safety of our house.

I walk with him. The sidewalk feels bumpy and cool beneath my feet. He doesn't say anything. I don't expect him to. He simply holds my hand, loosely, swallows hard, his eyes wide, searching the darkness for something I'm sure he sees but isn't there. I look into his face, into his eyes, but I can't see past the fear, glimpse behind the reflection of myself in his wide stare.

"Scary at night, isn't it?" he finally speaks. "So many eyes could be watching you. You're so vulnerable walking at night."

I struggle to keep up with him.

"Listen," he whispers. "Listen to the trees. How they rustle. Any one of those trunks could be someone."

He picks me up, holds me against his flannel. He smells of layers of sweat and dead skin, the faintest hint of sawdust. The street is quiet. No cars. Neighbors shut up safely in their homes.

"You're my best girl, aren't you?" he asks. "You're Daddy's girl. You always will be." He clings tighter to me. "Right?"

"Yes," I mumble. I want to go back home. It's too dark outside. I don't like having to answer his questions. I don't like not having a choice. He's my father.

We meander our way down to the gas station on the corner. A woman and her children fill their minivan. An old man glares at us, then streaks a squeegee across his windshield. My father puts me down, lets my cold feet touch the even colder pavement. He reaches into the pocket of his pants, and together, we walk through the glass doors.

The young girl behind the counter has copper red hair, dark eye shadow and her nose pierced. She barely acknowledges my father at the counter. I hold his hand, shift my feet to keep them warm.

"A carton of cigarettes," he says.

"Merit, Pall Mall, Marlboro?" she drones.

My father scratches at the crescent on his cheek. "Marlboro," he answers, giving my hand a reflexive squeeze.

She slides a carton out from behind the counter. She doesn't look at either of us. Doesn't smile. All but rolls her eyes at being expected to do what she gets paid for. My father sets the crumpled bills onto the counter. She presses hard on the cash register buttons, then hands him his change.

"This is wrong," my father says.

She blinks, looks him over, then at the register.

"You hear me?" he asks.

I tense.

"It's the price that comes up in the system," she replies.

"It's wrong."

"I don't set the prices."

"Yeah," my father answers. I stand on one foot, then the other. "I'm not leaving here until you give me the correct change."

"I gave you the correct change."

"Listen," my father grits his teeth, points his forefinger into her face.

Her hands disappear beneath the counter, and she leans forward, stares hard into my father's eyes. "I just work here," she says. "Complain to the manager. I don't have the time to argue. I don't have the time for any trouble, so you can just turn around and walk your ass out of here."

My father's jaw shifts. I expect him to blow up, to let loose with a string of profanities, to tell her that she's ignorant, that women shouldn't handle money, but he stays perfectly still, blinking fast, as though he is suddenly caught in something shrinking around him.

"Take it," he says, his voice quivers. "You just take it. Keep the change."

He reaches into his pockets and pulls out a few more crumpled dollars, tosses them onto the counter. When I look up, his face is red, eyes bloodshot, tears trickling down his nose. He swallows back a sob.

He might've stood there, sobbing in front of that girl, in front of those people, if I hadn't taken him by the hand and led him back out the glass doors. He's drunk. Through his sobs, he wipes the back of his hand across his eyes and mutters, "stupid bitch" to himself. "Everybody wants something."

I watch him now. He and my son drift downstream. They aren't anchored. I can hear Dane's voice. I wring my hands.

Before she passed away from ovarian cancer, my mother told me what she thought happened the night my father was mugged. She told me the story my father doesn't seem to have the words for anymore. We were wrapped together in her seaweed green afghan. I was twenty-one, pregnant with Dane. She was forty-six; her face ashen, lips violet. My father still drove the Rock Caterpillar, came home from work in time for dinner, still smelled of sawdust and earth. He rarely spoke, except to bitch about the cost of things and how the country was "going to hell in a hand basket."

"He was mugged," she said, stroking the hair from my eyes as I leaned against her.

We flipped through a photo album of when we lived in Ohio. Our memories framed by the camera's gaze: my father in his insurance salesman suit knelt in his garden—my eight-year-old self a sundress blur.

"What did they take?" I asked.

"Whatever muggers usually take," she answered.

"What else happened to him?" I asked, lifting the photo album to inspect a picture of my father in his treasured room at the top of the stairs. "Something else?"

"Else?" She took a deep breath.

I folded my arms and shrugged. "You know," I said.

"No," she snapped. "I don't know."

My mother stopped stroking my forehead.

"Why did he change so much?" I asked.

She flipped another page in the album.

"He didn't really change all that much," she answered.

I almost laughed. "Well," I said with a sarcasm I couldn't suppress, "did they ever catch the guy?"

My mother shifted her weight and coughed.

"The guy just got away?" I asked.

"I don't even know where it happened." She ran her hand over her face.

"And?"

"And," Mom replied sharply. "Some man stuck a gun in his face, your father got scared, and he was mugged."

"Mugged?" I asked. "I thought maybe he was—" The words caught in my throat; just then, Dane kicked.

My mother closed the photo album, patted my belly. "End of story."

I didn't believe her. Even now, sitting on the banks of the Maumee, I don't entirely believe her. The boat continues to drift. I want to hear the truth about my father. I want to know all that happened to my father that night—from him. I want him to explain to me what happened that night. I have to know, especially now, staring at my own boy on the verge of becoming a man—I have to know what that means.

I signal to Dane to steer the boat back. He obeys, dips an oar into the flickering surface and paddles back towards the banks.

My father stumbles onto the shore. I catch an arm. Dane catches the other.

"Time to go back, Dad," I say. "Dinner's in an hour."

"I didn't catch any fish," he grumbles.

I lead him up the narrow moss covered steps, exchange a look with my son. "The fish weren't biting."

At the nursing home, I guide my father through the double glass doors, past the gathering of old, gray-haired women cuddling dolls as though infants, towards his room near the back hallway. Dane follows behind.

The trees outside rustle but we cannot hear them in my father's room. He sits down slowly on the edge of his bed. He has Polaroids on his bulletin board of when he had a beard, when he looked strong, virile. On the stand next to his bed sits a ship in a bottle that my son made for him. An empty, green bottle of buckeye ale, the ship inside one of those that probably drowned under the currents of Lake Erie, something he found in one of his grandfather's books, I'm sure.

"I want to know what happened to you, Dad," I say, surprised at my own boldness. "What gave you that scar?"

He scratches at his cheek, at the crescent. "I don't know what you mean," he mumbles.

I hear my son shift his feet behind me.

"I want to know, Dad."

He stares out the window—his pale face stretched taut across his cheekbones. A cardinal sits on the windowsill. A female: brown wings, only the faintest hint of red on her breast. She's chirping.

"We always misunderstand birds," my father says. "She's not singing. She's calling." He holds his hands together, like he did that night when he removed the baby bird from his breast pocket. "Probably looking for one of her babies. Or something like that. Years of working in the woods teaches you the difference."

"Tell me, Dad," I press.

He clears his throat. "I was driving home and found a little bird in the middle of the road. It was still alive. Still calling out. So I stopped and placed it in my pocket. To keep it warm." His eyes begin to water. "Didn't work. I couldn't protect it, could I? Not even inside my pocket." He laughs a little. "Mother Nature is cruel, did you know that?"

I want to ask if he was really mugged that night, if that was all that happened to him, if that could actually be all that happened to him. I hear Dane cough, and I stop the words.

"That's what happened that night," my father says. "I was late because I stopped to save a bird that died in my pocket." He sighs, wipes his eyes. "End of story."

I stare at him, grit my teeth, rush forward and grab his arms.

He meets his eyes to mine. "End of story," he whispers.

This is a challenge.

"What happened to you, Dad?" I ask in a low voice.

"I already told you," he answers, his eyes darkening. "End of story."

This is the moment, I know it is. There are only so many moments in life when people have the chance for truth, to push through the layers of silence and lies. I feel like if I let him go, I will never know the man my father is.

93

"Come on, Mom," Dane says. His voice startles me.

My eyes stay focused on my father's downcast face.

"Dinner is almost ready," my father mumbles. "Spam and potatoes again."

And the moment goes as quickly as it came.

We give him our goodbyes, and I force myself down the hallway, back out those double glass doors. I turn around once we are in the parking lot and I see my father standing by his window, watching us, on the other side of those panes, too far away to hear the words the wind and rustling trees would steal from me even if I called them out to him.

"It's okay," I hear my son tell me, gently touching a hand to my shoulder.

I stop walking and hold him, tightly, as tightly as my arms will press him against me; I hold onto him. There are words I would say to him but none of those will do, so I hold him against me, hoping the beating of all that I have inside can communicate to him what it's too late to say.

"I think I know what happened to him," Dane says.

"What did he tell you?" I ask, my heart beating faster.

Dane pauses, sets his chin on my shoulder. "It was what he didn't tell me." Dane sighs. "He stared at Fallen Timbers, cried a little, I think."

Dane tightens his embrace.

"I think your grandfather was raped, Dane," I say. "All those years ago."

"Raped?" Dane asks.

"Or was hurt somehow, affected somehow," I answer, shaking my head. "He changed after that night, like he was afraid of something."

"Why didn't you ask him before?" Dane asks.

I move to shrug my shoulders, to tell him that I don't know, but I don't, I stop the impulse to dismiss this moment, this moment my father can no longer provide me, and I look my son square in the eyes. I see fear. I see past my own reflection in his eyes and see a little boy crouched inside, still vulnerable, still so fragile, and I answer, uncertain of what my eyes are showing him, "Because I was too afraid to know the answer."

He nods, looks back towards the nursing home. He gives my arm a little squeeze, and together, we walk back to the car. We won't speak anymore of this moment, I'm sure, but for the first time, we touched each other, not as mother and son, but as human beings, not too tall, not beyond reach, just two people with our guards down, doing our best to get through life without hurting each other or ourselves.

Off the Record

Lin Rice

I was hunched over my kitchen table, rolling cigarettes, when the Help Wanted ad shouted up at me. 'Experienced Interviewer Needed IMMEDIATELY.'

I picked off the shreds of stale pipe tobacco stuck to my nail polish and took a closer look. The ad was out of place in my hometown paper. I'd been absently scanning the 'Your Right to Know' section, taking in the names of old classmates who were getting married (or had been busted for domestic abuse) and was surprised to see something of genuine interest. "Interviewer needed IMMEDIATELY in the Southeastern Ohio region to conduct and record interviews. English speakers only. Must have Internet connection and own transportation. $1K per completed interview; half up front. Send inquiries to Jodi@haveubeenabducted.org."

I blinked at the number following the dollar sign. These too-good-to-be-true offers were a dime a dozen, but it was unusual to see one in actual newsprint. And for there to be a concrete payment amount, instead of the typical 'Massive earning potential!' hook.

How quaint.

I glanced at my old clunker of a laptop, hating myself for even considering it. The computer was nestled among a growing pile of neatly stacked, unopened bills. I might not have been able to pay them, but I could sure as hell organize the things.

"Rube," I said, and reached for the laptop.

I lit one of the home-rolled smokes while waiting for the computer to cough to life. The cigarette tasted like something you'd find in last year's winter coat, but at least it did the trick, and a whole bag of the generic pipe tobacco cost less than a single pack of cowboy killers. I'd save more money if I just stopped altogether, but my mama didn't raise me to be a quitter.

A quick scan of the ad's website did little to encourage me. Staring back at me was a mish-mash of topics you'd hear about on one of those late night, tin-foil-hat radio shows: Bigfoot, out-of-body experiences, men in black, some creepy article on the phenomenon of black-eyed kids, and even a handful of low-res photos claiming to be evidence of lizard people. Whoever had shot the pictures had at least angled the camera so the zippers wouldn't show.

The words "Have You Been ABDUCTED???" were scrawled across the top of the page in a quivery font. I took another drag and clicked through, ending up on a stylized map of the U.S., digital thumbtacks poked into dozens of small towns around the country, with smaller print describing the details of various UFO abduction cases.

I could see where this was going. But short of editing a few library newsletters and a disastrous tutoring session with some rich brat who was flunking English, my billable hours had dried up.

I pulled up my email. Aside from a few offers that made it through my spam filter and yet another dinner invite from my old co-worker, Paul, the box was empty. I fired off an email to the address listed on Jodi's site, resumé attached, and leaned back to think depressing thoughts.

A response pinged my inbox before my back touched the chair.

Thanks so much for your interest, the message stated in Papyrus font, the letters hunter green. *Could we please speak 'in person?' I'm a terribly wretched typist. Best, Jodi*

A link followed the message; it must have been an auto-reply.

I clicked on the URL, expecting a long wait as my old laptop limped into action. To my surprise, a video conferencing window popped up immediately. Staring at me through the screen was a hoot owl of a woman, her magnified eyes confused behind a pair of coke-bottle glasses.

I yelped and slammed the screen shut. I shot out of my chair and ran to the bedroom for a bra, pulling my hair back as I went.

Settling back into my chair, I peeked under the laptop screen. The woman was still there, eyes larger than before.

"Sorry about that," I said, fastening my shirt's top button. "You caught me getting ready for bed. It's almost three in the morning here."

"Oh that's quite alright, dear, nothing I haven't seen before." The woman's voice had a soft lilt to it, something that made me think of the grown-ups on *Sesame Street.*

Her face leaned in to fill my screen, eyes blinking rapidly. "I was just expecting Mr. Mitchell, is all. Would he be available?"

"I'm Anderson Mitchell," I said, going into the routine for the millionth time. "You can call me Anse. Don't worry; it happens a lot. All of the firstborns in the family end up with it."

"Oh, but I love it!" she said, the audio crackling in my speakers. "You're an old soul, I can see it already."

I fought the urge to roll my eyes.

"I saw your ad in the paper. You're Jodi, I assume?"

The woman cocked her head to the side, as if she was listening to something off camera. I tapped the volume button on the keyboard and made to repeat myself, but she spoke first.

"Yes, of course," she said. "I'm Jodi McTaggert, from the Sacred Constellation Project. You've heard of the SCP, I assume?"

If you can't say something nice, don't say anything at all.

Jodi tapped her thin lips with a lacquered nail. "That's alright, I suppose," she said. "Objectivity is what I'm after, and your resume is quite impressive. My apologies for taking so long to respond, by the way—I don't keep clocks in my house. They stifle the soul, as I'm sure you know."

I frowned. I'd noticed her ad in the paper less than five minutes ago, and she was apologizing for being slow to reply? I wasn't sure precisely how this woman was medicated, but her idea of time seemed somewhat skewed.

"What sort of services do you need?" I said. "Your ad didn't go into much detail."

Jodi tittered, her glasses sliding off her nose. "Right to the point, that's good, dear. It's a simple task, really, but I've got a number of irons in the fire, and my hay fever is simply atrocious this time of—"

"And that's where I come in?" This was starting to feel familiar. People looking for free work tend to bury the lede.

Jodi didn't break stride.

"Precisely," she said, pushing her glasses back. "I'm putting together a new compendium of abduction cases. Missing time, sub-dermal implants, mental suggestions…it's all quite exciting. It simply kills me to miss the Ohio Valley, I have so many theories on the Grassman, and don't get me started on Point Pleasant."

"Look Jodi, I don't know if—"

"In any event, I need a local, someone who speaks the language, as it were. Someone who can sit down with potential sources, get them talking, and record the whole thing for me. Once you're done you'll send the file to me, and I'll take care of the wordsmithing. I have the contact information and the list of questions all ready to send you. Oh, and your name will appear in the book's acknowledgments, of course."

There it was. "Your ad mentioned a set price, with half up front."

Jodi frowned. "Well of course dear, I told you I'm with the SCP. We're a serious operation. Check your email, you'll see."

I switched windows. A new message waited in my inbox, the address an ungodly long string of numbers and symbols. My hand paused over the mouse.

"Go ahead, it won't bite," Jodi said. I clicked the link. Again the old clunker jumped to light speed, and a command prompt window blinked open. A program kicked in, and green numbers flowed down the screen like something out of a Wachowskis flick. The command prompt closed, and my browser opened to my Paypal account.

Including the impressive funds already in my possession, there was exactly $514.72 in the account.

I'd worry about how Jodi pulled that stunt later. For now, money on the barrel was good enough for me. Clicking, I filled the laptop's window with Jodi's beautiful face.

"Lady, you've got yourself a reporter."

I slammed the screen shut before she could reply. I pushed myself away from the table, and gloated at the stack of bills.

It was time to work.

I dialed the number for Mrs. Jenkins, the first interview subject, on the drive to Columbus. When I'd signed for the package delivered at my door that morning and ripped open the heavy cardboard, I'd been less than pleased to discover a nearly three-hour drive waiting for me. Still, the money was worth it, so I'd completely topped off my old pickup's gas tank for the first time in months, and headed toward the big city.

"Hello, Mrs. Jenkins? I was hoping we could sit down and I could ask you a few questions about your abduction," I said into the phone.

A sleepy voice answered. "It's so early. Can't we do this in the afternoon?"

"Don't worry, ma'am, I've got a long drive ahead of me. I won't be there until the afternoon anyway."

I heard some dishes rattle in the background, and Mrs. Jenkins passed me some groggy instructions on how to pass the gate of her home owners' association.

"Sounds good. I'll see you at three."

I hung up the phone and squeezed the steering wheel until my knuckles hurt. I'd left the city to get away from this exact thing—interviewing entitled suburbanites who couldn't make it through a conversation without invoking the sacred words *property values* at least a dozen times. If she was on the damned zoning commission I was turning straight around—screw the extra five hundred.

I barreled along the straight shot of Interstate 70, and eventually the Columbus cityscape materialized on the hazy summer horizon. I followed the outer belt toward Mrs. Jenkins's suburb, flipping off my old company's shiny new glass building as I passed it. Exiting on the north side and working my way through a maze of cul-de-sacs and roundabouts, I had to check my directions three times before I ended up at the right neighborhood. For as much time as I'd spent in the suburbs, I still got turned around every time I ventured into them.

The surveillance camera at the wrought-iron gate to Mrs. Jenkins's neighborhood eyed my four-wheel-drive suspiciously, but I had the password, baby.

I cruised around until I found the right address, and pulled into the driveway of a spacious Cape Cod, complete with white picket fence and meticulous landscaping. I rang the bell, and a tall, middle-aged woman in a silk house robe greeted me, a small pack of those designer mixed-breed dogs yipping around her ankles.

We exchanged pleasantries, and she ushered me into the house. "Please excuse my mess," she said, leading me into a study. "Frank's been gone, and he's always such a dear about cleaning up after the little ones."

I dropped my bag onto a couch and marveled at my surroundings. It was like someone had transplanted the entire Area 51 gift shop from Roswell to Central Ohio.

An entire army of little green men salt shakers mustered on one mantel, next to a plastic statue of a classic flying saucer beaming up a dairy cow. A drawing pad sat open on the coffee table, displaying a clumsy effort at capturing a bug-eyed alien's likeness. In a frame on the wall was a copy of Mulder's "I Want to Believe" poster from *The X-Files*.

Oh boy.

Mrs. Jenkins shooed the dogs from the room, and sat opposite from me in an oversized armchair. She pulled one of those days-of-the-week pill carriers from the table drawer next to her, and tapped out a handful.

"It's so nice of you to come and see me," she said, pouring a glass of water from a pitcher on the table. "Most people think I'm some kind of a kook. Can you believe it?"

"The SCP is a serious operation," I said, pulling straight from the script. I pulled out my digital recorder and placed it on the table. Hopefully I could finish this up fast, before I was beamed up myself.

Mrs. Jenkins tossed back her pills and sat back in her chair with a contented sigh. I could actually see her pupils dilate.

"Oh don't mind me," she said. "It's my prescriptions. I used to have dreadful seizures, but the pills keep them in check. And I won't complain that they seem to make everything *just* a little more fabulous. But don't worry, I won't wig out on you!" She laughed, a hand covering her mouth.

"That's quite alright," I said. "But why don't we get started? First off, could you describe the nature of your abduction?"

Mrs. Jenkins nodded, leaning in. "It was all thanks to Dr. Aubuchon. Lovely young woman—she's the best psychologist in France, I'm told. Well, after she helped me get over my seizures, the psychic barriers in my mind were finally lowered. That's when the grays first began their communication."

I bet they did. I moved on.

"And how did they communicate with you?"

Mrs. Jenkins tapped her jaw. "It was quite simple. They've got people everywhere, you really wouldn't believe it. My dentist adjusted my partials, and I began picking up their signal from out in space. It was all quite exciting. They needed more of us to help pave the way for first contact, you see. To let the human race know that they're our friends, and that they're going to save our planet. It's so wonderful!"

"I'm sure it was," I said, eyes staying on my checklist. I felt my initial disdain for Mrs. Jenkins slip away. This woman wasn't trying to scam anyone. Meds could do all sorts of strange things to a person's mind. I'm sure Mrs. Jenkins received her fair share of derision, and there was no need for me to jump on top of the pile.

I mustered as friendly a smile as I could manage. "Have you been contacted by any representatives of the government?"

Mrs. Jenkins frowned, a finger on her chin. "Well, the postman seems kind of suspicious. He gives me the strangest looks whenever I sign for a package. But I've followed my orders—we're not to speak with the government about the grays' plans. They're afraid of intergalactic war, you see."

"Third question—have you told any family or friends about your experience?"

"Well, just the folks on the message boards, of course. There's quite a growing community on the Internet," she said. "And Frank's up there with them right now."

I paused. "Excuse me?"

She gave me an indulgent smile. "Yes, for about a week now. He went to Dr. Aubuchon's to pick up my prescriptions—he's always been such a dear about that, swinging by her office day or night to save me the trip. I never even have to ask him! Anyway, they beamed him up right there in her parking lot. Dr. Aubuchon told me the whole thing over the phone—I could hear the wind rushing in the background and everything. It was all very exciting."

I didn't have the heart to tell her it was more likely that Frank was shacked up in a cheap motel with the good doctor. If that was the case, she was better off without him.

Only one question left. I stared down at the paper, confused. Some kind of typo? *It's your money, Jodi*, I thought, and went ahead.

"Tell me, Mrs. Jenkins—what's the difference between the lightning and the lightning bug?"

She looked at me quizzically. "Excuse me?"

I repeated the question.

"Well, I guess a few million volts, dear." She began to laugh.

Jodi never said that the answers to her questions had to be good. The checklist complete, I packed up my gear, thanked Mrs. Jenkins for her time, and headed for the door.

"Won't you stay?" she asked behind me. "Frank's supposed to be back any time now. I'm sure he's had an amazing experience."

"I'm certain he has," I said, nudging one of her yapping dogs out of the way. Mrs. Jenkins waved from the doorway as I slammed the pick-up into gear and got the hell out of suburbia.

My phone buzzed on the way back. I'd uploaded the audio at a coffee shop around the corner from the True Believer's house, and half expected the message to be an alert of the remaining funds being dumped into my account. No such luck.

"How's it going, JT," I said into the receiver.

"Where are you, sis?" the voice drawled from the other end. "I stopped by your place, but you weren't home."

"Big city for the day. Picked up a new gig. Quick and easy."

JT perked up. "That's great, Anse. You should pick me up one of those Hound Dog's pizzas on your way."

I smiled. "Too late, I'm halfway back. What's up?"

He paused. "Same as before. The appeal's been held up, and Larry needs more money. You know how it is."

"You're sure he needs more money? He's not just saying that?"

"Come on, Anse—Larry's a good guy. You said so yourself."

JT had a good heart, but he'd never met a snake oil salesman he didn't like. His last 'lawyer' had nearly bankrupted him.

"What happened to the last check I gave you?" I said, juggling the receiver. "That should have covered it."

There was a pause from the other end. When JT finally spoke, the playful tone had evaporated from his voice.

"Peggy's car needed new brakes," he said. "A new window, too, after that time she went off the road. Nearly cleaned me out."

I could feel the bile rising in my stomach. "Why the hell did you have to pay for it? That drunk bitch needs to—"

"She ain't gonna take care of it herself, you know as well as I do," JT said. "And I'm not letting her drive Ava around in a car that's not safe."

I let out a sigh; I wouldn't argue with JT on that one, at least.

"I know you've had it tough lately, I just have to win this case, is all...Ava needs to be with me," JT said.

"I hear you. Turns out this new gig might just help with that."

You would have thought it was Christmas. "You're my hero, Anse," JT said. "Ava's, too."

"Love you, too." I hung up, and at the next red light, I checked my Paypal account.

Nothing.

The balance was the same when I got home, and three glasses of wine didn't seem to have an effect on it, either. It wouldn't have been a big deal for any other client, but considering how fast Jodi had been with the advance, I was getting twitchy.

I poured another glass, then fired off a short email. Nothing mean, mind you, or desperate. Just something to remind her I was still kicking.

Just like before, the reply pinged back almost instantly. I clicked the link, and like clockwork, Jodi's squinting face filled my screen.

"Hello dear," she said, her voice crackling with static. A bandage was visible on her cheek, wrapping under her glasses to cover one eye.

"Are you alright?" I asked. Jodi touched her face and flinched at the contact.

"No need to worry about me, dear. As they say, occupational hazard." Jodi raised a steaming mug and sipped gingerly. "How may I help you?"

I paused, not sure what to say.

"Well I was just wondering if you'd had a chance to listen to the interview."

Jodi set the mug down. When the china touched her coffee table, the hiss of feedback crackled through my speakers and the screen blurred into a cloud of pixels.

"I'm afraid I have," she said when the image cleared. "I thought I had been clear on what was required, dear. I don't believe I can compensate you for what you handed over."

Pinot noir shot out of my nose."What do you mean? I drove halfway across the state, and I asked every question from the list. Even the ones that didn't make sense."

"Yes dear, but don't you remember what I asked for?" Jodi paused to sip at her mug. "Someone who speaks the language, as it were. I need you to get the sources to really open up to you."

"And I did just that," I said. "Did you not hear her telling me about her husband? That was most decidedly off-script."

"SCP already knew all about that," Jodi said. "I need you to go deeper, to get me more. I'm sure you understand."

I wanted to stick my hands through the screen and wring Jodi's chubby neck. Instead I thought about my niece, and bit my tongue.

"Give me another shot at it," I said. "Now that I've got one under my belt, I know exactly what you need."

Jodi examined me with her good eye.

"Do you think you're up to it, dear? The SCP is—"

"A serious operation. I know. So am I. I'll do exactly what you ask, but we need to be clear on payment this time."

The screen pixelated again, and Jodi's voice sounded like a robot through the feedback.

"Alright then. I'll have another assignment ready for you tomorrow. But you really need to knock this one out of the park, dear—I've tried this abductee already, and he didn't seem all that friendly. Finish this assignment, and you'll be paid in full, including the remaining five hundred from the first one."

I hesitated, but went ahead with the question that had been eating at me.

"Jodi, there's something else," I said. "Don't get me wrong, I appreciate how quickly you've been responding to me, but *wow*. You've even got my computer perking up. What's the deal?"

Jodi laughed. "You've noticed that, I see. Well, the SCP places a lot of importance on making sure our technology is bleeding edge. We've got to keep up appearances for anyone who might be listening in, don't we?"

She raised her eyebrows and jabbed a finger toward the sky.

"Don't let it concern you," she continued. "Our network is mostly automated at this point. And as you can tell, I like to remain reachable at all times. We've got a very important mission. Anyway, must run. Good luck!"

The image faded to black, and my computer went through the crawl of symbols again. I pulled up my Paypal account to see a new deposit of $47.13—the exact amount I'd spent on gas getting to Columbus and back.

Jodi's hacker tricks were starting to concern me, but for the moment I didn't have any ideas. JT needed money fast, and it's not like my phone was ringing off the hook otherwise. She'd better not have put any weird alien spyware crap on my hard drive.

"You'd better be worth it, cat lady," I said out loud, and finished my glass of wine.

Waiting on Jodi's package the next morning, I killed time with a little research of my own. I called up my former co-worker Paul, a young business reporter with some impressive computer skills. I asked him to dig up whatever he could find on the Sacred Constellation Project. He promised to have a full profile for me by the end of the day, in exchange for drinks next weekend. What the hell—a little social interaction wouldn't be the worst thing in the world, and I felt bad about ignoring his emails.

It was late afternoon before the package arrived, and I ripped it open with determination. Inside was a black and white picture of an older man in a Carhartt jacket who bore a surprising resemblance to Neil Young. The picture had obviously been taken with a telephoto lens. Printed along the bottom of the photo was the name Karl Donegan. Beneath the picture was a topographical map, a red circle scrawled in one corner.

This guy really was off the beaten path, and that's coming from someone who grew up in Appalachia.

I grabbed my shoulder bag and checked to make sure my Ruger SP101 was easy to reach. I didn't expect to need it, but the solid heft of the .357 Magnum made me a little more comfortable at the thought of pestering a good old boy on his own property.

I headed down Route 78, winding through parts of the national forest as I moved toward the spot marked on my map. Asphalt turned to gravel, which turned to dirt. Eventually I was coaxing the pick-up down a road just wide enough for it, with branches clicking off the side mirrors. Grass grew in a strip as high as the bumper between the two wheel ruts.

After a while I turned off the radio, and just listened as the whine of the highway faded into the drone of cicadas and the squeaks of evening bats. Sometimes I missed the life I'd left in the city—but not on evenings like this.

The path ended at the edge of a broad clearing. The field rose gently into a small hill, with an old but well-kept trailer on top. A small outbuilding stood to the left of the trailer, and I could just see a pair of goats milling around inside it.

A length of cable, spray-painted blaze orange, marked the boundary between forest and field. Secured to two large oaks on either side of the path, a neatly printed sign hung from the middle of the cable—*No Trespassing*.

I killed the engine and made a show of slamming the door when I climbed out. If he was home, I had no doubt that Mr. Donegan had heard me coming up the road—no need to make it seem I was sneaking up on him.

A tall figure emerged from the trailer, the screen door swinging shut behind him. He stood in silence on the porch, arms crossed.

"Mister Donegan?" I called. "May I come up?"

"I told you, them goats aren't for sale." His voice was a deep baritone, but it had some quiver in it. "Not unless you want to come up and mow the yard your own damned self."

"I'm not here about the goats," I said. "I was hoping we could talk for a little while. About your abduction."

I could see him flinch from across the field. Before I could say anything else, he turned and stalked back inside the trailer, slamming the door behind him.

Well shit.

I leaned on my truck's front bumper and lit up a home-rolled smoke. It wasn't the first time someone slammed the door when I'd asked for an interview, but the goat thing was a first. I smoked in silence, trying to come up with a Plan B and listening to the first evening crickets.

I crushed out the cigarette and tossed the butt in the truck bed. I turned around to see Mr. Donegan stalking down the hill toward me. He wasn't moving in a hurry. But a 12-gauge pump hung at his side, the gun balanced by its slide in the cup of his hand.

Without making any sudden moves, I made sure my pistol was resting in the top of my bag.

Mr. Donegan stopped at the gate, staring at my license plate.

"Thought I recognized your truck," he said.

"You might have seen it around town," I said carefully. "I've lived here most of my life."

He nodded and looked up at me. His eyes were rheumy, but there was a clarity in them that bored into me.

"I figured I'd walk down and make sure I hadn't heard you wrong," he said slowly. "Most folks know better than to come around here lookin' for a freak show."

"That's not what I'm about, Mister Donegan," I said. "I got hired by a woman to record some interviews for her. Simple as that. I'm not looking to take advantage."

His face clouded, and I almost pulled the pistol when he switched the shotgun from one hand to the other.

"What, for one of them alien books? The ones that take people like me, and make us out to be toothless hillbillies? Who sleep with our cousins, and chase little green men? If you don't think that's taking advantage, miss, then you don't know what you're talking about."

"I'm not that kind of writer," I said.

He examined me in the fading light. "If you're helping someone use what happened to my family to turn a dime, then you sure as hell are."

I didn't have a comeback for that one. How many times had I railed about this kind of reporting when I still worked at the paper? How was this any different than sticking a camera in the face of a murder victim's family for the evening news? This was the exact reason I'd left newspaper work in the first place.

If it bleeds, it leads.

I felt a knot growing in my stomach. I was going to make sure JT had what he needed to keep Ava, but not like this.

"I'm sorry for bothering you, Mister Donegan," I said. "You're right. I don't know what I'm talking about."

I tossed my bag through the truck's open window and started to climb in.

"You're Sam Mitchell's granddaughter, ain't ya," Mr. Donegan said.

I paused. He had the shotgun cradled in the crook of his arm now, barrel pointed away from me. I nodded.

"I knew your grandpa," he said. "Come on, I might as well offer you a cup of coffee, for his sake."

He turned and headed toward the house. I slipped my phone and pistol into the pocket of my hooded sweatshirt, but left the digital recorder and notepad in the truck.

Mr. Donegan's trailer was small, but well kept. A small television and one lamp provided most of the illumination in the living room, the flickering light of the TV reflecting off dozens of framed photos hanging on the walls. The majority of the frames were filled with photos of an attractive woman and a boy with curly blonde hair, their clothing and haircuts straight out of the seventies. The others were grainy photos of men in Army green, posing next to artillery pieces.

Mr. Donegan emerged from the kitchen, a steaming mug in each hand. I took one and nodded my thanks before sitting on the couch.

"I forgot to introduce myself," I said.

"If you're Sam's granddaughter, I imagine your name's Anse," he said.

I smiled. "Word gets around, doesn't it?"

"Seems to be the case," he said. "It's been a while since anyone came back here asking what you asked. I'd hoped most people had forgot. Not too many around left to remember, anyway."

I set my mug on the coffee table next to me, next to a vase filled with lilacs. Their light scent almost masked the couch's mustiness.

"My wife's favorite," he said.

"They're lovely. Look, Mister Donegan, I'm sorry about earlier. You made me realize what I was doing, and that's not the kind of person I am."

I meant it.

"Call me Donny," he said. "And I figured as much. I could see it in your face. You don't look like one of those UFO chasers, anyway."

"I'm starting to wonder," I said. "It was just a job. No offense."

He took a sip from his cup. "You should write a book on them, instead. See how they like it. Who hired you, anyway?"

"They're called the Sacred Constellation Project..."

He snorted. "Oh yeah, I remember them. The 'serious operation,' as they like to say. They've pestered me a few times. I've always just fed 'em a line of bull."

He leaned forward, the mug cupped in his gnarled hands.

"They're the real problem, and folks like them. Tell me—where do you stand on the whole thing?"

"Well, I'm a reporter, and I deal in facts," I said. "I've never seen anything personally that I couldn't explain. But the official story is rarely the full story, in my experience. I don't know—I guess I haven't thought about it much."

He nodded. "That's a good way to approach it. Problem is, just because there's a thousand folks out there crying wolf, doesn't mean that one of 'em hasn't seen one. It's a pretty good way to discredit the honest ones, if you ask me—just have all the crazies start saying the same thing, and no one listens. Works in politics all the time."

I laughed. That wasn't very far from the truth.

"So you've seen a wolf, then?" I asked.

Mr. Donegan looked away, his lips pursed. "I didn't say that. Never have. People believe what they want to believe."

"But something had to have happened, if people like the SCP keep bothering you," I said.

He set his mug down, hard. "I never said it was any damned aliens."

We sat in silence for several minutes. I was too afraid to prompt him. But when I started to thank him for the coffee and leave, he began to speak softly, staring off.

"I still have no idea what happened. It's been thirty-five years, and...I was out back, on the other side of the hill. It was summer time, just starting to get dark. Sue was on the back porch, yelling for us to come inside. This was back when we had the house, before I had this piece of crap hauled up here.

"Ronnie was little, but he was big enough to ride the pony I'd gotten him for his birthday. Sweet-tempered thing, that pony—didn't mind him pulling on her ears, or anything like that. I was leading her around the yard with Ronnie riding, him laughing up a storm the whole time."

"Sounds nice," I said quietly.

He nodded. "It was. I don't know how long we were at it, but I remember that it was getting hard to see. Just when I went to lift him off, the pony shied away from me, like something had spooked her. Like I said, she was usually a real mild pony. About the same time, Gracie started whining something terrible from the shed."

"Your dog?"

"German Shepherd. That was strange too—she was always a real quiet dog. Never growled, hardly ever barked. But by the sounds she was making...you see animals act like that, you think they're hearing or smelling something you can't. Now that happens sometimes, especially if you live out here, and it's nothing to make a thing out of. I just scooped up Ronnie and put him on my shoulders, and headed toward the house."

"What about the pony?" I said. "Wouldn't she have run away?"

He looked at me with one eye, a hint of a smile showing.

"You don't have kids, do you." It wasn't a question. I shrugged.

"Anyway, I was almost to the house when this loud noise started up.

You ever heard a jet plane decelerate when it's getting close to the airport? How all of a sudden, it slows down enough for the sound to catch up, and it's like the plane's right on top of you?"

I nodded.

"Imagine that, times ten. I remember Ronnie squealing in my ear, and his little hands nearly pulling my hair out. He…"

Mr. Donegan sat for a moment, rolling the empty mug in his hands. I rose and gently took it from him. I found the little pot on the kitchen counter and filled it, and brought it back to him. He nodded, but didn't look up.

"I remember there being a light. Just soft at first, but it got bright real fast. So bright you could see the trees on the north ridgeline. For a moment it felt like the air was thicker, pressing down on me. Kind of like when you're in an elevator. And that's all I remember."

I frowned. "Where was the light coming from?"

He shrugged.

"I don't know. Everywhere. But it was just like that." He snapped his fingers. "The next thing I remember was laying in the grass, down by the trees. I remember it was the flies that woke me up—they were buzzing all around my face, and the sun was at high noon. Couldn't tell you how long I'd been laying there, but I felt like I had the worst hangover of my life. There was blood on my collar and crust in my nose—that's what the flies were after."

"How long had you been out?" I said.

He shook his head. "I don't know. I was pretty thirsty. I…I made my way up to the house, to see if Sue and Ronnie were okay."

I would have understood perfectly if Mr. Donegan had choked up at that point. I'd been a writer long enough to have an idea that the story didn't have a happy ending. What I didn't expect was the anger that began to fill his face, a slow burning rage that the years had failed to diminish.

"Before I made it to the house, I saw the pony in the back yard. For a second I was terrified that it was Ronnie—it had been tore up so bad that you could barely tell what it used to be. I ran in the house and yelled for them, but they weren't there. Both of them…just gone. Gracie, too.

"I climbed over every inch of these woods, calling their names until it got dark. When I couldn't see any more, I called up the Sheriff and we got a whole search party out here, probably three dozen guys with flashlights and dogs. We searched these hills for three goddamned days and nights. Nothing."

I examined him from across the room. I'd interviewed a lot of people, and I could tell when someone was trying to fleece me. Everything Mr. Donegan was telling me was the truth as he saw it. A chill crawled up my back.

"There wasn't any sign of them at all?" I said, carefully. "The dogs didn't find anything?"

He shook his head. "A couple times we thought they'd found a trail. They'd follow it for a mile or so, and then just sit down and whine. Couldn't get them to go any farther.

"I've never stopped looking. I called everyone I ever knew from when I was in the Army, guys in the FBI. Nothing. And once people like that SCP group of yours finally heard about it and started asking if I'd been beamed up, stuff like that, nobody official ever took me seriously again. I've never once made any claims other than what I've told you. It was them, not me."

"What do you think happened?" I asked quietly.

"*I lost my family, that's what happened!*"

I cringed at the fury in his words. Donegan's mug slipped from his trembling hands, and I flinched when it shattered on the floor.

"I'm—I'm sorry," I said, moving to pick up the broken pieces.

Mr. Donegan held his face in his hands, shoulders shaking. I hesitantly put a hand on his arm.

"I believe you," I said.

He looked up, reading my face. Finally he nodded.

"So is that what your Sacred Constellation Project wanted to know?" he said. "It's not much of a fairy tale, I'll tell you that."

I went back to my place on the couch. "Something like that," I said. "They gave me a list of questions to ask. Sort of leading questions, like how the aliens contacted you. And one that didn't make any sense at all."

He raised his eyebrows. "Like what?"

"Like, what's the difference between the lightning and the lightning bug?"

Mr. Donegan grew very still as the words came out of my mouth.

His jaw went slack, and the rheumy eyes that had stared at me moments earlier went vacant.

"Mr. Donegan?" I said, rising.

The old man slowly got to his feet. He took a few steps toward the hall to my left, and began taking his clothes off.

He left his shirt, pants and shoes behind him as he walked down the hall. I started to follow, until I heard the squeak of a shower nozzle and the spray of water start in his bathroom. The temperature in the trailer rose noticeably after a few minutes, and I could hear the familiar sounds of someone showering.

I was too shocked to move. I pulled out my phone, deciding who to call. No signal.

The water turned off, and Mr. Donegan walked out of the bathroom. The same vacant look gripped his face, and the old man was pink and naked as the day he was born. Walking past me as if I wasn't there, he opened the front door and stepped out into the night.

Not knowing what else to do, I followed him. I didn't have to go far. I found the old man sitting cross-legged in the grass behind the trailer, hands on his knees, and staring up at the stars. He was mumbling under his breath, some words I couldn't make out.

"Donny, are you okay?" I placed a hand on his shoulder, but he didn't seem to register my presence. I shook him a time or two, and he finally looked up at me.

"It's alright, I'll bring him in when we're done riding," he said. "I think Ronnie likes his present."

My throat tightened. Whatever had happened to Mr. Donegan thirty-five years ago, somehow Jodi's question had put him in some sort of hypnotic state. If she had known that would happen, we were going to have words. More than words, actually.

I hurried back inside and returned with a blanket. Throwing it around Mr. Donegan, I did my best to get him to his feet and help him back inside. He didn't fight me, but the old man never came out of his fantasy world. I turned down the quilts on the bed in his cramped bedroom, and helped him in. His head had barely touched the pillow before he began snoring.

I ran down the hill and fired up my truck, plowing over the underbrush as I turned it around on the narrow road. Whatever had been done to Mr. Donegan, odds were he needed a doctor. And if Jodi and her precious SCP had used me as their instrument to cause what had happened—so would she.

My phone finally picked up a signal when I pulled back onto the highway. Before I could dial the number for the local Sheriff, it started buzzing in my hand.

"Make it quick, Paul, I'm in a bit of a hurry," I said into the receiver.

"Hey Anse, sorry to call so late." His voice sounded tinny and far away. "Everything alright?"

"Right as rain," I said, doing my best to avoid pot holes at top speed.

"This Sacred Constellation Project you put me on is one strange group," he said. "I mean, they're a legit publisher, with a couple dozen paranormal titles."

"Apparently there's a market for it," I said. "What's so strange, other than that?"

"Well, I started to dig into their financials that are on public record. I found out that they're a subsidiary of that big government contractor you ran a story on last year. Know what I'm talking about?"

"Of course I do. What's the connection?"

He paused. "I'm not sure. Believe it or not, no sooner had I pulled up their damn web site, my phone started ringing. It was a lawyer giving me the whole 'cease and desist' spiel. How the hell does that even—"

His voice dissolved into a series of clicks and scratches. Cursing, I pulled off the road to see what the problem was. I fiddled with the phone for a minute, then tried calling back.

"Paul?" I said when the line connected.

"This is Gregor Smith with the SCP, Ms. Mitchell," a thin voice said. "Am I interrupting you?"

My jaw dropped. "I—how did you get on this line?"

"I believe you called me, Ms. Mitchell. Is there a problem?" His voice had almost no inflection.

I could feel my cheeks flush. "You bet your ass there's a problem," I said. "Where's Jodi? I need to speak with her. Right now."

"Ms. McTaggert is unavailable. Her instructions for you, shall I say, overstepped our parameters. I will be handling this account from now on. Are you ready for a new assignment? Your deliverable from Mr. Donegan was quite satisfactory."

I nearly dropped the phone.

"What the hell are you talking about?" I shouted. "I didn't record anything. And now the man's possibly had some kind of a mental break, thanks to you. Is that what you were hoping for?"

"The microphone on your mobile device proved sufficient to capture the needed audio. Do not worry. Mr. Donegan will be properly taken care of."

"If you touch him, you'll pay for it." The phone shook in my hand. "I don't know what it is you're doing, but I'll find out. And so will every major news outlet in the country."

There was a pause. "That would put you in breach of contract, Ms. Mitchell. I'm sure you wouldn't want that."

I flinched away as a high-pitched squeal burst from the phone. The line went dead.

The man's words rang in my head. *Mr. Donegan will be properly taken care of.*

I slammed the truck in reverse and sped back onto the gravel road. I tried calling Paul back before I lost the signal.

"The number you have dialed is no longer in service," the automated voice told me.

That wasn't good. I tried 911.

"The number you have dialed…"

I shoved the phone back in my pocket, and reached for my pistol. Try to disconnect *that*.

I turned a corner in the narrow road, and my headlights broke into Mr. Donegan's field. The knot rose in my throat again—the orange cable that had blocked the road was nowhere to be seen.

I didn't slow down. Instead, I coaxed the truck straight up the hill to the trailer, bouncing in my seat the entire way. I stopped with the headlights trained on the front door, and left them on. Pistol in one hand, I jumped out of the truck, climbed the porch and threw open the door.

The trailer was empty.

I don't mean there wasn't anyone there—it was empty. All of Mr. Donegan's furniture was gone, along with all of the photos and other mementos that had been on the walls. No curtains, no carpet. Nothing.

I went down the narrow hall, gun held in front of me. I called for Mr. Donegan, and was greeted by my own echo. His room was as bare as the rest of the trailer.

How could this be possible? I'd barely been gone an hour. I would have thought I was hallucinating, if it weren't for the faint smell of lilacs. This was indeed Mr. Donegan's trailer—at least, it had been.

Something moved through the beams of my headlights, throwing a long shadow on the wall.

"Hey!" I stepped hesitantly back into the living room, trying to keep my anger from losing its battle with the fear rising in my gut. The pistol shook in my hands. I peered out the door, blinking at the harsh headlights.

A boy stood on the porch. His hands were shoved in his pockets, and the hood of his sweatshirt was pulled up.

"What are you doing here?" The gun shook in my hands.

The boy looked up. He had rosy cheeks and a dimple in his chin like a million other little boys, but his eyes were completely black, just like the drawings in Mrs. Jenkins' sketchpad.

"Can I come in?" the boy asked, his voice saccharine-sweet. "I'd really like to come in. Please?" I slammed the door as hard as I could. My feet tangled and I went down. I shoved myself across the floor as far from the door as I could, panting as the fear took control.

This couldn't be happening.

The little boy's face appeared in the window beside the door. He grinned, his mouth stretching unnaturally wide, and pale blonde curls slipped out from under his hood. Another silhouette came to stand beside him. Then another.

Pounding boomed through the room, and the flimsy trailer door rocked on its hinges.

My phone rang.

I tried to pull it out of my pocket with numb fingers, and dropped it just as the door splintered. The headlights cut through the room, blinding me.

The phone hit the ground and turned on, its screen illuminating the terrible faces as they descended on me.

My phone was ringing.

I frowned at the half-rolled cigarette in my hands. The stale shreds of tobacco were dead and dull in the afternoon sunlight that streamed through the window and over my kitchen table. I must have nodded off—my throat was dry as hell.

I guess it didn't matter—the check for five hundred grand on the table meant I could damn well take a day off. Funny—it was more money than I'd earned in my entire life. This job had been…it had been…I was having trouble remembering exactly what it was that I had been paid to do.

The buzzing phone was making it hard to focus. I scooped it up and thumbed it on.

I couldn't place it, but the cheery voice on the other end sounded familiar.

"Hello, Mrs. Mitchell?" she asked. "I was hoping I could ask you a few questions about your abduction."

Faster Than I Could Follow

Anna Scotti

At the end of summer the year I was seven, my Aunt Elizabeth came to visit and I fell in love. Elizabeth was my mother's sister but you wouldn't have known it to look at her. She had a rope of thick, glossy black hair she'd twist around and around her hand while she was talking. When she got done talking she'd twist the rope up on top of her head and let it go, fluffing it out with her fingers as it fell to make it wild and big like a go-go dancer's.

Elizabeth had a tiny small waist hardly bigger than mine, and small breasts that poked straight out, separate from one another. You could see that if she took her clothes off her breasts would look the same, pointed and distinct, not like my mother's, which flopped into a wide low cushion beneath her robe at night. When I told my mother I was in love with Aunt Elizabeth, she looked sort of surprised and irritated and said, "You're not *in* love with her, you just *love* her, same as you do me and Daddy and your brother Scott."

"No, ma'am," I contradicted. "It's not the same."

My mother squeezed out a tight little laugh but I could tell she was aggravated. "You can't be *in* love with her, Amanda, because you're blood relations, and anyway you're both girls. And I don't want to hear another word about it."

I think Scotty was a little bit in love with Aunt Elizabeth, too, and I know my dad was. The first night she was with us she came to dinner with all her makeup on, red lipstick and a red dress, too, and a red scarf around her white neck. My dad looked up when she came into the dining room and said *well*, in a funny voice. *Well, well, Elizabeth.*

When my mom came in with a plate of pork chops she said the same thing, but she said it in the voice she used on me when I did something dumb that she thought was kind of cute all the same. Scott and I both wanted to sit next to Elizabeth but I got to, and I watched the way she ate and tried to do the same. When she finished she put her fork down face first at the edge of the plate, instead of tines up at the top of the plate. I did the same, and my dad shot me a look, but he didn't correct me.

"Well," Elizabeth said, pushing back from the table, "time to dance some of that off."

"Honey, it's too late to go out now," my mother began. "We've got to get up early in the morning."

Elizabeth pulled her hair up into a coil and looked at me and winked. She winked like nobody else, without crinkling her face at all. She just closed one eye and let the thick black fringe of her lashes rest against her white cheek.

"Not me," she contradicted. "Isn't this my vacation? Just give me a key and I won't make a sound when I let myself in, promise."

Mama wanted to argue but my Dad interrupted. "Elizabeth is grown, Billie, and she can take care of herself. Let her go on if she wants to."

I tried to wait up for her, but when I woke up, there she was beside me, curled up with the covers around her like a cocoon, hair spread across the white pillow. A silky scarlet robe was thrown over the foot of the bed, and a matching strap peeked out from beneath the twisted sheets. I touched Elizabeth's hair as lightly as I could but her green eyes opened and smiled at me. "Hey, snaggle tooth." Her breath was stale with sleep but I didn't mind. She had the whitest teeth and her eyebrows were like brown feathers across her forehead.

When I went into the kitchen Mama was at the stove turning bacon with a fork. She had on her blue robe with the stitches pulled out. I thought of Aunt Elizabeth's silky gown and my cheeks got hot.

"I don't want any," I said. Mama put down the fork and wiped her hands on her apron front. "Well, of course you do," she said. "It's Saturday, isn't it?"

My mother was right, eggs with bacon was a special weekend treat. But I didn't want to sit down at our battered old table with her in that faded robe with her big shelf bosom and morning smell and my father more than likely in his underwear. "Well, I don't want it," I said again. "Auntie said she'd take me out to eat."

I regretted the lie as soon as I heard it. But my mother looked pleased and when my father came in a moment later, not in his underwear after all, but with his chin still stubbled and his hair uncombed, she told him.

"Liz is a sweet girl," Mama said, and my father nodded.

"She's your sister, ain't she?"

When Scott came in he was dressed too, so my mother was the only one still in her nightclothes when Elizabeth wandered in, pretty and fresh in jeans and a clean white shirt.

She smiled around the table as she reached for the juice. My mother warned, "Now, don't fill up. Remember your promise to the little one."

Elizabeth looked confused but she must have gathered something from my undoubtedly miserable expression. "I told them you're taking me out to eat," I said carefully, leaving her an out if she chose to deny me, but

I was leaving the way open for her to rescue me, too. "Just me, not Scotty."

"How come—" Scotty began, outraged, but before Elizabeth could answer, my mother broke in.

"Because you and I have planning to do, young man," she said sternly. Her voice didn't fool us. She was talking about his sleepover birthday party the next Friday night. He was inviting four friends, and not one of them was me.

"Well," Elizabeth said brightly. She stood up and tugged on my pony tail. "Did you pick a spot yet?"

Gratitude washed over me.

"Never mind, Mandy. We'll just drive around and see what we like."

Aunt Elizabeth's car was the same shade as her lipstick, a scarlet two-seater with a white top that folded back, and a white leather steering wheel and dash. It was exactly like Barbie's convertible and I would have ridden in that curved bucket seat forever, with the wind burning my sun-chapped face and the black road narrowing to a point along the horizon, watching Elizabeth whistle soundlessly as her hair streamed out from beneath a nylon checkered scarf.

We ended up at the Cozy Corner on Decatur Street eating pigs in a blanket and Danish pastry, laughing out loud as much as we wanted, even when the other diners, gray looking people like my parents, turned their tired eyes to us—disapprovingly, I hoped.

"Are you going to live with us from now on?"

I knew she wasn't. I understood about vacations, but I asked her because it was the only way I knew to tell her how much I wanted her to stay. The bitter little smile that twisted up the corners of Elizabeth's red ripe mouth caught me by surprise. "Maybe I ought to," she said vaguely.

Hope turned in my stomach like a half-chewed meal. "You could," I told her. "You could share my room, I wouldn't mind. And—"

Aunt Elizabeth grinned. "Now, you know I can't do that, Amanda. What about your Uncle Bobby? Who'd look after him?"

I felt my face grow blank. This was the first I'd heard about an Uncle Bobby. Did my mother have a brother they'd never told me about?

"Your Uncle *Bobby*," Elizabeth insisted. "My husband." She put her coffee down and touched her mouth with the corner of her napkin. "Well, husband-to-be."

Jealousy made my heart beat fast. Still, I saw the possibilities. Husband meant wedding and wedding meant flower girls and bridesmaids, a new white dress and patent leather shoes for me. Maybe a crown of rosebuds or a wicker basket of creamy pink rose petals to carry over my arm.

I wanted to ask about the wedding but Elizabeth was in a strange mood. She leaned across the table toward me, talking low and serious, as if I were an adult. "I wouldn't leave old Bobby," she said, her eyes fastened to mine. "Not forever. But don't think I'm not tempted."

She looked up then, over my head, and gave somebody a brilliant smile. I turned around to see, but it was just old Mr. Andrews behind the counter. He lifted up his hand and wiggled his fingers at Elizabeth till he caught me looking. Then he blushed and turned away. I looked at Elizabeth and a laugh bubbled up out of me and spilled out between us.

"Come on," Elizabeth said, tapping the salt shaker with one curved red nail. "Show me the sights in this old cow town."

Every night Elizabeth went out in her red convertible and every morning she was there when I woke up, with her hair spread out over the pillow smelling of peaches and cigarette smoke. School started up and I had to go despite all my pleading. The fear that I'd come home and find her gone sat in my belly like a knot of dough. But day after day I'd hurry inside and find her waiting. We'd spend our afternoons watching television or driving around in her car sipping soda pop. Then after dinner she'd get up and go.

One night at dinner the phone rang. My mother answered and called to Elizabeth, but she bent over her fruit salad and pretended not to hear. Scotty and I stared at one another, clean amazed. You had to answer when spoken to. Least ways, we kids did. Adults, you just expected them to, without being told.

My mother called twice and then she came into the room and looked at my father, at Elizabeth. "You ought to take it, honey," she said gently, but Elizabeth shook her head.

"You ask him if he's got the house cleaned up yet," Elizabeth said defiantly. "You tell him I'll come home then, when he's got the window fixed and the door put back on its hinges. You tell him I'll come home when, when I can blink my eyes without seeing *stars!*"

Elizabeth shouted that last part and my mother stared at her, shocked, then put her fingers over her mouth and pursed her lips. "Little pitchers, Elizabeth," she said finally, and left the room. Elizabeth stood up and brushed imaginary crumbs off her lap. "I'm sorry," she said to my father, and he shrugged.

"You know, Liz," he said, "you don't have to go back. You could find a job here, or go back to school. It's not like you and Bobby have children to be concerned about."

"Children," Elizabeth said harshly, as if children were some kind of disease, a parasite, something yellow and crusted you find stuck in your teeth or in the corner of your eye after an afternoon nightmare. "Children!" Then she looked at me and Scotty and her face went soft.

My father got up and went into the other room where my mother was, and after a while they both came back. We finished our dinner and didn't speak of it again.

Scotty ended up letting me come to the party after all, when the boys had finished eating. They'd had pizza and potato chips and sodas and bowls and bowls of salted peanuts, Scotty's favorite, but I wasn't feeling too sorry for myself in the kitchen with my parents and Aunt Elizabeth. We had a pizza of our own, and Elizabeth was telling about her job selling makeup in a big department store. She said husbands would come over while their wives were shopping and fall in love with her, and then the ladies wouldn't buy anything. My mother kept interrupting and shushing but she was laughing as hard as we were. My father watched us with a funny, puzzled smile that made me feel, for the first time, like it wasn't always kids against adults. Sometimes it was boys against girls.

Oh, I wanted that. Remembering, I want it still, to be a grown up girl in a tight pretty dress teasing the husbands and making them fall in love with me. I would have given up all the years of childhood still owed me just to be there in that cool bright store, bare-armed beneath the lights, laughing with Elizabeth and trading lipsticks and flirting with the husbands, knotting my hair up on top of my head and letting it go, letting it go.

I didn't and did know both, the way kids do, that by the time I got there to where Elizabeth was, she'd be somewhere else altogether. I'd be the slim bare-armed laughing girl and she—the wife frowning sour-faced from the shadows? The dry-lipped woman testing hand creams at the bargain counter?

There was something there in that kitchen, moving away from me faster than I could follow after, and I wanted desperately to catch it in my two hands. I wanted to hug Elizabeth and my mom and dad all at once, and make us all promise not to change, to sit there every night laughing together, one girl, two ladies and a man, but all friends together trading stories and laughing. I was still laughing but I could feel myself about to cry, and my Mom looked over at me and was about to say something. But then Scotty came in for sodas and when he handed them out of the fridge to me he said, "Here, you can carry these in," and that's how I got invited to the party after all.

I liked sitting with the boys even though they were two years older and usually ignored me. There were two I especially liked, Michael Ray and Michael Patterson, and they both used to tease me, but in sort of a nice way. I pretended not to like it but I didn't mind. After a while my parents came in and said they were going out to a movie and that Aunt Elizabeth would be in charge. The boys were having a gross-out contest, everybody telling the most disgusting thing they could think of. Then Michael Patterson told about a séance his sister went to where they called up a spirit from the other side and it moved an ashtray clear across a tabletop.

"That's nothing," Michael Ray said contemptuously, and then he told about the roller coaster at Thrill World that's haunted by the spirit of a soldier who stood up on it and got his head cut off.

When Aunt Elizabeth came into the dining room all the boys looked at her and some of them got that sad, dumb look my dad had in the kitchen. But Michael Ray kept talking and their attention swung back to him. I'd heard his story before but it was making me kind of jittery anyway.

When Michael Ray finished everyone looked around, trying to think of something even scarier to tell. Aunt Elizabeth put her elbows on the table and lit a cigarette. "Did you kids ever hear about the boy and girl on Lovers' Lane?" she asked, exhaling a stream of smoke through her nose.

"Is that the one where the guy's fingernails scratch the roof of the car?"

Aunt Elizabeth shook her head impatiently. A strand of black hair flew onto Tommy Jergen's face and he pretended he didn't know it was there, but I knew he knew.

"That? That's not a true story," Elizabeth said. "This is a *true* story. It happened to a girl I knew back east."

The boys watched her expectantly but she took her time, tapping her cigarette against the paper plate in front of her. "Mandy," she said quietly. "Turn out the light. We have enough light from the kitchen, don't we?" The way she said it was all spooky but I got up and turned the lights out anyway.

"A boy and girl went to Lovers' Lane in the boy's car," Elizabeth began. She took a puff of her cigarette and looked around at us, and her eyes were big and frightened in the half-light. "They went up there to *kiss*."

Michael Ray began to laugh but Scotty shushed him.

Elizabeth put out her cigarette and stared at Michael Ray. "They weren't supposed to be up there," she said quietly. "They knew there was a maniac loose in the woods. They *knew*."

The way she said it, you knew something was going to happen to them, and that it would sort of be their own fault.

"When they got ready to leave, the car wouldn't start." Elizabeth laughed bitterly. "The boy had forgotten to get gas and they'd run out! So he decided to walk to the gas station, through the woods. He warned the girl to keep the doors locked until he came back. He told her don't you open that door no matter what!"

Elizabeth touched her lips with the tip of her tongue and looked at me. "Do you think she did what he said?"

"Yes," I answered quickly. "Yes, she did."

Elizabeth nodded. "Yes, she did," she agreed. "But then she fell asleep."

Stupid girl! But I knew it was possible. I'd lain in my own room more than once, paralyzed by a creak on the stairs or a sigh from the closet, and awakened with the morning sun streaming through the curtains.

"When she woke up," Elizabeth said slowly, "there was a light shining right in her eyes, right through the window. 'Open the door,' a voice said."

"It was the police," Michael Patterson shouted. "They told her to look right into the light and not look away. The boy's head, it was on the—"

I couldn't help it. The dining room window was behind me and I could feel things out there, policemen and maniacs and rustling, whispering things. Even the boys around the table looked scary, with their hollowed-out eyes shadowed in the half-light. Elizabeth's face was pale and bloodless as a fish, and I couldn't bear for her to say another word in that spooky, frightened way. I began to cry.

"No, no, no, Baby," Elizabeth said in her own voice then. "Someone turn on the light." She pulled me up onto her lap and pushed my face against her shoulder, hiding my face from the gang of boys.

"That's not what happened at all," Elizabeth said in a loud voice. "At first the girl was scared, but then she realized it was her own boyfriend come to take her home. He'd bought a gallon of gas and the man at the gas station had given him a flashlight to use in the woods. That's all. He drove the girl home and the next day they read in the newspaper that the maniac had gone back to the insane asylum on his own. Just walked right in and put on his own straight jacket."

"Oh, brother," Tommy Jurgen said, but Scotty told him hush.

After a while I felt better and Elizabeth put me down. "Come on," she said. "Let's let these boys tell their scary stories. We'll go in the living room and look at TV."

Aunt Elizabeth didn't sneak away while I was at school the way I'd feared.

I came home one afternoon and there was a strange car parked in the driveway, a big blue square-nosed Chevy with a chrome bumper. I went inside and there was Elizabeth curled up on the sofa with her shoes off, a beefy sort of good-looking guy next to her with his arm around her. I could tell she'd been crying because her eyes were all red and there were raccoon circles beneath them. But she looked happy and the guy looked pretty happy, too.

They hardly looked up when I came in, and I would have gone on upstairs to do my homework, but Elizabeth beckoned me to come over so I did. "I've been waiting for you, Amanda," she said quietly. "I want you to meet my Bobby, and I wanted to say goodbye."

"Goodbye," I told her. I felt like asking if she'd stopped seeing stars yet, but I didn't. Bobby looked like the boyfriend in the story, the one who'd got his head cut off.

Aunt Elizabeth started rattling off a whole bunch of messages for me to pass along to my mom and dad and Scotty. I tried to remember them all, but later I couldn't. I just remembered her fresh, soapy smell when she bent over to kiss the top of my head, and her hair falling over my shoulders, her scarlet nail polish and the jangle of her bracelets, and I remembered the way her red convertible looked following the Chevy down the drive and out onto the road: smaller, and tamed, somehow, like a bad dog that had been forgiven and was following its master home. Even when the Chevy was out of sight and I could just make out the taillights of Elizabeth's car, about to disappear around Buckeye Circle and be gone forever, I was re-membering her knocking that red convertible right into gear, me beside her in the front bucket seat, laughing with my hair blowing back in the wind, and somehow Bobby beside her too, his big hand on her white leg, real and not real, there and not there, big hands on her, big hands on me.

133

On Wilson

Brad Pauquette

My dog's hair will not grow forever. Each follicle reaches its terminal length, and then his body discards the hair, littered about in vacuum-clogging clumps on the carpet and pooled in the corners of every staircase. But each of my dog's hairs will not grow to the same length either, the short hairs on his snout gradually increase in length as they run over his head to the full shag of his German Shepherd back, and then the length tapers down again to his paws. No one directs them, but each hair follicle knows its exact length, every hair succumbs to the greater mission of his beautiful black and brown coat, none rebel.

My wife sits beside me, fiddling with the radio. My son, two-years-old, babbles nonsense in his car seat, positioned behind me.

I back out of the driveway, put the car in drive and pull forward. We aren't going anywhere important—out to lunch, cheap Indian food at the North Market or baked potatoes from Wendy's.

A short block from our house, Lyncroft Ave. deadends into Wilson Ave. On the left sits a broken pink dinosaur of a house, returning to dust by natural decay right before our eyes. It sits empty, with rain coming through blanket-sized holes in the roof, and grass in the yard that stretches four feet high. On the right, an imposing yellow brick house stands three stories tall, with six chimneys reaching towards the sky and as many pitbulls roaming the backyard. A right turn takes you into downtown Columbus, a left turn takes you into Eastgate, one of the better black neighborhoods in Columbus. Our neighborhood is neither downtown nor Eastgate.

If you were to pull through the dead-end intersection at Wilson, you'd run into a white duplex, where a sixty-inch TV blocks the only unboarded window on the left half. The TV is either picked up or delivered by the Rent-A-Center or Aaron's truck several times a year. It is apparent that the TV also partially blocks the front entrance, but there are many reasons "USE BACK DOOR" is spray painted in foot tall red letters across the front door.

A few times a week, I sit on my front porch late at night, dragging down a Turkish Gold as the cicadas compete with sirens and the sounds of casual domestic abuse. The foot traffic past my front porch never stops, no matter the time of night or day. Even in the wee hours of the morning, it never stops.

Jittery men, some young, some old, almost all of them black in this neighborhood, walk down Lyncroft Ave. and disappear across the street, behind that white duplex, their eyes jumping back and forth, nervously checking behind them. Fifteen minutes later they emerge again, heading back up Lyncroft Ave. to a vacant garage most likely, but now with a smooth, rhythmic gait, their eyes staring straight ahead, focused—mellowed, yet alive.

In the afternoons, when I pick up litter out of my yard, I see young men wearing coats, regardless of the weather, travel from that white duplex to the yellow brick house across the street. These young men know the pitbulls at the yellow brick house by name, but it doesn't stop the dogs from barking each time the boys cross the street, the pockets in their baggy coats imperceptibly heavier or lighter, depending on whether they're going to or from, determined by the relative weight of cash to crack and quarters to meth.

I don't normally drive towards Wilson after noon, instead, when I need to head downtown, I'll head north out of my block, and circle back around to Mt. Vernon. This particularly Tuesday I'm feeling frisky, or I'm tired of having the direction I can travel determined by an external authority like I'm nine years old, or perhaps I'm just careless.

I see them as soon as I pull out of my driveway, six black teenagers, looking up towards the white duplex, hollering at a girl on the porch of the right side. All six wear red, it must be a special occasion.

Neighborhood patrols don't usually wear colors anymore. It only took the police fifteen years to figure out which color belonged to which organization, and then it took the young men who run the crime in the neighborhoods fifteen minutes to switch to subtler methods of team identification. Except for the kids. Kids always wear the colors—like children in the suburbs wear a t-shirt with the name of their favorite band, or the jersey of their favorite MLB star.

Yet, on special occasions, when it's absolutely critical to determine who belongs on which team, the young men wear their reds in my neighborhood. It's been a special occasion for a couple of weeks now.

A week earlier, I'd seen six boys between the ages of fourteen and seventeen, suited up in their reds, traveling East towards Pointdexter, ready to help a nearby neighborhood push off the "MS-13" or the "Rolling 22" tags I'd recently seen pop up north of Broad Street.

Just a couple of days ago, I saw the young men of the neighborhood, dressed in black, dispersing to their homes during the hour I sit on my porch, returning a few minutes later to roam towards Mt. Vernon in their red adornments, pants hung low, filled with instruments of exhilaration and destruction.

Red socks peek from beneath Daryl's black basketball shorts, James wears a red hoody, Darius wears a red stocking cap. Alone, these colors wouldn't look out of place, but it's unlikely that every single one of them might have chosen to wear that color by coincidence.

On this particular Tuesday, these six boys making a ruckus with their backs to me, standing in front of the white house on Wilson where Lyncroft dead-ends, they're wearing their colors. These teenagers aren't in charge, they don't get paid—they're pawns, they get addicted, they get trapped. These ones in front of this house, every one of them is already lost, and most of them will never gain anything for their sacrifice.

These boys aren't even trusted with guns. Most of them in this group of six are fourteen or fifteen years old. They could get a weapon if they needed to, but they're not trusted to carry them regularly.

These boys should be in school, but instead they'll stand in front of a convenience store somewhere to take the group's numbers from two to six, two of them will be placed on a street corner two blocks down with a cell phone and be told to watch for cops and the right kind of hooptie. At this moment, they could be in school learning to read, learning basic math, but instead they stand in front of a shitty duplex—suited up, hitting a pipe, waiting to be told where their hopped up, hormone-addled brains should go stand—go stand and look like something, but be nothing. At least they know some math, it's industry specific though, mostly revolving around fractions of an ounce, and the metric gram.

We could count off these boys—ten years from now—prison, drug lord, dead, hopeless addict, prison, dead in prison.

My wife coughs twice in the seat next to me, breaking me from a trance.

"Are you gonna stop?" she asks me.

"Sorry," I say, and apply the brake.

I shouldn't have gone this way, not this week—not ever. But today their backs are to me and they don't look like they'll notice. I click on my right blinker and pull to a stop at the sign. I turn my wheel and accelerate. Clairvoyant, or possessed by the devil, one of them turns, looks me in the eye and shouts "Hey Bitch!" Spit dribbles from his blue lips, his glazed red, half-closed eyes look into mine. He lifts up his black sweatshirt, and slaps his naked, ashen belly with his flat hand.

The others turn slowly and snicker, evil eyes peak out from under hoods.

I should complete my turn, I should continue on my way and go eat Indian food with my family. But today I can't.

They hate me because I'm white. They hate me because I take care of my yard and try to improve my house. They hate me because they can't touch me, their Lords watch over me like guardian angels. Nothing would bring the cops crashing in on their operations like harming an articulate white family, but they still want me gone.

They steal from me. They come up on my porch late at night and run off with my furniture, they throw rocks through my windows.

Not today.

I pull to the left side of the street and park facing the wrong direction. I reach under my seat and pull out my Sig Sauer P226 9mm pistol, I flip open the center console and take out a loaded magazine.

"What are you doing?" my wife asks, clutching the armrest.

"Not today," I tell her as I snap the magazine into the grip, and lock it in. "Not today," I tell her as I stick the gun in my jacket pocket and open my door.

"Stop…" she says, but I can't hear her, my foot is on the sidewalk and

I elbow the car door shut behind me.

I walk directly to the group of six, they are forty feet from me. They turn and congregate to face me like a wall. They laugh. Corporately, they can not decide whether they are more confident or amused, their eyes shift and change.

I walk quickly, but not hurriedly, with my eyes fixed on the boy in the black sweatshirt with the blue lips. When I am twenty feet away, I pull the gun out of my right pocket, and pull back the slide to load a bullet into the chamber.

The boy's name is Jared. He is seventeen. I know this because I know all of them. I know this because I had a functional basketball hoop, a rare commodity in this neighborhood, and I learned all of their names before I let them play.

The others see the gun and their eyes widen, bright white eyeballs glaring between their dark brown faces and their dark brown eyes. Their feet begin to hint of shifting. But Jared stares at me coldly, he smirks with only half his mouth.

I am fourteen feet away now, and I pull the gun up and level it at his eyes, still moving forward. The younger boys around him begin to back away when I pull back the hammer.

"You gonna shoot me crack—" he begins to say, but I refuse to hear him call me a "cracker" one more time, and the deafening blast of the 9mm cancels out the rest of his word.

The steel slug exits the muzzle of my Sig at twelve hundred feet per second, and my hand jerks upwards and slightly to the right. The round whistles through the air for the two-hundredths of a second it takes to travel the six feet between my outstretched arm and Jared's forehead, the muzzle flare chasing close behind it.

The bullet splits Jared's forehead just above his right eye, splintering his skull, immediately bruising his eye. Jagged fragments of bone chip from his forehead and the bullet forces them into his mushy, drug-addled brain. The once spiraling bullet now fragments into two pieces, each of which tumbles through the mass of nerve tissue, tightly orbiting the other like a satellite moon.

The hole in his forehead was tidy, but the mass of bone and matter and bullet fragments tear a ragged hole in the top of the back of his head, his matted hair and unwashed skin tears away and lands on the sidewalk behind him.

As the slide on my pistol recoils, the expended bullet casing ejects from the barrel, and the slide pumps another round into the chamber. The empty brass casing tumbles to the ground, ringing on a rock and tumbling through the grass to my right.

Jared's body follows his matted hair, and he slumps backwards to the ground.

I hear my wife scream from the car, I hear the girl on the porch scream, but their screams are indistinguishable from the terrified shrieks of the teenage boys as they turn and run. Two of them bolt between the houses on this side of the street and I hear their feet beat down the alley, their voices trailing off. Two stupider and younger ones turn and run down the length of the sidewalk with their backs to me, and the one remaining hoodlum, Darius, tries to back away but trips over his heels. He lies frozen and silent, hyperventilating on the sidewalk in front of me, his narrow chest heaving.

I am tempted to shoot Jared's lifeless, draining body where it lies on the sidewalk. I am tempted to shoot him in the chest for the basketball hoop he stole and destroyed, though he could have used it at my house every day. I want to shoot him because I can't leave my son's three-dollar plastic toys in the front lawn overnight and expect them to be there in the morning. I want to shoot him for every time I've been accosted while walking my dog because of the color of my skin. I want to shoot him for every thug kid who's called me a cracker, for every bullshit gangster who's threatened to shoot me, for every son-of-a-bitch hoodlum-rapper wannabe who I've had to kick off my back porch—smoking blunts on the cement steps when I pull into my driveway, threatening to hurt me because I don't know "the rules."

But I don't have enough bullets for all of that. And Jared's already dead.

For once I am glad that it will take the police twenty minutes to arrive.

I rest my index finger on the outside of the trigger guard and lower my weapon.

I turn to Darius, and look him in the eyes. I see only fear, I see only panic. I take two steps, bend over and snatch my discarded bullet casing from the grass.

"Not today," I tell him, and I turn to walk back towards my car.

When I reach the silver station wagon, I slip into the driver's seat. My wife is terrified. She's scared of me, she's scared of the gun in my hand, she's scared of the neighborhood who will soon be here. I look in the rearview mirror where my two-year-old son is perplexed, his brow furrowed, yet he is silent.

I place the gun on the floor in front of me, put the car in drive and pull across the road to the correct side.

After three blocks, I pull down an empty alley, roll down my window, and toss out the spent casing. It glitters in the sunlight midway on its arc to its new home, hidden among the alley's trash and vast collection of other spent bullet casings. Suddenly there is a pain in my neck, my arms shake robotically as if the world is a vinyl record player stuck in a scratch.

The bullet casing's tumbling reverses and it glistens in the sun at

141

the top of its arc again. Before I can comprehend what is happening my hand closes around the shell once more, and my car is traveling in reverse through an empty and gray world. All of the people, the traffic, the noise is gone. My wife and child are no longer with me, and the sun, the only source of color in the world, burns scarlet.

I am alone, paralyzed, trapped moving backwards in my car to an unknown destination. My car roams backwards through the streets to Wilson Ave. Jared, the only other occupant of this gray world, stares blackly at me through sunken dead eyes, standing in front of me on the sidewalk like a marionette held by strings. His matted hair and bits of skull lie in the gray grass behind him, and a pool of black blood stains the sidewalk.

My gun is in my hand again, and I am looking down the sites at Jared's forehead. The pool of black recedes behind him. A cylinder of steel less than a centimeter in diameter escapes from his forehead, the skin closes neatly behind, and the bullet approaches my paralyzed body.

The Sig's muzzle swallows the bullet whole, and I suddenly realize how cold the weapon's steel grip is in my hands. I exhale in this gray world, my breath condenses and falls to the ground in front of me.

The scenery around me is the only living thing, still rushing past me. I continue traveling in reverse, paralyzed, until I am back in my car. I blink and the world fades, I blink and the blackness moves in closer still.

My wife coughs twice in the seat next to me. I look up and the sun blinds me, reflecting off the dull red stop sign where Lyncroft Ave. dead-ends into Wilson.

I look over at her.

"Are you gonna stop?" she asks me.

"Sorry," I say, and apply the brake.

I signal my turn at the corner and stop, and begin to pull away.

One of the punks on Wilson, Jared, turns to me with his blue lips and ashen face, and yells, "Hey Bitch." He lifts his black sweatshirt and slaps his ashen belly with his flat palm.

I neither look at him, nor do I look away, I simply execute my right turn, and depress the accelerator.

My wife sniffles in the seat next to me, and I shake my head. I look over to see her eyes turning red before she covers them with her hand.

"Not today..." I mutter to myself, and continue on my way.

Resetting

Kelsey Lynne

Dying, by itself, wasn't particularly inconvenient. The amnesia that
went with it, however, was. It was precise, like the memories had
been cut away with a knife. There were no fragments or images like the
leftover pieces of a particularly vivid dream. The memories were simply,
absolutely, gone. Two years removed. A surgeon's knife was a butcher's
job in comparison. I had only my notes to go by, bound up in a journal
that I'd found tucked inside my jacket, sealed in a Ziploc bag with some
car keys. There were stones in my pockets, river stones, heavy enough that
I'd had to pull them out, one by one, wallowing at the bottom of the river.
The water filled my lungs and my chest convulsed, trying to breathe in the
bracken silt, until the last of the stones fell away and I was free to find the
surface. It was dark there on the bottom of the river, but my bare feet found
the bottom, and I shoved away. Found the surface. Clawed my way to the
bank.

Two years, my journal said. I still worked as an accountant and I'd
earned a raise but no promotions. Same house. New car. I'd find it parked
up the path where a small lot had been cleared away in the trees to allow
people to overlook the river. It was late in the day, the sun slipping towards

the horizon, and I wondered what day it was. I hoped it was a Friday. I could use the weekend to catch up on my life. The stones in my pockets—the careful notes of my journal—this was not a murder. This was suicide. A futile gesture, since no one had died for about three years now. Just forgot. Died, came back, and forgot everything that happened, all the way back to the first time they'd died. Like hitting the reset button.

I'd run my car off the road that first time. Through the guardrail, tumbling it down the easy slope and into the river. The impact had knocked me unconscious and I'd drowned by the time the rescue crew pulled me free. That was my reset point. A dark night, the river, and a car ponderously filling up with water. I'd killed myself in almost the same place I'd died the first time. I wondered why that was. The person that threw herself into that river was a stranger now, lost, and I was left wondering what had driven her to such desperation. We shared a name, muscle and skin, but I didn't know who she was. All that I had was this journal in the Ziploc bag.

My house was not empty when I pulled up into the drive. I entered the kitchen, coming in through the garage, and had just set my car keys on the table when I heard a creak from the hall and someone said my name. I screamed and threw myself back, hitting the wall. I stood there—paralyzed—and stared at the stranger that regarded me. He moved warily, as if I were a startled animal. I noted his black hair, brown eyes, careful layers of muscle—very little stubble on his rounded jawline.

"Sandy," he said again, his voice low, "You're soaked through."

"Who are you?" I whispered, edging back.

He froze, one hand raised as if to reassure me. I huddled in on myself, arms pressed in against my stomach.

"I just died," I said, "in the river."

"Shit."

He took a step back, put his hand half in his pocket. Stared at the ground. When he spoke again, his tone was bitter and my blood ran cold. I was shivering violently now, muscles jerking like they remembered the water in my lungs.

"That's twice now. Twice you've done this to me. Us. I'm Dean. We're engaged."

I looked at my hand in reflex. It was bare of a ring. His was not.

"I—but—why?"

"I don't know." He threw his hands up and turned away from me. "We met a few months after your car accident. Why don't you go get cleaned up and put on some dry clothes? I'll go pack my things. I don't think you'll want a stranger sleeping over here."

"Do you—"

"I have an apartment. I'll just go there. Call you tomorrow, okay?"

I nodded, numb. He vanished off into the living room, clearing the way between myself and the stairs. I took them at a run, fleeing the stranger that was in my house, bewildered and afraid. He came up to the bedroom after I'd turned on the shower and I could hear him moving about, jerking open the closet door and dresser drawers, kicking them shut. I stood there under the flow of water until I could no longer hear him. It reminded me of the river. I turned my face up to the nozzle, held it there under the spray, wondered if that was how it felt with the river stones holding me down, letting the entirety of the river's mass press on my limbs and steal away my memories.

My journal had no mention of Dean. I read it sitting there on the floor of my bathroom, wrapped in a towel, the mirror covered with condensation. It talked about my job, things I needed to do, meetings, people. Everything that would help me recover from losing two years of my life. My relationships with my friends, my family, current events. Passwords to my computer, my bank account, online shopping. There was nothing about

Dean. I read through twice, and on the third attempt I tore one of the pages, frantically thumbing through them as if I'd somehow missed something, a letter tucked between the thin paper that would explain all of this to me. Nothing. I threw the journal and it banged against the closed door.

Then, I cried. Sandy-before was a stranger to me and she'd taken my memories away, left me alone in this terrifying world—familiar enough to feel right, but with objects and scents I no longer knew. Cologne, an additional towel on the wall rack. A fiancé and no ring on my own hand.

There's no explanation for why people stopped dying. The animals still did. Humanity did not. Our population was frozen—there were no more children born—and science was still waiting to figure out how the aging process would work. It upset everything. Death was far more common now that there were no consequences. The police force was overwhelmed with murders, to the point they could only investigate the serials. The sporadic ones, the moments of anger that only escalated once in a while—the restraint had been removed from those. Like cutting the brake lines. The suicides, too, had increased, as had the accidental deaths. Nothing was final. We were no longer afraid.

I wondered if my first death had truly been an accident. Dean's wasn't. It was a mistake, he said, when we talked over the phone. He regretted it. During the first year, when the world went insane and people were testing out this newfound immortality in droves. He'd shot himself and revived gasping, his bathroom wall sprayed with blood. It had been a nightmare to clean, he said, as if that was the worst part of it all. Drowning was much cleaner.

We went out for dinner a few days later, once I had my feet on the ground. I wasn't sure if I truly understood the world I'd woken up to, but

Dean was confident. I'd done this before, he said. The last time it had only taken a few days for me to readjust to my life. I kept such meticulous notes at work, it was easy. The restaurant was generic Italian and I found the sauce heavy and insipid, as if the kitchen were afraid to try anything for fear of offending someone's palate. Dean talked about his job, about the promotion he was angling for. He told me of our times together, how we'd go to baseball games and what I'd wear when we went to clubs. He loved horror movies and told me we'd go see one soon. Maybe this weekend. I did not say much of anything. I told myself that it was because I was still so unsure of myself, of my place in everything around me. I felt adrift. Like I was still caught in the river and the current was pulling me along, that the stones had slipped from my pockets and I was lost in the tumult. I could only keep treading water and hope that the surface would appear.

After dinner, Dean dropped me off at my house. We stood on the front porch and I wondered if I should invite him in, if I could at this point. He didn't say anything, just looked at me with a furrowed brow, like a dog at the window. Then he leaned forwards and I felt his lips on the line of my jaw. They lingered there and I didn't move, aware of his hands at my hips, not quite touching just yet. My back was straight and I could only think of my own breathing. Then Dean drew back, leaving a cold spot of moisture from where his lips had touched my skin, and he stepped away, down off the porch.

"I'll pick you up this weekend for the movie," he said, "Around eight, I guess."

He turned and walked away. I stared down at my hand as his car backed out of my drive. He'd bought me a new ring as I could only assume I had lost the original in the river. It was a plain gold band. Cheap. He didn't say it, but he was waiting to see if this would still work. He didn't want to waste his money on a broken relationship. I'd thrown away years of effort when I threw myself into the river.

I turned and fled back into the house and locked the door behind me. I checked the backdoor and windows as well. I told myself that it was because crime was up since we stopped dying, that there was a higher chance that a home intrusion would result in the homeowner being killed. Then I went upstairs, to my closet. I had stowed my journal in the back, in an old shoebox. I took it out and sat on the floor, cross-legged, and thumbed through the pages. I did take such meticulous notes—there were lists of the movies I'd seen and the places I liked to shop. My favorite restaurants. I skimmed that page, searching the entries. I did this twice. The Italian place was not listed. We'd gone there for our anniversary each year we were together, Dean said. We loved it.

I returned the journal to its hiding place and stood. I looked through the shirts, flipped through my blouses, one by one. Studying them. I found, at the back of the closet, a number of t-shirts for a baseball team. Their fronts emblazoned with the logo, the backs either bare or sporting an unrecognizable name and number. There were four in all. I stepped back and looked at these for a long time. I did not really like baseball. This, I knew, without the help of my notes. I'd never really cared much for sports.

Didn't people change in a relationship?

I asked my coworkers about Dean. They talked to me carefully now and I thought that perhaps they knew something happened, but did not want to bring it up directly. I was caught up on my work. The adjustment was almost seamless. There were notations of important life events—how Jessica married three months ago, how David's son was now four years old, and how Eric had tripped on the stairs and broken his neck last month and was still trying to dig through his archived e-mails to understand what he was doing here. It was enough to get by, the details of their lives would

149

be obscured by the casual detachment that the workplace fostered. I saw the looks though, the wary glances in the hallway that said not everything was right. Perhaps they knew the signs better than I did. I'd done this twice now, after all.

They told me I'd had my difficulties with Dean. That I was often stressed by our relationship, that I worried about the two of us a lot. We'd fight and break up, then he'd show up that weekend with all these plans for a romantic trip and talk me into going with him and it'd be better for a few days after that. I'd be happy. Then he proposed and that put an end to our regular breakups. He'd send me flowers sometimes, have them delivered to the front desk and I'd go down there and bring them back to my desk. I'd leave them there until they wilted and someone else would throw them out after I'd gone home for the day. It was more detail than I expected and this was why I thought they knew I'd killed myself. There were clues here, subtle signs that could help me understand why I'd done this. This, and the journal. I brought it to work with me and read it over my lunch break, sitting at my desk with my pasta half-eaten in front of me, flipping through the pages and re-reading every word. My doctor was located on Elm St. My air conditioner had been repaired the previous summer and I was putting back money for when it finally broke for the last time. I'd changed which church I went to. All these little details in my precise script, little phrases with no embellishment. No explanation. Just facts.

I was starting to hate the before-Sandy.

Dean was passive in his anger. I learned this in bits and pieces, how he would look away and sigh—a sharp gesture—when I did not react to his advances. How he would move away from me and excuse himself to his apartment shortly after. Even that seemed like an accusation. He never invited me over and he never returned to gather the rest of his belongings. Like it was just a temporary thing, that we were on hold until I came around. He'd tell me that we would do this together, that we liked this and enjoyed doing that. Together. As if I'd suddenly remember and it'd all be okay if he just said it often enough. I would look in my journal after he left, even though I knew most of the entries by heart now. I didn't have the park we'd go to on weekends listed as my favorite place and I didn't write down any of the horror movies as ones I'd seen since the first time I died.

I didn't see him angry until some months into our struggling relationship. I was cooking dinner, my attempt at reconciliation, at saying that this house was his house as well and we could pretend and be normal for a little while. I made stir fry and I put peanuts in it, and when I set down the plates at the table he recoiled, standing and stalking to the other side of the kitchen. I stared at him and he leaned up against the back wall, letting out his breath in a huff, arms crossed. I knew the posture. He wasn't looking at me.

"Dean," I said, "I didn't make it spicy if that's what you're worried about."

"I'm allergic to peanuts."

I was quiet a moment.

"I-I forgot," I said, reaching for the plates to take them away, "I'll order something instead."

"Yeah. Do that."

My hand stalled in mid-gesture and I stared down at the steaming food, the brown noodles and the pile of vegetables, littered with the offending item like slick insects.

"I'm sorry," I said, "I'm really trying here."

"Yeah, you're trying." He didn't keep the bite out of his voice. "We shouldn't even be having to do this at all. And all you say is you're sorry."

"I don't know why I killed myself," I whispered, "I don't know what else to say."

"Don't know why?" He threw his hands into the air and turned his back to me. "You were being selfish! Did you even think about what that would do to me? To us?"

"Were we fighting just before? Like this?"

"No! I don't have a clue why you killed yourself. For kicks, I guess. Oh, I'll just go pop in the river for a swim and not come up for air."

"You shot yourself." It came out with more of a sting than I intended, like the crack of a whip. I regretted it instantly. Dean went still.

"I wasn't in a relationship," he said, each word measured. I could hear the heat behind them. "I didn't have anyone who cared about me."

I couldn't find a reply to that. Maybe I was selfish. I hadn't even written down his peanut allergy in my book. I hadn't written down anything about him.

"You know what?" he sighed, running his hands through his hair, "I'm going home. Just forget it. We'll try dinner some other night."

I let him go. The door fell shut behind him, hard. When the engine of his car died away in the distance, I stirred to life again. I returned to the kitchen and took out a bottle of hot sauce. It was from a local farmer's market. I'd written that down in my journal, which day to go, which vendor to see and what flavor to buy. I poured this liberally over both plates and ate first mine, then his. I felt sick after, my stomach full to the point it hurt.

The peanuts were the best part.

I talked to Jessica the next day. I went to her cubicle and sat there and we held the conversation in a low tone. I asked her how her relationship with Ben was, how things had changed for her after she'd gotten engaged. She was quiet a moment, studying me, then she put her hands in her lap and composed herself. It was a deliberate gesture, an indication that she was giving me her full attention. That she took my question seriously, that she understood it was more than just idle talk.

"This is about Dean, isn't it?" she said.

I looked down at the ground.

"I don't like to interfere in other people's relationships," she said, "but Sandy, you've killed yourself over this before—and I think you've done it again. You don't have to tell me if I'm right or not. But I think that says a lot on its own. Have you asked any of your friends about this?"

"I didn't find any notes left in my journal," I said, "and all the ones I have in my address book...we haven't talked for a long time, they said."

"And isn't that kind of telling?"

She said it with an air of expectation. I just stood and returned to my desk. I sat there a long time, staring at the computer monitor, until the screen went into hibernation and I was forced to stir the mouse to jog it awake. I thought, then, that I understood before-Sandy. She'd given me a blank slate. All the important details, the things I needed to establish myself. Nothing else. A second chance, to do things differently this time.

To decide for myself on Dean.

He was like a wart, I decided, on my drive home. Stuck there, part of my flesh, and I saw it every time I looked at myself in the mirror. I had to get rid of it. It was a blemish and I picked at it, constantly, and tried to pretend it was nothing. Like a stain on my skin that I could cover up if I was just skillful enough with the concealer and blush. Something I could put a bandage over and pretend it wasn't there, that it wasn't a problem. That everything was fine or that I just needed to try enough. It had to go.

I left my house after dark. I'd never been to his apartment but I called one of his friends and got the address. I took a longer route there so that I would drive past a construction site on the way. I parked the car in one of the gravel turn-offs beside the road and walked along the fence surrounding the site until I was out of sight of the street. Then, I climbed up and over the fence, landing hard in a crouch. There were neat piles of building materials stacked in rows. I found what I was looking for at the end of one of these lanes, where scrap material was piled to await disposal. There was a length of rebar there, about the length of my forearm and the width of my thumb. I took it with me.

Dean's apartment was on the second floor. I bought a bouquet of flowers with the longest stems I could find from the grocery store down the street, and I slipped the rebar into the middle of them. Then I waited at the outside door to Dean's apartment building until someone came along and I begged them to buzz me in, I told them that I wanted to surprise my fiancé. For our anniversary. He recognized Dean's name and knew that he was engaged, so he let me in. I saw him look at my hand, noting the ring. I hurried upstairs and then hovered there outside his door, listening to ensure the other resident had gone inside and the hallway was empty. Then I knocked.

Dean was surprised to see me. He glanced backwards, at the living room beyond. Uneasy. I wondered why he'd never brought me here. It was curious.

"Sandy," he said without much enthusiasm, "I didn't think we were doing anything tonight."

"I wanted to surprise you." I clutched at the flowers nervously. "Can I come in?"

"Well—okay—but I don't have much furniture. Just cheap stuff. I never really built this place up because I thought we were going to live together."

His voice had taken that hard edge again. I didn't reply, just let him turn around and start to move inside, through the entryway. The door slipped shut behind me with a heavy click and I pulled the piece of rebar free. He didn't realize it, didn't realize anything. There was surprisingly little effort involved. The weight of the metal was enough, gravity pulling the rebar downwards, like it was eager to be reunited with the earth and only needed the slight push I gave it. I felt the muscles in my arm all too clearly—how the bicep strained a moment, how the forearm seemed to twist and the wrist gave a sharp bite of pain as it rotated around. I felt the impact up through my elbow. It made my fingers go numb. There was a heavy sound, like I'd dropped a sack of potatoes on the tiled floor, and Dean sagged as his knees folded under him. His body was squat, lax. His head draped against the wall and lolled there, eyes open and unfocused. I raised the piece of rebar up again, the metal protesting at the movement, as if it didn't want to leave the earth. I let it drop again and Dean shuddered and slid further towards the ground. There was blood slipping down his forehead, like fingers caressing his hair. I'd not touched him back, not in the entire time we were together since I died in the river. He'd stroked my hair, kissed my face, touched my shoulders. I never moved.

I raised the rebar. Let it fall. I did this, mechanically, watching with a sort of detachment as the blood puddled in the hollow of his neck and overflowed onto the floor. How the side of his head seemed to bow inwards. Like a waning moon. My muscles hurt and I stopped a moment, letting the tip of the rebar touch the tiled floor. I was panting. My shoulder ached.

I wrapped the rebar in plastic bags and put it back into the flowers. I cleaned the floor and the wall. Dean was right—blood was messy. I couldn't imagine what it had been like to clean up after a gunshot to the head. This was bad enough. I threw the soiled cleaning supplies into another plastic bag and tied it up. I'd take it with me. Dispose of it elsewhere. The entryway was now relatively clean, the only blood spots were close to where he'd fallen. He'd think he had slipped and fallen, perhaps, when he came around in a few hours. I didn't really care. I wasn't feeling much of anything at the moment, just a sort of light-headed sensation, like

I was floating. I walked through his apartment and looked at each room. There was little furniture and fewer personal belongings. Pictures of himself with his friends, some memorabilia from his baseball team. I found a few framed photos of us, shoved off to the side. They weren't recent. They were the before-Sandy. My smile looked strained.

I left with the flowers and threw the bag of bloody rags in a random dumpster in a parking lot on the way home. I threw the engagement ring out the window of the car as I drove away. When I reached my house, I put the flowers in a vase of water on the table. I put the rebar at the back of my closet, still wrapped in plastic. I left it there, letting the blood dry, resting in the corner next to the shoebox with my journal. The flowers remained on my table until they wilted and then I threw them out. I threw out the rest of Dean's belongings as well, his cologne and his toothbrush and the woman's sized baseball t-shirts. The bottle of fragrance broke from the fall and the garbage can stunk of spice and the sickly-sweet perfume of half-rotted lilies.

After that, I did not see Dean until almost three weeks later, while grocery shopping. I stopped at the mouth of the aisle, staring, and my heart tumbled over itself. He was standing there, by the jelly, trying to decide between apricot and blueberry. I could go up to him. Introduce myself. Smile, flirt. Start over. I'd know all his favorite things, what movies to suggest we see, which baseball tickets to surprise him with. He wouldn't know that I'd killed myself twice before. He wouldn't blame me for it, again and again. I could be perfect and he'd love me for it, for understanding him and knowing and liking all the things he knew and liked. I'd know not to cook meals with peanuts.

I walked down the aisle, stopped next to him. Reached in just beside him so that he was forced to side-step out of politeness.

"Excuse me," I murmured.

I picked up the the first jar of peanut butter my fingers closed on. I dropped this in my basket, turned my back, and walked away.

Let Me Know

David Armstrong

The paranormal investigators arrived at our house the same day I was scheduled for an abortion at the East Columbus Planned Parenthood. Two of them were men and one was a woman with a purple birthmark near her right ear that looked like a burn. The heavyset man wore a digital recorder with a purse-strap. He kept touching the small gray knobs and repositioning his headphones. When he asked for quiet, the only thing I could hear was the whir of the refrigerator and the shrill whistle of air moving in and out through his nostrils.

They were making a documentary about their investigation. The director was a man named Charles Everett. He said to call him Charlie.

He shook my hand and looked at me funny when we met in the kitchen.

"How old are you?" he asked.

"Fifteen," I said.

"You're going to be a heartbreaker."

Mom and Dad were all smiles.

Charlie continued, "So what we need is some background. Maybe about the house, the area. Is there a history here?"

My dad swiped some crumbs off the countertop. "You know more than I do."

"Fair enough, but for the documentary we want to get some footage from the horse's mouth."

"I got it," said Dad. "You want me or Karen?"

"Probably all three." Charlie was maybe thirty, with an elongated, childish face. He pushed his hair off his forehead, and it all fell back into his eyes.

Mom pulled a trashbag out of the can like a magician with a rabbit.

"Sorry about the mess," she said. "We just finished breakfast."

My mother is shy and pretty, and Charlie smiled at her differently than he did at my Dad. I don't think this meant anything except that Mom and Dad are different people.

"Can we fix you anything, Charlie?"

"We're fine. Mostly we'll shoot in the den. But we'll set up some other shots at the door to the attic. And maybe for Amy's interview we'll film in her room, if that's okay with you."

"Seems reasonable," said Dad.

They positioned the lights in the den and got some close-ups of Dad's signed Ernie Banks baseball and his collection of Appalachian Trail books. They also recorded room tone with the wheezy sound of Justin, the sound man, in the background.

Lydia, the gaffer, cracked jokes when the sound wasn't rolling. She plunked a dime in Justin's crack when he was crawling on all fours searching for the "hum" that turned out to be from our computer's power strip. He rose up and smacked his head on an end table, and it made me shoot orange juice out of my nose. From then on me and Lydia were tight. She showed me how to tilt the LED panel to make the shot "ominous" and how to sandbag the tripod. I stopped thinking about going to the doctor for a while.

When it was my turn for the interview, Charlie positioned a few of my old stuffed animals on the bed behind me and pulled the curtains. Lydia put a dense black canvas over the window and placed a rectangular bank of flourescent bulbs in front of it. These were supposed to give the impression of cool sunlight seeping in. Lydia said fake light was better than sunshine any day. She put a translucent blue "gel" inside my lampshade, and the whole room got spooky and hot. Charlie said to try not to sweat, so I stood out in the hall when we weren't shooting.

For filming I sat on my bed and Charlie asked the questions.

"Just look at me, and forget about the camera," he said. "When did you hear the noise first?"

"Seven weeks ago."

"Remember the date?"

"February. It was in February."

I remembered the exact date, but I pretended not to. It was February fifteenth, which is the first time I ever had sex, and it was with Joseph Salzberg in our attic. I remember because it was the day after Valentine's, and Mom said she was bummed because she thought it would be more romantic if the Ballroom Winter Festival at NorthPointe had been one day earlier. Then my parents left and Joey came over and we climbed up into the attic where I'd put down a few quilts and laid out some flower petals that I'd ripped off some daisies in the foyer. The petals looked a little sad and uncomfortable and lonely in the moonlight through the circle window with its beam like a target right where we did it.

We didn't talk much. And right after is when Mom and Dad came home and started yelling for me, which is when Joey and I ran to my room. To lead Mom and Dad away from Joey, I told them I heard something in the attic. We all went up. They found the quilts up there, and the flower petals that hadn't really gone anywhere, and at first Mom thought a squatter had been in our attic. But then Dad found some old boxes, which were the same boxes where I'd found the quilts, and there were black-and-white pictures of faded people in there who were sitting on that same quilt in a field of daisies, and they were smiling, and I felt my stomach kind of flip, then I threw up.

Everything happened fast after that. Dad and Mom got hooked on the ghost angle. They tried to find out who the previous inhabitants were. To keep them going I said sometimes I heard movement over the thin set of stairs that rose to the attic, and it was always at night, and my father checked every evening before we went to bed so that it couldn't be anything but supernatural, or at least a trick of the house.

"Like two people laughing. Like they love each other," I said. "That's the sound."

"And that's all?" Charlie said.

"Maybe kissing." I thought of Joey.

"Kissing?"

My neck suddenly felt hot and itchy.

"Can we take a break?"

"Sure."

Lydia handed me a cold bottle of water from a little cooler my mom had supplied.

Then Mom called everyone for lunch, and Justin and Lydia turned off the lights and went downstairs, and when I walked back into my room Charlie was near my dresser with an off-white thing he called an EVP listener that looked like a baby monitor in his hand, and he was waving it around like he was checking for radiation, and in his other hand he had my fake license that said I was eighteen and the papers that the abortion counselor gave me before I signed the medical forms.

"It says you have an appointment today," he said.

The little detector hissed in his hand and squealed. The sound was very quiet, like a newborn puppy.

At first I couldn't think of what to do. I thought about running downstairs and lying, telling everybody Charlie touched me, but I didn't.

Then he did touch me. He crossed the room and put a finger on my belly, just lightly, for half a second.

"How far along are you?"

I wanted to lie about that, too. But again I didn't.

"Seven weeks."

I looked at my feet. I was wearing purple ankle socks that day and didn't remember putting them on.

"So, since—"

I was about to nod when the detector crackled. Through its pinhole speakers we heard a baby crying. Very small. Very far away.

Charlie stepped back.

The crying stopped. Charlie reached out and put the detector near my stomach. The crying started again.

Baby and I have turned the detector into a little game.

I say something like, "Hello, baby," and then I put the detector up to my stomach and sometimes it makes a little giggle because it heard me. Very faint. Sometimes I read my brochures about bodily health and a woman's rights under federal law just to see what baby thinks. Mostly baby is quiet.

It's been a week since the paranormal investigators interviewed us, and they're scheduled to come back tonight. Charlie said I could keep the detector if I promised not to go to Planned Parenthood. He gave me back the carbon copies of the papers that I signed with the counselor, but he kept my fake license.

The crew is in the driveway now. My mouth is as close to my stomach as I can get, and I am humming a lullaby about the mockingbird, but I don't know the words, so mostly I just hum, and sometimes out pops a "heard" or "word." I straighten up when my Dad opens the door to my room.

"Hey, pumpkin. Want to say hello to the crew?"

Somehow I feel like if I get up I'll leave baby in this room here in the chair, and we're getting along so well.

"No thanks, Dad. I'll wait."

I hear them downstairs, and the first one up is Charlie.

"Did you decide?"

I feel bad because I've been using his detector all this time, but I say no, I haven't decided. Plus, he has my fake ID.

"You think this is a game?" He's angry. He's pointing a finger at my stomach. "That's a baby in there. And we can hear it. Do you want me to tell your parents?"

I put the detector up to my stomach, and the baby makes a new sound. Smacking tiny lips in amber liquid that make a syrupy hiccup. And then another, and then a hard sound like a bubble bursting in tar.

"You see," says Charlie. "She's trying to talk."

"I don't see how you know it's a girl." But I think he's right. The voice is like glass bells.

The detector clears its staticky throat, and then there it is, my baby's tiny voice gurgling, but also stringing sounds together, and then, zip, just like that, a word: *Beb-beb.* Or maybe *peb-beb.*

"What? What's she saying?" Charlie's on his knees, sliding across the floor to my feet. "She's saying words."

Peb-beb. Behhb-pppppppp.

"Pebble?" Charlie says.

"Bed, maybe."

"Have you been getting enough rest?"

"This is stupid," I say. I throw the detector across the room. It doesn't break because it hits the bed and falls off with a soft whump onto the carpet.

Now Charlie is very angry, and he shakes that finger. The crease between his eyes is off-center, and I can't help wanting to roll it over to make a symmetry of his face.

"I'll tell your parents if I have to," he says.

"They'll probably want me to get rid of it," I say, though this isn't true.

I want things to go back to the way they were so I can stop worrying about having a baby or not having a baby. Somehow the question—yes or no—feels like it's changed everything already. Sometimes I wish I could fall down the stairs and I would lose the baby, and then it wouldn't be my fault, and I wouldn't have to make the decision, and I could also go back to doing whatever I want.

Charlie goes and picks up the detector off the floor. He hands it to me and says, "Just tell me if she says anything."

I take the detector, but I only look at his knees.

Lydia and I have a great time again. She makes me forget there's a baby inside me trying to say something through a ghost detector.

When Justin, the sound guy, tries to record the groaning I told everyone I heard on the stairs, Lydia hides her phone under some blankets near the attic door. Last night she downloaded fart sounds off the internet and made a playlist and plays it on the phone's tiny speakers under the blanket. You can't hear it over everyone talking. Then Justin tells us to leave the house so he can listen for ghosts. This is at six in the evening, and everyone is feeling a little spooky because it's getting dark and the ghosts might be moving around. We sit on the back patio in the dark and drink lemonade in quiet sips and whisper.

It's a little cool, and my father builds a fire in the fire pit, and Lydia and I sit next to it, joking and trying not to laugh at the idea of Justin tracking the farts. But then the fire makes us somber. The air feels dry and humorless with woodsmoke. Lydia stares into the coals and I suddenly know. She's the one I want to talk to. About this.

"Have you ever had a baby?" I ask.

She has a hard time looking away from the fire. She puts on a smile.

"I got pregnant once. Do you want to have kids someday?"

"What did you do?"

"You mean, did I keep it?"

I nod.

"I kept it. I wanted to. But he didn't stick around." She shrugs kind of comically by raising her elbows off the chair.

"Did you fall down some stairs or something?"

"No. Nothing like that. It just wasn't a good time. I had low iron. That may have had something to do with it. Maybe not. Sometimes little babies just aren't meant to make it. One in five, or something like that."

She looks very sad to me now.

I want to tell her I'm pregnant. But just then Justin opens the window of the second story bathroom and yells at us. His head floats between moving streamers of smoke from the fire.

"Very funny," he says. "Very funny, Lydia." He holds up her phone. It's still farting, and we can all hear it now.

Lydia turns in her chair and makes a half smile, but the fire is keeping her sad. The smoke won't let her lips rise all the way.

"And by very funny," Justin says, "I mean not funny at all."

He throws her phone down onto the stone sidewalk my father built two summers ago. The plastic pieces bounce and roll, and I wonder which parts are the case, which are the phone, and which are its guts popping free and wobbling into the grass. Everyone is quiet. Justin shuts the window.

Lydia doesn't get up, and my dad walks over and picks up the pieces in the dark.

Lydia whispers to me.

"Justin was the dad."

Then my father brings the pieces of the phone to her and says he's sorry. We're all trying to keep the blank expressions that people keep when two people are fighting between themselves.

There are no noises other than the farts on the digital sound recording. Justin says that our house is a bust, very loudly, in the hallway so we're sure to hear. My Mom and Dad look ashamed that their ghosts didn't perform well.

Charlie hands me a bright green Gideon's bible before he leaves. It is small. Smaller than my smallest notebook. He whispers in my ear, "I'll let you off the hook. Those detectors pick up baby monitor frequencies. That's what you're hearing. Your neighbors probably have one in their kid's room."

He smiles and tilts his head like, *forgive me, it was harmless.* Then he taps the bible. "Read it," he says. "Hope you make the right choice." Then he's out the door.

Lydia flips up my pony tail so it hits me in the forehead. She says, "Stay funny."

Then they're all out the door and Mom and Dad are in the kitchen washing up the lemonade glasses.

Back in my room I see that Charlie put my fake license in the bible. I put both things in my sweater drawer and turn on the detector.

I feel like my baby was sitting in this chair waiting for me to get back.

I hunch over and whisper.

"What do you think, baby? You a keeper or a go-er?"

The static is a tiny gray ocean on a marble-sized planet.

"What about it, baby? Speak up or forever hold your peace."

Then I hear it. Babbling at first, but then making words. Whole sentences. Spelled out in whispers as light as corn silk.

Harvest

Ann Brimacombe Elliot

We are bringing in the wheat. In the more remote areas of southwest England, it is still some years before the advent of the combine harvester. The rust-mottled red tractor chugs slowly around the perimeter of the field, puffing clouds of pungent blue exhaust and dust. The old binder rattles behind it. Its turning vanes chop off the stalks at stubble level and steer the ripened grain into the machine's maw, where it is swallowed and regurgitated as neatly bound sheaves. We children—five or six of us—and a bevy of uncles follow, stacking them into what my Devonshire relatives call *stooks*—round dozens of sheaves forming miniature wigwams.

It is August and hot by English standards. I am eight years old—more or less—and tired, sweaty, thirsty. My hands are sore from the stalks of the grain, the harsh binder twine, and the thistles that inevitably hide within the sheaves. My exposed skin prickles with sunburn. I am from the town but I am determined to keep up with my bronzed and toughened country cousins.

In addition, if I work hard, Uncle Fred has promised me a ride on the broad back of Violet, the bay Shire draft horse who, with the younger mare, Jessie, drowses in the meager shade of a hawthorn tree. The horses are fully harnessed, ready to take over if the tractor fails, as it so often does.

Above the tractor's steady chug and drone, a skylark spills its end-less cascade of sweet song. It is a sound that I forever and perversely still associate with the scent of my uncles—a heady masculine perfume com-pounded of cows, dried sweat, mud and manure. The uncles goad and tease me with rough affection. My face grows hotter and redder and I trot and stack, stack and trot.

At noon the aunts arrive with our lunch wrapped in checkered cloths and carried in wicker baskets. Among them, Auntie Win—distilled kind-ness, tall and ample with arms like fleshy hams; Auntie Frances—birdlike, tiny and neat, quietly energetic; Aunt Phyllis—a witch if ever there was one, skinny, sour and scolding. I avoid her and her acid gaze if humanly possible.

A boisterous group, we sit in whatever shade we can find, fidgeting in our attempts to find comfortable places on the prickly stubble. The food is unwrapped: generous slices of Devon pasty burst with potatoes laced with nutmeg, parsley and bacon fat; spicy homemade sausages wrapped in more heavy tough pastry; hard-boiled eggs; raisin-stuffed rock cakes. I eat and eat. The uncles laugh and urge me toward yet one more slice of pasty. I am famous for my capacity, but the sun is so hot that the food is making me slightly queasy, and I must disappoint them. The men drink rough cider and mugs of strong milky tea. For us children, there is scalded milk, whose taste and floating gobs of congealed cream I cannot bear; or we are offered bottles of carbonated liquid in virulent shades of red, green or yellow. The cousins consume this poisonous pop with glee. I try to follow their example but I have difficulty with such sweetness, and the bubbles tickle my soft palate, rise up the back of my nose, and cause me to choke and splutter. I long in vain for a glass of plain cold water.

After lunch, the standing grain is much reduced. The tractor puffs in ever-decreasing circles. One by one, the dogs arrive. Collies, terriers, and other mixed and motley canines from surrounding farms congregate around the field. They pant and gaze with fierce intensity at the shrinking circle of wheat. I pat a sheepdog named Sam, a usually responsive multi-colored mutt, but he does little more than twitch a burr-studded tail, and does not take his eyes off the diminishing island of grain. The dogs are waiting. Some of the cousins have given up stacking, and have taken up stout sticks. They too wait.

The first rabbit appears; it streaks for the hedgerow, frantic white cottontail bobbing. A black dog is onto it in a trice. A thin high scream, and the rabbit lies disemboweled and bloody, the dog tearing at its corpse. More rabbits and an occasional rat break out, dogs, cousins and uncles in hot pursuit. Swiftly the air becomes heavy with the rusty smell of blood and spilled intestines. For a few minutes I find myself swept up in the frenzy. I have no weapon, but I yell wordlessly, and run this way and that. The circle of grain shrinks and shrinks. Animals and humans dart in every direction. The tractor chugs steadily. When a veritable flood of desperate creatures bursts forth, safety in numbers is briefly afforded. A few make it to the hedgerow, some disappear beneath the wheels of the binder.

A very young rabbit careens toward me and halts at my feet. Its black eyes bulge with panic, its small sides heave in terror. With a rush, the last of my excitement vanishes. I bend to snatch up the little animal and save it—but a cousin is there. With one savage blow, he cudgels it into oblivion.

I turn away and walk over to the horses. Tears of loss and sadness spill down my cheeks. I bury my nose in Violet's warm, sweet-smelling hide and cover my ears to block the sounds: the barks, the pitiful shrieks, the thuds and yells. Violet chomps lazily at a nosebag of grain, ignoring me, my sobs and the mayhem in the field.

The sound of the tractor suddenly ceases. I turn around, wiping my eyes with a grubby fist. It has driven to the edge of the field and stopped. The uncle who has driven it is clambering stiffly down from its metal seat. It is over. The field is nothing now but stubble and stooks, blood and fur, dogs squabbling over small corpses. Cousins and uncles laugh and shout; they slap each other on the back in collective triumph and exultation.

Unnoticed, I pass through the gate out into the lane. The lark is still bursting with song. I am alone. I am from the town.

Twilight of the Revolution

Justin Hanson

I'm on the phone with Henri, his Gallic voice strangled with emotion, and his news strikes me like ice water on naked flesh.

"It's Grant," Henri says to me. "He's slipping in and out. The doctors can't be sure about anything. Godammit, Herb, I can barely get a straight answer out of them."

He keeps talking like this, dispensing theories and analyses, perambulations of speech meant more for him than for me. Henri is just doing what so many do, dealing with the specter of death in his own way, and his way is talking. I don't mind though. I haven't really been listening since I answered the phone and heard Henri telling me that Grant Peterson, his lover for the past fifteen years, my first love, is at death's door.

I hear Henri as if from a distance, like his voice is a scream's last echo. I mostly hear the tap dancing sound of the rain pirouetting in a kind of dark whimsy, its footsteps resounding throughout my cavernous flat in Union Square, which seems ancient and empty in its loneliness. I observe the artwork that adorns my apartment—paintings and sculptures I bought but never understood. Now I am their only witness, like the last living acolyte in an undiscovered Egyptian tomb.

Henri repeats the things he's heard from doctors and nurses, things like "we'll know more when the blood work gets back" and "there's no way we can be sure until we've narrowed down all the possibilities." Clinicians words these, calculated words. I've heard them many times before, words crafted for their precise ambiguity.

"Herb, can you hear me? Herb?"

I'm coming back now, back to reality.

"Yes, Henri. I'm here."

"Well," stammers Henri, and I can almost see him thrusting his hand through his hair as he speaks, "if you want to see him again, Herb, you shouldn't wait. That's what they're saying. Some others I've spoken to will be coming by soon. We're hoping to time it right for when he's awake. Mornings have been best."

I hesitate slightly, thinking of all the times I've been offered such an invitation, all the times I made some excuse to avoid seeing another friend wasting away into nothing. Every older gay man in New York knows this feeling, and I, at sixty-two, remember the worst of phone calls like this.

"Yes," I hear myself say.

"You'll come?"

"Of course," I say, collecting my thoughts. "I'll be in as soon as I can, perhaps not right tomorrow but Thursday if possible. I'll have to check flights. Summer usually isn't bad to get to Toronto."

I hear Henri's muffled speech in the hospital. No doubt he has pressed his cell phone against his shirt for the sake of propriety. I wait.

"Herb, that's wonderful. I know you and Grant haven't seen much of each other the past few years, but he talked about you all the time, always spoke with such fondness for you."

I notice the change in tenses but make no comment.

"That's good, Henri. That is very good to know."

"Have you thought of where you'll stay?" Henri asks. "I'm sure you'll be fine. There are plenty who can put you up. I would offer myself, but—"

"Yes," I say. "But mentioning that, I should be off—so much to plan for and pack for."

Henri has muffled his phone again. I wait.

"Of course, Herb. It will be good to see all of us, I think," he adds, tentatively, as if wondering if it's an appropriate thing to say, "all things considered."

"Sure," I say.

Henri is crying again. I think of crying too but don't.

I arrive in Toronto the next day. I take a cab into the city, noticing that here, like on all things, time has done its work. I see the neighborhoods that were once slums have been gentrified. Yongue Street, once the pillar of vice and impropriety, a playground for Sodomites, has been warped and twisted, transformed by Coke and Pepsi, Kentucky Fried Chicken, and Taco Bell. It reminds me of Times Square. But that's the way of things— the heroic rise of civilization.

Toronto was a very different place when Grant whisked me here, away from the gloomy town I called home. I'll forever owe Grant and Toronto an enormous debt for that. In Columbus, Ohio, where I grew up, it was hopeless to be queer. Until the age of twenty-one, that was all I had, the despair of my plight, to have desire without possibility, my body and mind in thrall to invisible forces. Sometimes, under the courageous influence of whiskey or wine, I would travel to the town's only gay bar, Larry's. I can scarcely remember seeing more than twenty men in there at once. They always had fugitive looks about them, suspicious eyes that raked the bar and each other, massaging the finger they'd freed of their wedding bands, somehow tumescent in their terror. No one would enter through the front door. Speech within was subdued. Larry's allowed my first clumsy forays into sex, surreptitious affairs usually resigned to the backseats of cars and hurried, embarrassed acts of fellatio. It was an unhappy time.

That all changed when Grant—with three friends down from Toronto, a vague spot of geography to me then—charged into Larry's one night in October of 1970, riotous and cheerful as a group of post-victory athletes, and began buying drinks for the entire bar and singing show tunes. Grant spied me nursing a drink and made his way toward me, smiling the whole time. Never before or since have I been so struck with a look, so engulfed by the sight of another that, for a moment, I forgot to breathe. I think I fell in love right then.

Grant was a radical, speaking at length of politics and revolution. His words, to me, contained the sweetness of fine candy, words that worked magic passion on my young mind. We ended the night in a clasp of lips that seemed an hour in length. He left for Toronto, promising to write and return. For days my heart convulsed in wild acrobatics with every thought of Grant. I privately relived that first night a thousand times, sometimes during conversation with my family over dinner, other times while I taught my high school course on democracy, allowing Grant's words of revolution to slip into my lectures, lectures that then became powerful orations which shocked and intrigued my students.

Grant did come back, and he took me to Toronto, where he was putting together a gay rights magazine called *Brave Queer World*, which would later become a hit periodical. I made limited explanation to my parents—my father a stone mason, my mother a housewife and piano teacher—who, in their aloof ways, allowed themselves to be politely puzzled by their son's disappearance with a young man to another country.

Today Toronto drinks in sunlight, and my nostrils taste the clean, chilled air swept in from Lake Ontario. It seems impossible to think of death. I arrive on the doorstep of Al Cynthe's place off Queen St. in Brockton Village. Al is an old friend from the seventies. He wasn't much of an activist, him not being terribly social. Al was, and remains, an eccentric: an oddball who consistently maintains, against all established medical opinion but with an extraordinary knowledge of archaic medicine, that HIV is a mutation of syphilis rather than a new epidemic.

"Why if it isn't Herbert Roth," Al says, greeting me in his grand way and approaching for a hug.

I direct myself into his path for fear he might miss me. We embrace.

"How is old honest Al?" I ask.

"Surviving one winter at a time," he says. "And how is Handsome Herb, best-looking guy in New York?"

Despite my age, I blush at this, modesty still being an affectation of mine.

"Old and feeble, losing my charm and looks with every day."

"Not you," says Al, leading me to his car. "I suppose we should get going right away then. I'll set your things inside and we can be off to St. James."

Al spends the drive trying to distract me with a lengthy monologue about the history of his automobile, its fuel economy and performance in various climates. I appreciate this tactic, but it is of little use. I dread hospitals. My visits to them have always been brief affairs, with a ready-made excuse to leave just as soon as I can. It's the feel of the place, the mood: the lingering scent of bleach, the fluorescent lighting, the paper gowns patients are made to wear. An audition chamber for death.

Al and I enter the hospital and proceed to the third floor. We navigate the hallways and approach Grant's room. I try to compose myself.

Henri is here, standing outside the room looking weary and biting his fist as he scrolls through his cell phone, oblivious to the goings-on of the ward around him. He's wearing something predictably outrageous, a shirt adorned with a tiger set against a yellow background whose brightness rivals a halogen bulb. Henri is modestly handsome, though: very neat and trim, a runner, and quick with a smile and his signature high laugh. Still, I always told Grant—in whispers after a few drinks—that he could do better.

"Henri," I say, quietly because this seems appropriate.

"Oh, Herb—thank goodness," Henri says, in his characteristic melo-drama, and throws his arms around my body. I'm taken aback a bit—I've never been much at comforting—but I recover and allow Henri his hug. When we break I see that my presence has reduced Henri to sniffles.

"Grant's awake," Henri says. "He's in with a few people now; some of the old gang has been dropping by. Gerry's in there, Sammy too. Others have been coming and going, but Grant sleeps a lot, so most of the time people just sit around and talk."

I sneak a look around the door frame. Inside, I can see two figures standing over a hospital bed, Gerald Douglas and Sam Perfidon, both writ-ers and managing editors for *Brave Queer World* that I once lived and worked with, fighting and writing side-by-side in the revolution.

"It's been testy in there," Henri explains. "Even in here, in his condi-tion, Grant won't let up on poor Sammy about the parade thing. I keep tell-ing Grant to let it go for a bit and save his strength, but as soon as Sammy walked in it was all politics and what-not for Grant."

"That sounds like Grant," I say.

Over the past few months, trouble had been brewing in the Toronto queer community regarding the annual Toronto Pride parade, one of the year's largest and most lavish events. A certain group demanded to protest Israel during the parade, but the commission overseeing Toronto Pride denied the group's request for a permit. This opened the floodgate of criticism towards the parade commissary. Charges of censorship were hurled, editorials written defaming the Pride Commission and *The Other World*, the offspring of *Brave Queer World*, operated within a gay media conglomerate run by Sam Perfidon. Grant, of course, was in the thick of it from the beginning, writing furious bits of calumny against Sam, *The Other World*, the Pride Commission, and the corporate interests in the revenue and advertising that Pride Toronto produced. Grant had phoned me a couple months back about it giddy as a schoolboy, just like in the seventies, with an injustice to fight and a cause to champion. Who would have ever thought, back then, that it would be each other we'd be fighting in our dreary senescence with talk of rights and revolution?

Listening outside the room, I hear my Grant's voice ring out in perfect outrage—

"Well," I say, "perhaps now is as good a time as any."

I enter the room and Sam and Gerry look up. Grant is the last to notice me, turning his head after he sees that Gerry and Sam have ceased listening to his indignation.

"Herb," says Gerry, bespeckled and still sporting the same mustache he's had for three decades.

"Hello all," I say.

I embrace Sam and Gerry, big hugs from both and kisses on each cheek.

"It's so good to see you again, Herb," says Gerry, beaming and stepping back to have a look at me. "And still the handsomest of the lot," he says, laughing.

"Only to eyes as bad as yours," I reply.

I turn and look to Sam. He's held up well, a little pudgy, but then again we're in our sixties. He's still got a head of fuzzy hair, now gone white, and he wears pointy, stylish glasses that suit him.

"Sammy you look wonderful. How's the paper doing?"

"It's still my mistress," he says, grinning. "Business is good. We've been growing every year, trying to do as much online as possible—you know, like everyone else, everyone in the mainstream, that is."

"That's grand," I say, doing my best to sound enthusiastic.

"Yes, indeed," Sam says, beaming. "Should come by the new space some time, Herb. We've got new offices now, very modern, and we're preparing a special layout for the anniversary."

"Anniversary?" I say.

"Come on now, Herb," says Gerry. "Time doesn't move any differently in New York. It's the fortieth anniversary of *Brave Queer World* at the end of the month, two weeks away."

"Oh," I say, nodding now, recalling that summer I came to Toronto in 1971 with Grant, who, two weeks later, took me to the first secret meetings that would spawn *Brave Queer World*, Toronto's first and arguably most influential gay magazine, a feat that I consistently forgot belonged on my resumé.

"That's right," said Sam. "And *Other World* will be putting on quite the spectacle, and a special edition to commemorate it. Come by the offices this week, Herb. We must work you in somehow. Who knows, maybe we'll even throw you on the cover again."

"Again?" I say, genuinely perplexed.

"My God," says Gerry. "You really have sailed off into the waters of dotage, haven't you? You were on the cover of—of—"

"Nineteen-seventy-six, June edition," I hear Grant murmur, a sound that needles my heart. I haven't looked over at the bed yet, avoiding it like it contains a light that might blind me.

"Right before he sailed off to New York, actually," Grant adds.

I feel Sam and Gerry melt away from my sides, leaving me, and the hospital room comes into better focus. With the blinds half drawn, sunlight slips into the room in a wan glow, the pearl-white walls and floors reflecting the illumination. To the left of the room, a few feet from the entrance, Grant lies in his bed. I move closer to him, barely aware of my footsteps propelling me forward as I finally look into his face.

Nothing quite prepares you for this, though I've seen it many times: the cruelty of the disease upon living flesh. Grant, once an Adonis himself, looks emaciated and withered as a dried plant. His complexion, always a deep manila, has turned pale, almost translucent in the sweat that bathes his face. I see his arms have lost their vitality, limp as unformed dough, their strength and life expended. I fear going near him to learn how he might smell, for I always cherished pulling him close to me and burying my nose in his black curls. These have remained intact. Yet his body doesn't belong to the man I knew, a body inching towards expiration.

"You still look good, Herb," Grant says. "Even now, you still have something of your old self."

"How...are—Grant?" I feel my throat tighten just to look at him, and I fear my eyes might bubble past my control.

"Come on now, Herb," says Grant. "You were always such a tough-guy."

I rush forward, my fear of hospital germs evaporating, and envelop him. Grant holds me closely too and I hear him sigh. I wrap my arms around him, caring, perhaps too little, for his comfort. I smell his hair. It smells the way I remember it: a deep mix of soil and coffee. Grant smells like home.

"Come on now, you lug," he continues. "How have you been?"

"Me?" I say, almost hysterically. "To hell with me, Grant. Tell me about you."

"Well, hell," he says, and within moments Grant launches into politics, into Sammy's refusal to make a deal about Pride and the censorship thing, about how the community is on a downward spiral and the old ideals are leaving us. I listen to it all and nod, reassuring him that it's not all doom-and-gloom like he says. He doesn't mention the disease. To Grant, it's as though we're having the conversation in a cafe on Church Street, sipping afternoon tea, enjoying the sunlight, unburying all the old politics and wondering at intervals where we might take supper.

"Honestly, Herb," Grant says towards the end of a speech, "what might come next once our own community leaders have censored us? Hell the mainstream media and society used to do that, and now it's the gays that are silencing the gays. Who'd have thought we'd live to see the day?"

"Yes," I say, doing my best not to sound parental. But it's nothing doing: Grant senses this.

"Don't do that, Herb—don't trivialize things the way you do."

"Well," I say, "it's a pretty sensitive subject, and I can understand Sammy being in a tight spot."

"No," says Grant, closing his eyes and shaking his head from side to side. "Sam's doing what he's doing for business. He doesn't want anything to upset the millions Pride makes for those friends of his."

"Well, they're gay businesses, aren't they?"

"Christ, Herb," Grant says, looking exasperated in a way I haven't seen him look yet. "I know you stopped being political a while ago, but can't you hear yourself? Can't you hear how that goes against everything we believe?"

"Use to," I say. "People change." I slide off the corner of Grant's bed.

"Yes," he says, looking up and into the lamp above him. "You changed, of course. I never understood why you stopped being political, Herb. You were so damned good at it—the articles you used to write, the speeches you would give at meetings. When you went for New York, we were all happy to see you do well in business. Lord knows we treated your apartment like a private hotel. But, secretly, I always wished you hadn't."

My heart rolls at this. I glance and see Henri in the doorway, eaves-dropping.

"Well," I say. "I loved the movement, but I left for me."

"I know," Grant says. "I don't blame you. I guess, for a while, I thought it would be the two of us, taking on the world, changing things, trying to build something. It's easy to think like that when you're young."

"Time has its way with dreams," I say and kiss him on the forehead, allowing myself a moment's pause.

"I'll be back soon," I say.

"Okay," says Grant. "And Herb," he calls as I walk towards the door. "If you talk to Sam, see if you can get him to come around and print something bloody critical for a change."

"No promises."

Later that evening, back at Al's, I peruse some old copies of *Brave Queer World* that Al, perhaps a bit too suggestively, has left out. I thumb through old issues and smirk at the articles, whose topics now appear horribly abstruse. We wrote against the suburbs, the State, corporations, medicine, psychiatry and especially the nuclear family and marriage. Fresh from university with Humanities degrees in hand, our minds aswim with Leftist dogma, we took for our muses Marx and Engels, Trotsky and Che. We even lauded that crackpot Laing and the hack Marcuse, trumpeting any idea that contributed to our Revolution.

Grant was a demon about politics and philosophy, always musing about the root causes of oppression, of how things might get better. Grant nurtured *Brave Queer World* from the start. From an original few dozen issues of the first edition, the magazine ballooned with a readership in the thousands. We became the gay voice in Toronto, and the community looked to us for leadership. *Brave Queer World* even made its way to Europe and across the urban gay circles all over the States. It was how we communicated then with no email or cell phones. *Brave Queer World* wasn't simply the voice of one or two editors—everyone had a say and a vote on what went into the paper.

When I came to Toronto, I moved in with Grant straightaway. He found me a job teaching English as a Second Language, a task that I was horribly ill-prepared for but enjoyed nonetheless. Grant took his time with me, not wanting to traumatize me with too strong a push towards sex and professions of love. Our relationship progressed slowly, perhaps gracefully in comparison with my future affairs: reading Housman and Auden in a park during the day, dining on North African food in the evening, seeing the latest Truffaut by night. When, at last, we made love, Grant was gentle and loving.

For the next few years Grant and I could hardly be separated. We lived together throughout, often with the company of friends or temporary boarders, who always considered us the model couple. I took odd jobs, taught or worked in retail, while Grant manned the helm at the magazine, eventually bringing on Sammy to help professionalize things. We talked movement politics at all hours, always developing the next strategy or article series. I can scarcely remember Grant being in a bad mood, such was his animation for his work. Even the magazine's frequent financial worries only exhilarated him further. For Grant, no task was too small, every difficulty a welcome challenge.

Five years into the relationship, when *Brave Queer World* was at its zenith, two things occurred: at twenty-seven, I began to feel the terror of age, and I found my eye wandering. I had also, for quite some time, found solace in the gym. In exercise, I found meditation, a place of worship, and the workshop where I could craft the essential tool of my life—my body. I took to the bodybuilding life like a zealot, a Spartan, training twenty hours a week and devouring proteins, examining myself in the mirror to see if I resembled the men in magazines.

I also noticed other's eyes, men and women both, sweep over my body with lust or envy. I felt the thrill of being beautiful when all I had ever felt back home was common, everyday, ordinary.

Grant barely noticed this. How could he have, being so wrapped up with changing the world? By then, late in the relationship, around 1977, I had taken to frequenting Manhattan, occasionally for weeks at a time. Something about the city ignited my spirit. Here was possibility in every form: every lust could find its object, every fantasy its reality and every dream its fruition.

I planned my flight carefully, began putting my finances together and attempting to find the right words to tell Grant. Timing with these matters, I've always known, is crucial.

Grant came home late one night from working on the paper, which was the norm rather the exception. He registered only mild surprise to find me waiting for him at our kitchen table.

"Grant," I said. "Can we speak?"

"Sure, sure," he said, unloading his valise, which was packed with papers, and walking into the kitchen. Grant made his way towards me, looking worn but happy, expectant at whatever I had to say, perhaps anticipating me to yank him out the door for an impromptu night out.

"I don't feel happy here anymore," I said. "I feel like I'm missing something big, something important, and I need to follow it." I remember sighing, shrugging, wiping my hand over my mouth before, "Grant, I'm moving to New York."

I noticed then, perhaps for the first time, Grant frown, his eyes drop, and saw him rub his face with both hands and bend over at the waist.

"It's just—" Grant stammered, "I thought you were happy here, Herb. I thought we were happy, that you enjoyed yourself here, and your work on the paper and your teaching. I just—"

It went on like that for a bit, I reassuring Grant that there was no simple explanation, no cause to boil down to, no great way to explain it, just that I was moving on. He took it well and cried a bit. For the sake of being the put-together one, I didn't cry, clinching up my eyes when necessary. A few weeks later I was off for a vast and thrilling new life.

I awake early the next morning, in part due to Al's calling from the kitchen, "Herb, Herb, I've got breakfast." Reluctantly I pull myself from bed, don a robe, and proceed downstairs to quell Al's calls. Unlike many my age, I'm still a very late sleeper, but Al always rose early, even as a young man, much to the displeasure of his housemates.

"*Ecce Homo,*" I say to Al, settling into the dining nook of the house's open and flush kitchen. Located at the back of the old Victorian, the kitchen opens into a screened-in patio that abuts a plush garden that Al and his partner have nurtured into a pastoral wonderland. The Lake Ontario wind whistles through the screen and into the kitchen, filling the place with the smell of sage and rosemary, mint and pepper. For a moment I feel a great calm.

Al places before me a plate arranged with an omelet, toast drizzled with honey, wedges of melon and slices of banana, and a cup of coffee. Like most that possess a mind and hands for craftsmanship, Al is a wonderful cook, and I enjoy my repast as Al settles opposite me.

"Sammy called asking for you," says Al.

"Oh," I say. "What of it?"

"He said you should come by the offices downtown today."

"Oh," I say again, sipping my coffee. "What do you suppose he wants?"

"He probably just wants to show you around, maybe show off a bit is more like it, and I think he wants to take your picture and get you to say a few charming things about *Brave Queer World* for the memorial edition coming up."

I consider this and allow myself a small upsurge of excitement. It's been a while since I've been featured anywhere, on a posting or in a magazine. Aside from the one cover issue of *Brave Queer World*, I'd been featured in a few advertisements and queer mags in New York. I'd never attempted or cared to be a model, but a few friends in the media business asked me to lend my face and physique to their cause. Flattered, I obliged, but that was a long time ago.

"Okay," I say.

Al, appearing a bit startled at hearing me speak as he pored over his morning edition of the *Toronto Star*, looks up at me and asks, "Okay what?"

I arrive on Church Street late that afternoon at the offices of *The Other World*. The offices reside in a lean, historic building in the gay district of Toronto. The facade is a deep, rusty brick, lending an aura of history to the place, as though it might be some kind of proletariat factory.

I enter the building and ascend the stairs to the second floor office. There's a foyer, contemporary and official looking, complete with plasma televisions and cushy furniture, abutted by tables groaning with magazines, copies of *The Other World* and various pornographic issues whose titles I don't recognize. Left of the room, situated before large glass doors that lead to the main offices, rests a desk with a muscled youth in a bright yellow *Other World* t-shirt, who sits in complete unawareness of my presence as he blankly negotiates his cell phone and bites his lip. I approach, somewhat awkwardly, and voice my presence.

"Excuse me," I say.

The boy looks up. He has bleach-blonde hair combed straight up and studs in his ears. He looks like a child to me, a muscled, bewigged toddler.

"Yes," he says.

"I have an appointment with Sam Perfidon."

The bemused expression on the youth's face shows no affection. He lays down his cell phone, gazing at it with a pained expression as though it was an amputated limb. Next, the boy punches a few keys into the office phone and says, "I have a Mister..." He looks up at me here, expectantly.

"I'm Herb," I say. I've always been useless in official-type conversation.

He nods knowingly and continues, "A Mister Herb here to see Mister Perfidon." He nods again, the receiver moving up-and-down along with his head. "Okay," he says, and hangs up.

"Mister Sam will be right out to see you," he says. "Please have a seat."

No sooner have I done so then Sam comes bouncing through the glass doors with a wide grin on his face, beckoning me inward, saying, "Herb, Herb, come on in," coaxing me as one does a pet kitten.

"And Tyler," Sammy says, placing his hand on my back and gingerly patting me like a piece of memorabilia, "we never keep *Brave Queer World* royalty waiting—Herb was a founding member."

Tyler's eyes widen theatrically in reverence, paying his due to the antique visitor, this queer fossil, and he returns to his cell phone, this time biting his tongue.

Sam leads me back through the offices, describing me with similar auspicious introductions to the hurrying writers, web technicians and editors who each express the same mild, polite interest in my involvement with their vaunted antecedent. Next, Sam leads me through a maze of cubicles back to his office in a secluded corner of the place. The aesthetics of the office strike me as decidedly dull: a pale desk centers the room, adorned with a computer, and behind it is Sammy's chair. A few books occupy the grooved, in-wall shelves behind Sam's desk, and a rather perfunctory fern languishes in the corner, yearning for the few strips of sunlight available to it. It provides the only hint of color in this chamber of gray.

"Herb," says Sam, as though seeing me for the first time in this visit, "I'm glad you could stop by."

"Yes," I say. "I don't seem to make it back here much, and people don't come to New York quite as often as they used to, but it's good to be back."

"All a part of age, Herb," says Sam, adopting an air of wisdom I'd never heard from him when I knew him in our twenties. Back then, Sam was a hard-line Marxist, moving to Toronto after studying history at Cornell eager to get high, get laid and change the world. And now here he is, a Chief Executive Officer.

"You get older and you get wrapped up in business or new people that you don't care for but have to pay attention to. It's that spiral downward, you know?" He sighs here, satisfied with this dissection of middle age and its social workings.

"Something like that," I say. "But seems to be doing well here."

"We're booming," Sam exclaims. "*The Other World* is just the tip of the iceberg, Herb. We're online now, and that's where the future is for everything. We only keep printing paper copies of *Other World* because old fogies like us still buy them. They'll be gone in twenty years. Kaput."

"And to think," I say, "it all started in a basement in Kensington Market with us begging the lefties at UT to use their printing press."

Sammy nods and forces a laugh. While Sammy is the reigning CEO of *Other World* and a healthy chunk of queer media in Toronto, Grant always maintained that Sammy feels ashamed he missed the first rough-and-tumble years of *Brave Queer World*, that he skipped the war and arrived for the peace treaty.

"Well," Sammy says, slapping the table as though time is imminent, "let's get you downstairs and take a few photos of that famous face of yours, you prince of New York, and we'll have you on your way."

This occurs, much to my embarrassment, as I spend the next two hours having my body arranged and manipulated by a pair of hissing photographers, who twist and shape my figure into poses as if I was a storeroom mannequin, giving such intermittent advice like, "More natural," "now be serious," and simply, "contemplate." I silently give thanks to the small mercy that allowed me to remain clothed for this bodily parade, my physique not being what it once was.

Afterwards, Sam leads me through the foyer to walk me out. We stop in the entranceway as I make to leave.

"Well," says Sam, "that's that. Photos will be fabulous. You have no idea what our guys can do with computers these days. They can take ten years off you like that," he says, snapping his fingers.

"If I write you a big check can they take off thirty?"

Sam laughs at this, somewhat too loud and forced. I see him raise his foot a bit, as though about to stamp it to add some percussion to his mirth.

"Anything for you, Herb," Sam says. "Now there's just one more thing, the editors will have a little bio of you as a headliner, boilerplate stuff—who, what, when, where—that kind of thing, but we'll need a few reflections from you to add some personality. Let's say three hundred to five hundred words."

Sam rummages in his pocket for something and produces a business card.

"You can email it to this guy, one of our associate editors," he says, handing me the card.

"About what?" I ask, almost too forcefully, putting quite a bit of breath into the what.

"Oh," says Sam, looking a touch startled by the question himself. "About anything, really. Whatever you like. Most people opt for the 'way it was when I was a young queen' and the like. You were big in movement stuff and *Brave Queer World* at the beginning, Herb. Jog the memory a bit—write what you know."

Later that night I think about Grant, about my leaving. I arrived in New York early in 1977. The city churned with life, drugs and sex that could be found anywhere. This was before the great cleanup, before Times Square became Disneyland, before porn shops and best clubs folded, a time when you could go out for groceries or a pack of smokes and get laid once on the way there and once on the way back.

I got myself another retail job at a bookstore. The pay was livable, and my only expense was myself. I hit the docks and bars with regularity. At the docks you could walk into a carrier crate, screw, and be on your way. At the bars you could be more discriminating: survey the crop and take your pick of the litter.

I learned, very quickly, the hierarchy of the gay world. In this world, beauty was the only currency, and it was accepted everywhere, in every language, regardless of politics or religion. I saw that beauty made you powerful, made it acceptable to enter rooms thought to be exclusive, clubs whose guest lists did not contain your name, and private parties where you were but a distant acquaintance.

I found men easily. Sometimes, I could go for several weeks sharing my bed with a new person every night. I'd only quit if I was near exhaustion, taking a few days off to recharge myself for the next adventure. At one point, I went with an older man whose business was real estate. We became business associates, and I acquired some properties and became moneyed. I stopped doing anything professional whatsoever, allowing hours at the spa or salon, the cinema or the bookshop, the cafe or strolling in the park to fill my day.

I made friends, perhaps a few hundred, as I became a star in New York, a jewel in the coterie of desirable men. Nights I spent at the clubs. The Anvil. The Peppermint. I was one of the originals at Studio 54, convening with Steve and Ian, bearing witness to Travolta and Donna Summer, even shared a drink with Roy Cohn. Finally, I felt that I had arrived.

The crowd from Toronto visited often. For a while, I was the golden boy of the old circle, the apple of their eyes, the one who had got off to the real big city. Grant came when work would allow. I noticed Grant grew handsomer with time, obviously committing himself to his own fitness regimen. We always slept together when he came to New York. Afterward, I would wrap my arms around him, resting my head on his chest, and listen to him breathe while he stroked my hair in odd circles. We never spoke much of it.

I did, from time-to-time, take a regular lover, a boyfriend. Such instances punctuated my wild lifestyle only occasionally, providing all the depth and sustenance of cheap candy. At such moments I would select a man—always young, and practically at random from my harem at the time—to go steady with for a while: going to dinner and the like, introducing him to friends at parties. Such dalliances never lasted long and always ended poorly, sometimes becoming the seeds for Midtown gossip. After a while I would grow bored with the state of things, find the affair monotonous, reeking of pallid domesticity, and lacking in the excitement that accompanied my evening trips to the bars. Thus, I would end the relationships with some tired, ambiguous excuse ("I'm feeling trapped," "I think we're going in different directions"). They were always hurt, these men. They would, on occasion, take the opportunity to stab at my psyche in grand soliloquies describing my various flaws, striking like miners for psychological gold. I offered no rebuttal, always nodding my head and making no argument, which I'd learned was the best way to bring such events to a close, allowing my adversary to create and verify whatever story suited him best and leave.

Things progressed like this, more or less, for many years. Then came the eighties, that chiaroscuro of a decade, a time that my memory inveterately assigns the colors grey and black, its fashion that of funeral suits, veils covering stony faces. All too well I remember how it began. It was at Fire Island, the closest thing to gay paradise, that we first noticed something was wrong. It began with whispers, rumors of unexplained deaths of hale young men, their lives just in bloom. The prettiest ones went first, their beauty betraying them, proving itself a curse, and only later would we understand why.

Soon, bit by bit, our knowledge evolved. It was a sickness born from love, from loving too much, from love gone awry. Quickly, like winter night falling, fear descended on the city. Where we used to appreciate the passing glance, the too-long stare, we now grew wary, frightened of our own desire, of what might be churning through our veins, infecting us, making us creatures of illness.

I lost three out of every four friends I had, slowly, torturously over twenty years. I came to dread the sound of the phone ringing, of the door knocking, of any friend's voice even, because of the words that might enter my mind and, for the freshest time, lay siege to my very soul.

Yet despite all the warnings, despite Larry telling us to give up sex for good, despite the pure common sense of the matter—I couldn't stop. I acted as though nothing was afoot, as though no reality lurked in every blowjob, in every screw. For years I carried on, hitting the same clubs, the same bars, picking up strangers without discussion of a condom. I can't explain myself for it. Even now that behavior shames me. I thought that, perhaps, if I could die, all of it would be so much easier. It would be others who would visit me, burdened with keeping the gallant face for a dying friend. No more pain, no more misery, the burden of health relinquished.

But it never came for me. I remember sitting one night at home in the fall of 1997, getting the call from Grant. By then, such fears had become manageable. Grant made chit-chat, talked politics in his usual way, and then he told me the news. As I recall it, I feel myself nodding along with whatever I must have said at the time, assuring him that things would be "all right" and "okay," that what was needed was a positive outlook, a strong constitution and the wherewithal to endure. I made a joke or two, I knew he'd like that, something about at least he had a health care system instead of a syndicate. A proper Canadian, he loved to hear an American bash his own. When we hung up, I wrapped myself in blankets and wept.

By then just about everything in my life had changed. I had just celebrated my fiftieth birthday in a sumptuous festival at my flat. And yet, while I routinely heard that I could still pass for thirty-five, I began to observe the menace of advancing age. First I saw it in my friends, many of whom had settled in a committed relationship and sedentary lives, allowing their muscles to soften, their bellies to grow slack. I still kept at my routine, trying my best to keep age at bay. But time gnaws away at you like the tide upon rock. It begins with something minor, a sore shoulder or knee, infirmities that become advanced, keeping you out of the gym for weeks at a time. Wrinkles appear where there were none before. There's a procedure. A second procedure. But how many more?

These facts come home at last, and no rage can alter it. Rage at the feeling that the best is passed, that the final act of life is about to play, the curtain soon to fall. Friends and family enter hospitals en masse, this time from natural causes. The body's various ailments anchor conversation, reminders of the mutual journey to the grave. Sex becomes a memory, and though the desire is still present, the act seems now a chore, and former flames give no solace in the here-and-now. People begin to die from simple things, a flu or a short fall. Friends and relatives slip away almost imperceptibly, with only dim memories to prove they were alive at all. "They are not long," a poet said, "the days of wine and roses." All that's left are the noiseless hours and small distractions as the candle burns down—until, at last, you take the final sleep.

Several days pass by unnoticed and without purpose, as imperceptible as the turning earth. Al gets the call early on the second to last Thursday in June, one week before the Pride ceremony, that Grant is barely holding on, not expected to last much longer.

"Herb," Al says. "It's time."

Al and I race to the hospital. The drive is silent, our faces contorted into an image of quiet and determined solemnity. Grant's room is filled with friends and a few relatives. The volume of the room has been brought low, the occupants communicating in hushed drones of information. Grant is very weak. He has an oxygen mask fitted around his face. His color has faded to parchment, his body has compressed to the size of a child's doll. People approach Grant, bending down on their knees to whisper a few words, to make our last peace as we've been instructed to do. I've been in this position before as well, usually resorting to platitudes so cheap I could barely spit them out.

Henri approaches me, rests his hand lightly on my shoulder and pulls my ear to his face.

"Herb," Henri says, "Grant would like a word with you. People are going to step outside for a few moments, okay?"

I stare at Henri blankly, hoping my face betrays no terror. Henri, who seems uncharacteristically composed, anticipates some action, and I comply with a single nod. I stand and wait as the people file out, some giving me half-smiles of encouragement.

I will my limbs to carry me forward, to sit down at Grant's side and take his hand in mine. He has removed his oxygen mask and speaks in a quiet, cracked voice.

"I'm at the end, Herb," Grant says.

"Yes," I say.

"Herb—are you happy?"

I cry now. Great, effusive tears slide down my face, and my voice erupts in sobs and chortled words. I notice, through his ashen face, Grant's surprise.

"Don't cry," Grant says.

I can't help myself now. The indifferent plainness of it all rushes upon me: my only love dying, my wasted life, the way he thought to phrase it like he did and how it lacerates me so.

"I'm sorry," I manage to say, those two horrible words, full of vagueness and elusion. "I'm sorry for leaving. I'm sorry for thinking you weren't enough. I'm sorry for turning my back on the best thing. I'm sorry for being such a disappointment."

Grant does his best to console me, and what power he has left he uses to grip my hand. I see tears froth in Grant's eyes and feel ashamed. I've asked a dying man to comfort me.

"You didn't disappoint me," Grant says. "I was hurt, but then I realized you were going to New York to be happy. I want you to be happy.

That's all I ever wanted for you."

Grant looks away from me now. His eyes move up. I want him now more than ever. His every word has become treasure. I want to ask him how to be happy, why it has evaded me for so long. I want him to give me some truth.

"Grant?" I say.

"That's all."

Grant dies late that night after most of us have left, leaving only Henri and Grant's sister at his side. I skip the funeral, citing business in New York. The truth is far more cowardly. Since I left Grant in the hospital room, I can scarcely stand to breathe, my every thought an artwork of my ignominy. It is a feeling beyond tears, beyond tremors, beyond all the poetry of old men and soldiers fresh from hell. Grant is gone, and so is another life I might have led. I live with that every moment, and will for the rest of my life.

Back in New York, I stay in my flat and listen to old records, go for long walks if I suspect my phone will ring, or take a copy of the *Times* to a coffee shop, sit down and gape at the issue without taking in a word. I do this today, a few days after the funeral, and when I check my mail I see a package postmarked from Toronto. It's square and brown, about the size of a cutting board. Inside, I open the package and find a large frame containing a photograph featuring myself with Grant on my side, and a copy of the first edition of *Brave Queer World* on the other. Beneath the pictures, at the bottom of the frame, there is a tiny sterling placard, etched with spindly words that read: *Long Live the Revolutionaries.*

Staring at the placard with the odd sensation of my memory working new mechanics, I notice that the package also contains a brief note from Henri:

Herb,

Grant wanted you to have this photo. I think he meant to give it to you a while back, but he must have forgotten to bring it on his last trip to New York. We found it buried underneath a pile of his papers at his desk. You remember how clumsy he was with those things. Again, sorry you missed the service. It was quite moving. Grant's nephew read Whitman. Anyway, I'm off to Paris for a few weeks—I need to shake free my mind for a bit, take in the sight of Montmartre once more while I still can. All the best to you, Herb. My door is always open if you find yourself in Toronto again.

Cheers,

Henri.

P.S., Sammy mentioned that you still hadn't sent in your anniversary bio. You might want to do so quickly to avoid Sammy inserting his own version, which might be what he was counting on all along.

Without really thinking much of what I am doing, I walk directly into my study, sit down at my computer, and write the following:

In the early 1970s, I was, in the practical meaning of the term, a founder of *Brave Queer World*, the predecessor to this magazine and one of the first and finest sources of queer media in Canada. Those were grand times, times when love, sex and the struggle for justice comingled in a thousand ways, and the entire world seemed ready for the remaking of revolution. But I won't wax poetic, for we all know the truth of the thing: gains have been made, but the spirit has been lost, our community having grown to admire expedience rather than struggle, the material rather than what's true. But I cannot claim righteousness. It was I, a founder of such a pioneering magazine, who was the first to make the trade, exchanging happiness for pleasure. But there are those, both then and now, who remain true to the original ideals of the great era of change: equality; justice; freedom from fear, tyranny, and exploitation; but above all the freedom to question, to focus the lens of critique upon anything that could threaten our essential liberties, even if the lens focuses upon ourselves.

Grant Peterson—my truest friend—continued to voice these ideals until he died, observing that our very own Pride Committee has become the new censors. There's an irony here, I'm sure, but also the old feeling of discomfort. *The Other World* would not print Grant's objections, even though it was his tireless work that allowed *Brave Queer World* the lifetime and eminence it maintained. I encourage you to read his blog to view those objections, and ask that Mr. Sam Perfidon, managing editor of *The Other World*, include them in a future issue and on his website.

I remember once, sometime during the 1990s, when I'd expressed to Grant, quite cynically, that our old beliefs were dead and buried, that commercialism and materiality were all that remained. It was then that he reminded me of Sartre's old definition of the difference between rebels and revolutionaries: rebels preached the good word, but they couldn't stomach actual change, for then there would be nothing to complain about. Revolutionaries, on the other hand, would endure and continue, struggle and promote the vision for a truly New World as not just a matter of nominalism, but because they meant it.

I think it high time we ask ourselves in which group we should be counted, lest the revolution slumber too long in the graves of people like Grant. My time is at an end; it is too late for this old queen to take up the cause again. I look now, with optimistic eyes, to the young, in the hopes that they might continue where Grant left off, and succeed where I have failed.

I do a quick edit, and without changing much, I send those lines off to the junior editor Sam had indicated to me previously. I walk out into my living room, observing some of the artwork that I acquired in the eighties but never studied nor contemplated. I tear it all down, every effete piece of nothing I bought on a whim and pile it on the floor. I pick up the frame Grant has sent me and feel light, energized in a way I haven't in a long time, and hang it in the center of the wall. I leave the flat, walking down Park Avenue, thinking vaguely of stopping into some bar and having a glass of Cabernet, tossing wistful glances towards the door in expectation of some wonderful stranger I might meet. That thought, which would have seemed silly and probably sad just a few hours prior, I now find promising.

Walking through town, with the sun just setting behind the Hudson, I feel my old love of New York, the thrill of adventure, the endless dance of possibility, of the movement of never-ceasing life. I stop at the corner of Park and 32nd and, feeling the wind at my back, start moving west. Held up at a cross, I spy across the street, in front of a small old church, a young man, mid-thirties and handsome, eyeing me with what appears to be some intensity. I find myself startled. Could he be giving me one of those looks? Could I really still have something?

The look holds, and, feeling a boldness quite forgotten, I cross the street and approach him.

"Good Evening," I say. "Beautiful evening, in fact."

"Yes," he says, looking down, sheepishly, nervous. I see now that he can't be much older than thirty or thirty-one. His complexion, which from a distance I thought merely tan, reveals Latin descent, possibly Puerto Rican or Cuban. He has an accent that tickles and chills, one filled with the flavor of Spanish wine.

"I'm Herb," I say, and extend my hand.

"Javier," he says, clasping mine. "Are you here for the meeting?"

"I could be," I say, not wanting to appear foolish. "What meeting?"

He regards me oddly for a moment, as though suspicious.

"It's a support meeting," he says, "for people that are trying to come out."

"Oh," I say, somewhat surprised, looking back at the church with new understanding. "We used to have those all the time in my day. I wouldn't think that many would be around now, especially in New York of all places. I thought that's why people come to New York—to come out."

Javier appears almost scandalized: his eyebrows arch almost all the way up to his dark, pomaded hair and he appears to stifle his contempt.

"Of course there are still meetings like this. You wouldn't believe how many people show up confused and scared, looking for answers or just someone to talk to. Our members are old and young, and we have all peoples: gays, lesbians, bisexuals, transgender and intersex people, and sometimes straight people come in just to listen."

"I see," I say, genuinely amazed. "I had no idea. I've been out a long time. I guess I sort of forgot what the first step is like."

He continues to give me a hard look of appraisal.

"Why don't you come in?" he says. "You can meet some new people, see what's going on these days."

"No one will mind?"

"Of course not," Javier says. "And first timers have the option to share or not share, to tell us about themselves or not."

As he says this, Javier places his hand upon my elbow and begins to lead me down the stairs to the church activity rooms. I've missed people, and I can't remember the last time a stranger has taken my arm in friendship.

"Why don't you come in and tell your story," Javier says.

I tell him that I'd like that very much.

Blood Off Rusted Steel

Brooks Rexroat

It's awful as hell to see a set of flashing lights off in the distance and know immediately that they're coming for someone who shares your last name. I was barely even out of the driveway, on the way to school just before dawn broke when I saw them: red and blue flickers off in the distance but moving fast, and I wondered what it was he'd done this time, which of those poor creatures had got loose. Instead of heading straight down Birch Pond Road, I took a left onto the state route because lights moving that fast toward his place meant school would be canceled without question. I figured I ought to go over and see what the damage was this time.

I was steamed, too, as I drove, because we had a game that night against Clear Valley. That game had been circled on my calendar for months; they hadn't won in two years, so it was almost dead certain I'd finally get to play varsity. The night before, Coach even let me practice with the offense instead of playing dummy defense like I had every practice for three years. I'd been working on my three-point shot in the driveway, ready to impress Dacie Lindt—ready to play some string music if the ball found my hands, ready to prove I existed, even if my heroics came during garbage minutes at the end of a blow-out.

I had it all planned out in my mind: I nail a few pretty shots, enjoy the concept of having some sweat from my own palm involved in the hand-shake line, then clean up and bolt toward the cafeteria and the post-game dance where Dacie would stand at the center of a crowd, still in her pleated orange and black skirt, and I'd walk up to her and ask her out. I didn't bother to daydream her portion of it—the result was her business. But I knew my part and I was ready.

Of course, whenever school got canceled, whether it was for snow or flooding along the river or one of my uncle's animal escapades, it meant games were canceled. And meaningless three-pointers at the buzzer. And dances. And daydreams.

I took the turns too hard that morning, my old Ford swaying side-to-side as I fumed about how Uncle James found a way to ruin things one more time. I turned the radio to something fast and loud, cranked it up to keep from thinking hateful things about him.

When I pulled around the bend and saw all those lights, all those cars, saw the distant pinpricks of light coming from the ends of shotguns, my gut curled up into a ball.

Again and again, the pinpricks came, some in isolated flashes, others in the small bursts of an automatic. The sun was starting to rise in earnest, but it was still dim enough that each flash was shocking. Each flick, I knew, was another one of those poor, ridiculous creatures catching its end. The first one I saw was right at the edge of the property, before I even got the truck stopped. A Bengal tiger, endangered as hell, and there he was with his head in the ditchwater and a dozen red pockmarks staining his belly. I swallowed back a gag then took a deep breath to pull myself together because the guns were still popping and I figured I was about to see a lot worse.

Sheriff Martin stood in the middle of the road with his hands up.

Even in that small of a town, most people my age only knew the look of him from his reelection posters, except maybe the serious delinquents. I brought the truck to a stop and he came to my window, pointed a flashlight at me. "Morning, Davis," he said. "You can pull on through, but I have to tell you it's ugly. Your aunt's over by the first barn with some of your folks. You need to go see them first, you understand?"

"It's not just the animals, is it?"

"Like I said, son. You need to go speak with your kin."

I parked between two of the satellite trucks—there were dozens lining the road, which was a new thing. An escaped bear or two usually fetched just the local newspaper and a couple of cops—guys I knew from school, a few of them classmates of mine who dropped out and took the GED so they could get on with becoming a cop before someone else beat them to the open job. If you didn't get on with the force and wanted to stay in town, your best options were trash collector, fast food cook or car salesman. Being a cop was the dream gig for a lot of the guys I knew: walk around with a loaded gun and a uniform, look tough, and occasionally shoot at one of my crazy uncle's animal herd—maybe even get your picture in the paper standing hero-like over a lion or two.

That day, they all got their pictures taken. And even though they tried to act later like it had been a solemn and regrettable occasion, I knew better. Those boys made like they were on safari and blew away everything they could, whether it was legitimately dangerous or not. All those animals were just deer-in-season for them, and Sheriff Martin was handing out licenses. They hit everything that moved, even a couple rabbits, a squirrel and Aunt Linda's cat.

That morning, all those boy-deputies got their moment of glory, got a big story to exaggerate for their eventual grandkids and newspaper clippings to validate it. I can just picture one of them retelling the story to some dumb kids, turning a sweet-tempered tabby named Princess into a vicious panther, coiled and ready to pounce.

Before I got to the barn where my family was gathering I saw mixed in with the cop cars and ambulances a black sedan with white letters on the side: County Coroner. I decided to skip the chat with Aunt Linda, decided I'd seen enough of the whole mess. I got back in my truck and drove fast toward home, those little flashes following me in the rearview mirror the whole way.

It stinks like hell burying the week-old corpse of a tiger, a monkey, a leopard, a bear, a tabby, a horse. Each body has its own tint of rotten and when the sun does its work on a six-acre killing field, it's the embodiment of foul with different stinks blending from different directions. By the third day of work, I could pick apart whether I was near a cat or a monkey without even looking. I got stuck with the bulk of the cleanup duty when I proved to be the least skilled at evacuating. The professionals did it first, put their trucks into gear as soon as they could and hit the interstate. Sure, the cameras hung around for a few days. The reporters with their thick make-up got real practiced at saying the word *tragedy* and talking about how *this small Ohio community will be forever changed*, as if they knew a damn thing about what it was like before. They should've asked me. Instead of wilting on cue and talking about how *I never imagined something like this happening here*, I would've said the truth: this place is and always has been weird, whether it's dead animals or live people. Nothing's going to change that.

When the humane society people came in a day later, they shook their heads a lot and said *Oh, how terrible,* but couldn't figure out anything productive to do. In the end, their best guess was to spray paint a big black

X on each bloated body to prove the animals were actually deceased, then they tacked an embossed license on Aunt Linda's front door that showed we had permission to bury the bodies.

The county engineer's office sent out a couple men and a backhoe to dig a pit, and the state Environmental Protection Agency showed up long enough to line the pit with thick black plastic so the decomposing tigers didn't foul up anyone's drinking water. Then, the important people left with their equipment and their rules.

"I'm afraid you'll have to take it from here," one of the EPA workers told Aunt Linda, who nodded and evacuated into her house. Everyone else in the family claimed they were busy preparing for his funeral—one the rest of the town was thinking up reasons to avoid. Dad said everybody was really more worried about protesters at the cemetery than they were about proper grieving. My folks would've helped, I suppose, if I'd really pushed it. But they were three weeks behind getting ready for spring planting on our own farm, and I wasn't about to beg them away from that.

I asked a couple guys from the team, and in the cafeteria they thought the project sounded cool—but I guess once they told their parents where they were going it all got shot down, because no one showed and there I was, left alone with the mess. Just me and the shovel, some lime dust, a saw, a straw baling hook and my poor old truck.

I could describe the whole operation, but let's leave it at this: animals of that size can't be moved in one piece. There were tools and a strained elbow, two days of coughing afterward from the lime, a couple of mistaken steps that led to regret and a pair of perfectly good hoops shoes getting burned off in a wood pile.

It's irritating as hell when nobody wants to talk to you anymore, except about one thing. Take Billy Thiggens. He'd been in my math class all the way through school (even though he was supposed to be two years ahead of me). Now, Billy strikes me as the sort who would cower in a corner if a white bunny rabbit got too rambunctious within five yards of him. But he was one of the first ones on the scene that night, and to hear him tell it he was fierce as Rambo out there. He may well have been, too: with those night-vision goggles on, it must've seemed like one big, hilarious video game.

He used to be an okay guy—a little goofy, but the type you'd be okay talking with now and then if you passed each other on the sidewalk or something. Now, though, all he ever does to try and start a conversation is shape his hand into a fake pistol and point it at me, then wink. I guess it's his moment of glory and I should let him live it. But what really irks me is this: just about everyone else at least has the level of decency to start off their recollection with something about how awful it had been, how sad that the man unlatched each and every one of those cages before he turned a gun on himself. Everyone else had some empathy about it. But Billy just used misery to turn himself into a hero, and every time he points his index finger my direction, I want to snap it at the first knuckle. Instead, I've gotten good and practiced at nodding and giving a fat, fake smile that says, "Yeah, Billy, you're real clever, and I'm just going to keep smiling so you don't follow me around looking for excuses to write me a ticket."

My teachers weren't any better than Billy, writing "Okay" next to answers that were clearly wrong so my test scores got bumped up.

"Let me know it there's anything I can do for you," Miss Henderson said in passing at least once a week. She said this because she was a freshman science teacher, and there was absolutely nothing she could possibly do for me. Coach Thornton didn't give me any playing time, but he took to patting my shoulder a lot at practice. Mr. Anderson, the guidance counselor, pretended to check his watch every time he passed me in the hall. I guess he was afraid that if we ever made eye contact, I'd ask him for an appointment so I could spill my guts. Thing is, I've never seen the man actually wear a watch. These were the people in charge of my future, and they couldn't even be bothered to let me finish high school without treating me like I was as broken as that poor tiger in the ditch.

It's hard as hell to scrub blood off the rusted steel of an eighty-four Ford pickup. I know: it sounds useless, scrubbing blood off rust. One of them's no better than the other. In fact, you'd have to be strangely attentive or maybe a little deranged to even notice the difference. I would've left it there, except for that one spot, that one splatter on the top of the left side-wall, positioned just so that I couldn't help staring right at it every time I looked in the rearview mirror, as if the crazy cook and all his animal mess was chasing me around.

I doubt people will ever stop asking me to tell the story, so within a couple days, the reality set in that my uncle's final streak of madness will always follow me around. But I didn't want it *actually* following me, especially that weekend. And so I scrubbed at that truck, scrubbed until my shoulder and elbow were numb, tried to rid myself of every trace of it. Tried to make myself as normal as possible.

By the time things calmed down, I lost my shot with Dacie. They never rescheduled the game—both teams were so bad it didn't really matter. Consequently, I never made it off the bench, never had my moment of glory except the last home game when all the seniors got to start, and then as soon as somebody caught the tip-off, coach called time-out and people clapped and our parents took pictures while the senior benchwarmers trotted back to our rightful places and the skillful sophomores took back the court for the remainder of the game.

Even if that moment had produced equal parts glory as it had embarrassment (at least Mom let it rest with the camera once I took a seat and put back on my nylon pullover), it wouldn't have been worthwhile to bother with Dacie. By then, she was already seeing one of the senior wrestlers, a squat little muscle-bound guy named Logan whose senior year was just a big countdown to the army. I guess Dacie had her sights on escaping the town and seeing the world one base at a time, so she latched onto him hard, and from the start it had the look of something permanent, hand-holding in the hallways and the exchange of various stuffed animals and so forth. I was busted up about it for a couple days after I heard, but that's the sort of thing you can't let weigh you down too long. In a town this size, if you don't go off to college or find someone to marry by the end of high school, chances are you'll have to wait a good four or five years before the first round of divorces kick in, and even then you're stuck dealing with someone else's brats and you're probably handling four or five years' worth of pent-up bitter—anger you didn't put there, but that you've got to live with every day.

So I took after Abbie Greenway. She wasn't blonde with big, pouty lips like Dacie, but she had cute brunette ringlets and she was the sort of kind, quiet girl you can see yourself getting along with for a good long while, the sort you don't imagine ever having to pick up from the bar at two in the morning because she's taken off all her clothes and started swinging her stiletto heels at the bouncer.

I pressed and scrubbed with Brillo and Scotch-Brite pads and torn-up t-shirts and even a little heel of sponge. I tried solvents and detergents and vinegar and that orange smelling stuff with lava rocks in it—I tried everything I could to erase that spot and to remove it from my rearview, to put it as far out of site as all those poor decaying beasts. I scrubbed until my shoulder and elbow went numb, then I switched arms and scrubbed some more until Mom came out and shouted, "Shouldn't you be getting ready?" and I looked up to see the sun had already slipped halfway below the horizon.

It was time to shower—to clean myself instead of my truck. I stopped before I pulled open the screen door, though, and looked at the deepening tone of the sky, a sky that within the course of moments had turned itself from clear and pristine to deep and foreboding red. Like rust, like blood. The things that surrounded me, encapsulated in that sky. For a moment, I considered calling Abbie Greenway and thinking up the kindest way to tell her to forget it. But I did what I do—what we do around here—I shrugged it off and pushed forward, showered and dressed, and looked around the basement for an umbrella big enough for a pair. I picked up her corsage from the Kroger on the way to her place, even bought a couple of sodas while I was there, since I figured we'd be facing a solid wait at the Olive Garden.

I waited for her to say something about the truck, about how clean it was maybe, but I guess it was too dark by then for her to notice. As we drove and the drops started to fall and the wipers started to swish she just wanted to know things like what I thought might be on the geometry test and where we might work once school finished for good.

She didn't ask me why we took the roundabout way to the prom, the three-mile detour that had become habit in the three months between. Abbie just kept up the conversation through the ride and through dinner. On the last stretch before we got to the school she reached with her left hand and held onto mine. The purple-dyed carnations that circled her wrist tickled my arm and I told her it felt nice. We reached the parking lot, full already of SUVs and pickups and a couple of rented limousines. After the dance, there would be new and important things to consider, large things not easily undone. But for a moment we sat quietly, said and did nothing. It's comforting as hell to sit next to someone who can ignore what your last name means to the rest of town. Who doesn't see the difference between blood and rusted steel. I peeked briefly into the rearview and saw nothing important.

"Ready?" she asked.

I nodded and got out to open her door, to help her down onto the asphalt in those precarious heels of hers. I lifted the umbrella over her head and as we walked past the truck bed and toward the doors of the gymnasium, all I saw was rust.

A Test of Faith

Alice G. Otto

Charles and Maggie lived deep in the hills of Kentucky. They had an old tractor and an orange ATV and a cellar stocked with smoked meats and canned vegetables, so they rarely worried about the distance to town—a gas pump, a country kitchen and a church.

The snows, though, could be a cause for worry. The county-run plow wouldn't risk the four-mile dirt and gravel drive ascending from their cabin to the mountain pass, which took another twelve miles to meander into town. Charles rigged a corrugated metal roofing panel to the front of the tractor and strapped chains on its tires, and that rudimentary plow served well when God was kind for the winter. But, though the people of the hollers were kind to God, in prayer and services, He didn't often return that kindness in the cold months, when ice draped the trees and snow piled thick in the valleys.

As Maggie's pregnancy became apparent, the December sky roiled and heaved into slivers of steel, and winter's first blanket settled itself early. Maggie washed pots with a rag by the kitchen window and, with a small, calm smile, watched the menace building outside. She trusted her body as she trusted God. She felt wonderful, beautiful, and since spring, when

Maggie's church friends first learned she and Charles were trying for a baby, they had passed along vitamins and onesies and bottles, nursing pads and rattles, a crib and a Johnny Jump Up, a portable food masher and little jars, booties and bibs and books. Their home was ready, and Maggie was ready, but Charles desperately wanted her to see the town doctor before the weather got any worse. He wanted the reassurance of facts, of medicine, but he only had the timeline for comfort—Maggie being three months along in December meant a June birth, most likely, which meant most any potential crises would fall outside winter's grasp.

The clouds murmured, dusted themselves, and by the second week of December began to salt the earth in earnest. At first, Charles spun out his makeshift snow plow once a day, then twice a day. He'd chopped wood all through September and October, stacking logs high in the den, piling them on the porch, along the outer walls, in pyramids between the shed and the cabin.

There was nothing Charles could do when the snow won, as it did for at least a short while every winter. Later, normally. January or February. The third week of December unfolded, and he awoke one morning to a bright white square where the sky and spruce trees typically showed through the window. He squeezed Maggie's arm.

Peeking over the down comforter, she said, "Mercy." The light was strange and muffled, as if the house were sunk in cotton batting.

"I don't imagine the tractor's gonna do a lick of good against that," Charles said. He pulled Maggie close, relishing her heat, the soft curve of her belly.

"How much of that was just the wind, do you think?"

"A fair portion, I'm sure." Charles looked at the window, like an oversized note card—so white! "But a draft that high, just on this one side, well…that still has to be a few feet all around, I imagine."

"My. Guess this means Christmas alone?"

"Just the two of us," Charles agreed. "Three of us, that is."

"Mmm...good."

Any thoughts of productivity laid to rest, the couple slept three more hours, happy to be warm, abandoned on their quiet homestead.

Charles heated handfuls of rags to press along the front door's edges, and jimmied and plied the door until it finally pulled open—to reveal another wall of whiteness.

"Mags. Come look at this."

She padded around the corner in her slippers and thick bathrobe, her long black hair in tangles and knots. "Well I'll be. How deep? Is it just another draft pushed up?"

Charles grabbed the broom by the fireplace and, holding the bristled end, drove the handle into the wall of snow. They peeked down the narrow tunnel: no sky, sun, or trees. Charles tried driving the handle up high, at an angle: no light came down.

"We're buried. I don't believe it, but we're buried."

"But the chimney?"

Charles nodded, "It'd be bad if the fire wasn't going all night. I mean, I have to think the snow couldn't go *that* high...but I don't know what to think, I just know it's good we had it going, 'cause even if the whole cabin's under, the heat kept that passage open. We'd be dead of carbon monoxide by now if it hadn't."

"That's very comforting, dear. Do you want potatoes?" Maggie asked.

They ate potatoes by lamplight, then read by the fire, taking turns feeding logs to its crackling orange tongues. They passed their sleepy days that way, aware of time only in that it had to be passing, and the grandfather clock clicked away the hours and nights in place of the sun.

Charles was checking the smoked ham hock in its pot on the fire, ladling the meat's juices over the potatoes to tenderize them, to make something like a holiday meal. It was Christmas Eve.

He heard a whimper behind him, and the sound mounted to a scream of instant, furious pain—"Charles!" He dropped the ladle and sprinted into the bedroom.

"Mags—Maggie!" he shouted when he reached her. "Oh, God. Oh God, it's gonna be okay, Mags, hold on."

Blood soaked through her nightgown and stained the sheet beneath her thighs, an inky maroon puddle in the oil lamp's glow. Maggie's eyes were wet, the nightgown clung to her skin and she clutched at the blankets with bloody fingers.

"Charles, I'm sorry, I'm sorry—help me I'm sorry, what's happening—"

He grasped Maggie's shoulders and pressed her forehead to his lips, kissed her cheeks, guided her hair behind her ears, off her shoulders, off her face. "It's okay. I'm here, Mags, we're fine. I'll be right back, okay, I'll be right back, we're fine."

Charles tore through the cabin. He pulled the ham hock off the fire and grabbed a large pot from the kitchen. He opened the front door and piled snow into the pot with his bare hands and shoved it directly into the fire to let the snow melt, then boil, and he grabbed a lantern and held it to the bathroom medicine cabinet, pushing bottles aside with shaky fingers, his mind stumbling to keep up with its instincts and reason. Maggie was in pain. *Aspirin. Aspirin thins blood, she's bleeding, she'll bleed out—bleed out? Jesus, bleed out. No aspirin. A muscle relaxant. Wasn't a miscarriage something to do with contractions, with muscles—miscarriage. Miscarriage.* Charles dug his shaky thumb into the cap of the muscle relaxants, fighting the childproof top. The pills scattered across the sink. He picked up one. Two. To the kitchen, poured a cup of water from the pitcher they'd been keeping on the counter, back to Maggie.

She looked sallow and desperate and primal in the unstable light. Charles put one hand behind her neck, craning her head up, and eased the two pills into her mouth, grabbed the cup and held it to her mouth to drink. The water dribbled between Maggie's lips and down her chin. She sobbed.

"It hurts. Charles I'm scared it hurts, it hurts, it hurts—"

Dizziness threatened his knees and heart. Charles told her to keep pressure on the wound, knowing that made no sense but having no idea what else to say, and ran to grab dishtowels from the kitchen and drop them into the water simmering in the hearth. The cloth squares bubbled and undulated in the pot like sacs of fish eggs ready to pop. Maggie moaned in the bedroom. Charles looked over at the pot on the floor with the ham hock and potatoes. A thin layer of fat was congealing on the broth's surface. He leapt up and squirted dish soap onto his hands in the kitchen, scrubbed it into his calluses. He picked at the permanent oily stains about his short nails, plunged his hands into the water pitcher and shook them furiously until they rinsed as clean as they could be. He pinched the dishtowels from the boiling water and barely registered the pain.

Time slowed for a moment, looking down at his beautiful wife, his wife, lost and suffering in a fortress of snow. It slowed for a moment. Sanitized rags were for childbirth, weren't they. They weren't for child deaths. Charles had no idea what to do: surely and calmly, he realized this. He peeled Maggie's nightgown away from her thighs. He pulled down her panties. He'd first done that ten years before. They were wet then, too; she was nineteen, had waited nineteen years for him, and she was beyond ready. He'd waited twenty for her, and when he first saw it—saw *her*, glistening, pink—it nearly sent him over the edge before they could consummate the marriage.

Now, there was nothing of that pinkness; all the colors ran red and black. Since it was the only coaching Charles could remember, he commanded, "Push." And Maggie did, and it was messy. Charles pressed the moist, boiled dishtowels against her inner thighs, around that opening from which this hell was springing.

"Push." What in God's name was he saying?

"Push." Push what, blood until she dies?

"Push." And Maggie was screaming again.

"Push." And Maggie was quiet.

Charles said, "Push," and there was something in his hands that wasn't blood.

She pushed one final time, without his guidance.

Charles looked at what lay partially cradled in his hands. The dizziness was back. Maggie was out: eyes shut, inert. That was best. He looked down again, and what he saw wasn't the bare beginnings of a baby.

It was puppies.

Charles gathered the puppies in his arms and set them before the fire in the den. They squirmed and gargled. He walked to the laundry room and opened the pantry which had been the baby closet since spring. He picked up a small knitted blanket. Charles returned to the hearth, knelt, arranged the yellow blanket into a nest, and transferred the puppies to the blanket-nest individually. One. Two. Three. Four. Five. Five puppies. Their eyes were sealed and they wriggled atop and between one another, their little mouths parting and closing in search of milk.

Charles walked back to the bedroom, where Maggie lay motionless, her legs still splayed. He gently cleaned her thighs with a wet dishtowel. He placed another towel between her legs and straightened them, then pulled down her nightgown and tucked the comforter around her chest. Her breaths were even. Charles kissed her forehead and extinguished the lamp.

He grabbed the washcloths from the bathroom and tossed them into the pot on the fire; the water was still boiling. The wind blew outside. It transferred through the snow-insulated cabin as a low thrum. Charles crossed the den to the bookshelf and picked a selection from the shelf Maggie had labeled "MOMMY'S CORNER" in blue glitter-glue on a piece of pink construction paper cut in the shape of a stork. He flipped to "D" in the index. "Daddy's Checklist. Decorating the Nursery. Delivery Options. Diaper Changing Essentials." He flipped to "P" in the index. "Packing for the Hospital. Pelvic Pressure. Pet and Animal Safety." Charles flipped to that. It turned out dogs could carry bacteria such as campylobacter and salmonella, which a pregnant woman ought to avoid, and that it was wise to accustom a dog to a newborn by bringing back a blanket carrying the baby's scent from the hospital. Boundaries had to be set for the dog once the newborn was home in the nursery. Charles returned to "P." "Placenta, Preeclampsia, Premature Birth." Charles flipped to that. Useless. Preemies were prone to underdeveloped lungs and feeding troubles, but according to the book, they were not prone to being puppies.

Charles replaced the book and returned to the fire. He wrung the boiled washcloths out on the rug and shook them to dissipate the heat. The puppies appeared to have fallen asleep. He picked up the least entangled puppy and wiped its face, its belly, its little legs and tail, cleansing the blood and mucus from its fur. It suckled the air and whined until he put it back in the nest. Charles carefully pulled another puppy from the pile and wiped it off. It was dappled gray, with white feet. He put it back in the nest. He cleaned the last three puppies, changing washcloths as they soiled, and watched the fire as the quivering pile of puppies fell into a quiet slumber.

The grandfather clock chimed. It was Christmas. Charles put the ham hock and potatoes back on the rack. He stirred the broth, now and then, and stared into the bricks of the hearth.

When Charles awoke, the fire was weak, just an intermittent flame and the ashen glow of logs carrying their last heat. His back crackled from sleeping on the hard floor. It was too dim to read the grandfather clock, but Charles saw two dark shapes about a foot away from the blanket-nest on opposite sides, and he grabbed them, terrified to feel how cool the puppies were. He realized they were crawling into the darkness in search of their mother. Charles edged closer to the fire, stoked it, and tucked the two puppies under his sweater, atop his belly. He hunched over and pushed slow, hot breaths through the sweater, massaging the puppies through the yarn. A tiny haunch extended, a little head shook side to side: they were okay. The other puppies voiced aggravation as Charles lifted them to tuck the voyagers at the warm bottom of the mass, but they settled quickly, and he fed some kindling and a hearty log to the fire.

Charles lit the lamp by the bookshelf and turned to the grandfather clock: quarter past five, in the morning, he assumed. Grabbing two wash-cloths from the floor, he pulled out the crusty, burnt Christmas Eve meal. A mewling from the nest. Charles jabbed the charred ham hock with his thumb, licked it. Definitely ruined. More mewling. He grabbed the lamp and crossed to the bedroom door.

Maggie was still buried beneath the comforter on her back, arms atop the blanket with her pale palms upturned. Her head fell to one side on the pillow, her lips barely parted; she would have looked peaceful, if she had ever been the type to sleep on her back, but she always slept on her belly with her elbows hitched out at awkward angles that threatened to oust Charles from the bed. He thought she looked clinical, exposed. Dead. Charles touched her lips. She rustled.

"Charles..."

"Shush. It's okay. You're okay." He rubbed her shoulder and stroked her arm. "You're okay, Maggie. How do you feel?"

"I feel awful. Is our baby okay?" Maggie opened her eyes and her mouth danced a quavering line between hope and desolation. "Can you tell? There was so much blood."

Charles stared at the comforter. Maggie was much better at getting stains out of the wash than he was. He wasn't sure if it was okay to put a down comforter in the washing machine. The machine wasn't working, but never mind that, was it okay to soak a blanket filled with feathers?

Maggie touched his arm. "I lost the baby, didn't I?"

"There isn't a baby. Get some rest, honey. You rest up. I love you." Charles fetched another muscle relaxant from the bathroom for Maggie, tucked her in. When her eyes shut, he closed the bedroom door.

His hand rested on the cool knob; blood crusted his nails. It would be different if Maggie had agreed to see the doctor when Charles first asked. And he hadn't just asked. He had begged her to go, but she replied that her body was the dominion of her husband and God alone. Humbled by Maggie's pure convictions, flattered by those words, Charles had backed down, but he now understood how weak he had been. He hadn't protected his wife.

And what now? A pillow pressed deep into the blanket-nest until nothing moved beneath his weight? A systematic wringing of soft little necks? Charles couldn't back down this time, couldn't fail as the protector and provider, so when he turned to the growing fire, and the five fuzzy shapes within the nest, he thought: food, clothing, shelter.

Charles scooped more snow into the water pot and set it above the flames. The mewling was louder. He pulled two pink onesies from the baby closet and some scissors from Maggie's craft box and cut off the leg and arm sleeves at the shoulders and thighs. He folded the remaining torso sections of the tiny outfits and laid them in the craft box. Charles fetched bottles and nipples from the baby closet and hesitated by the simmering water, fairly certain he was meant to sterilize them first but aware of a yipping near his right foot. He dropped the bottles in the pot and stepped over the nest to search the laundry room pantry for powdered formula, where he found that the box provided detailed instructions for mixing formula according to human nutritional standards, but lacked a conversion chart for his current needs.

The omission seemed negligent—*but why on God's green earth does that seem so*, Charles stopped to think, and into this pause slipped a memory. When Charles was a boy he had a little beagle mix named Bratwurst who survived on table scraps alone and never ate a kibble, and he was the happiest, healthiest dog—

And Charles stopped thinking just as quickly. He stirred the powder into a jug of water and grabbed the five cutoff sleeves. The puppies' faces were tiny pink things, eyes glued shut, ears just miniscule flaps. They squeezed and looped into one another like fuzzy gray and white intestines, with one pup jet black. Charles picked that one up first. It was the runt—he carefully turned it in his palm—*she* was the runt. He guided her into one of the pink sleeves and set her in the nest. The next puppy had a smushed face and steely coloration about his head and tail, and he arched his back and cried and cried as Charles slid him into another sleeve. He rubbed the puppy's tummy as the others began to cry. The water was boiling. Charles fitted the rest of the puppies into their sleeves.

Their mouths wouldn't open wide enough to take the bottles' nipples in fully, so Charles had to cradle each puppy on its back in his hand and let the milk dribble past their thin lips. The meal quieted them, and they drowsed together in a warm pink lump.

Charles pried open the front door. Snow. He tore back the curtains in every room. Snow. He thought about dousing the fire and wriggling to the rooftop but the passage wasn't wide enough; he would only lodge himself and suffocate, and assuming he snapped his skeleton apart to fit through the chimney and somehow came out operable on the other side, the ATV and tractor would still be buried in that thick, ungodly pallet of snow, with no way to locate them or get them to the surface. He opened the front door one more time. Snow.

He remembered playing outside during winter breaks as a child, digging deep in the snow and channeling through the compressed powder, carving intricate webs of frosted passages invisible to anyone on the surface, and how his mother used to call him back inside each day to peel away his wet, frigid clothing and warm his hands around bowls of soup or chili. And now, Charles saw the impenetrable white wall beyond the doors, the windows, envisioned the four-mile journey to the pass and the twelve-mile stretch to town, and there was no one, there would be no one, to call him to the surface.

"What are these?"

Charles had been on a vigil, feeding the puppies every couple hours, kneading them into releasing themselves atop open cloth diapers he'd spread in a mat on the floor. He had plucked a scant meal of burnt potatoes for himself and fallen asleep on the rug. He moved to stoke the fire.

"Charles—what are these?" Maggie stood in the middle of the room, her hair limp with sweat, the gray nightgown stiffened into wrinkles around her bloody groin. She wrung one hand about the opposite wrist and curled and uncurled her toes, awakening into her numbed body's sensations.

"They're puppies."

"Well…okay. Good." Maggie struggled to open the front door. Her hands were weak. She stared, and the snow glared back, as concrete and impassable as before save the laughable dents made by Charles to boil up water. "Well..." Maggie scratched the corner of her eye. She glanced at the puppies, swaddled in their nest and makeshift cozies. "They're cute. They're little, aren't they? Look like newborns. So you got the back open."

As Maggie walked to the kitchen, Charles stood and said, "No, Maggie," but she continued to the back door and tugged it open: white.

"You crawled out a window? What were in those pills, anyway?" Maggie returned to the den and carefully lay down by the fire, wincing and pressing a hand to her abdomen. She took a deep breath and reached out to stroke the black puppy's neck. "Puppies on Christmas. You're amazing." She smiled.

Charles sat by Maggie and put a hand on her knee. "They're not strong. We only got that powdered formula, and I don't know that it sits well." He paused. "I've been up with them most of the night. They're hungry little guys."

Maggie turned to Charles and asked, "Where's their mom?"

Charles shook his head.

"Well she got in somehow and she got out somehow, where'd you burrow out? The bathroom? Is there a way out the laundry room? Did you get to the ATV?"

"Snow's got us piled in. We're buried. There's no way out."

"But—" she waved a hand at the puppies, "there's a way *in*! Way out, way in."

Charles closed his eyes. "It's only been you and me, Maggie. It's only been a day." And he looked at the puppies. He looked at her stomach. "No way in or out."

Maggie stood, steadied herself against the wall, and clapped her hands. "C'mere girl." She whistled. "C'mere girl." She weaved window to window to door to window, just as Charles had done. She looked under the couch and bed and in the dryer and oven and even the toilet tank. "Where's the dog?" Maggie dug her nails into Charles's shoulders. "Where?"

"There's no dog. I didn't know how to tell you when it happened—"

"Charles."

"—And you were scared and all that blood, I couldn't tell you when they," he motioned weakly to her hips, "well, when they came out."

"You're not saying that."

"It's gonna be okay." He paused. "It's like you say, when God gives we receive, and we love. He works in mysterious ways, and He gave you these to give to us, and…they're healthy. I love you, it'll be all right."

Maggie clenched her nightgown in her hands and released it and touched her belly and snapped her hands back and then held them away like a poison. "I lost our baby not my mind. Oh God I lost our baby—" Maggie sobbed.

Charles picked up the dappled puppy and held it out, "But you didn't. You didn't lose our babies."

When Maggie collapsed, Charles carried her to the bed and put a glass of water on the nightstand.

As the grandfather clock ticked away the final hours of Christmas, Charles constructed the bassinet by the fire. It had been dissembled into slats and legs, stored by the dryer to save space until the baby came. He tried to nail the pieces together quietly, shaking the bassinet to test its sturdiness before lining it with yarn blankets and depositing the swaddled puppies. They looked content in there—they wriggled less. Charles fiddled with an old fishing vest and, between awkwardly stabbing himself with a needle and stopping to reassess the logistics, succeeded in jerry-rigging a nursing vest. The malleable bottle liners dropped into the vest's many pockets to attach to sewn-in nipples poking through holes in the pockets' bottoms. With the puppies in a pile on the rug, he could lie on his side and guide them to the nipples. Their little paws kneaded the pockets and dinner was served.

They looked so fragile in the orange glow—their soft bellies, their tiny awkward legs, their blind, squirming movements. Charles had to make sure that the smallest, the black one, had her fill of milk each time. She tended to get jostled away from the teats. The puppies were back in the bassinet and Charles was just unbuttoning his vest when the bedroom door opened.

Hollow-eyed, Maggie looked at the bassinet, but Charles wasn't sure she really saw it. She had changed into her pink bathrobe.

"Maggie, you're up."

She walked to the kitchen, picked up one of the pitchers of cold water—Charles had been melting containers of snow throughout the day—and turned into the bathroom. Charles heard the water splash into the tub. She brought a kettle of water to the tub, then a mixing bowl of water.

Charles touched her arm as she returned for another pitcher. "Let me warm you up some bath water, Mags. Just a few minutes, let me get you a warm bath ready, that's all cold."

She put the pitcher down and returned to the bathroom. Uncertain, Charles put two big pots of water into the fire and checked the puppies, whose chests rose and fell in slow unison. He finally took a deep breath, picked up the lantern and went into the hall. He felt Maggie's bathrobe under his feet as he stepped into the dark, chilly bathroom. There were only a couple of inches of water in the tub; she sat there naked, knees pulled to her breasts. Her skin looked shiny, her hair gooey. Charles saw an empty body wash bottle cast aside on the tile and realized Maggie had poured its entire contents on her head. She rubbed the gel up and down her arms, up and down, up and down. She hadn't wet her skin first. The gel spread around like jam.

Charles knelt by the tub with a cup from the sink and dunked it in the shallow bath. He tilted Maggie's head back and carefully poured water along her scalp line, letting it run through her hair. "Come on, help me rinse this. You got too much soap here." He poured cups and cups over her head and tried to massage the soap out with his other hand, but the water quickly turned to pure lather and her body was still sticky all over. "You're freezing, this ain't working, I'm getting the pots off the fire, you stay here."

As Charles wrapped towels around his hands and reached in to grab the first pot, he heard laughter. It was almost like the laugh she had when she looked out the window in spring and the fat squirrels were clinging to the chickadee feeder, rocking it around, shaking seeds to the ground to fatten themselves up even more. She'd laugh and say "Poor chickadees," but what could be done? And it was kind of like the laugh she had the time she was knitting a cardigan for an older lady in her church group who'd fallen ill and she got through nearly the whole sweater and realized she had somehow counted ten more stitches per row into the left sleeve than the right sleeve, and Charles assured her you couldn't tell—you really couldn't tell—but Maggie kept imagining that poor old woman tugging and picking at the smaller sleeve wondering why she felt so lopsided, and on top of being sick? Maggie had no choice but to laugh as stitch by stitch and row by row she undid the entire sleeve, winding the yarn back into a ball as she tugged her work loose. It was almost like those laughs.

But it wasn't. It wasn't those laughs, and the difference iced Charles's blood even with his hands plunged into the fire. Naked, legs dripping, the soap crusting on her breasts in white scabs, Maggie laughed and laughed as she returned to the bedroom, pills rattling in her hand.

On New Year's Eve, one by one, the puppies opened their eyes.

The dappled gray girl with the white feet was first. "Well look at you," Charles whispered. He was sitting in a rocker beside the bassinet with a bowl of stew in his lap, chewing hunks of beef and cabbage. He rubbed her ears with his thumb as she looked around with quiet cries. "A lot to see. Those are your brothers and sisters." Charles held up a spoonful of stew. "This is cow. It's good, but you can't have cow just yet. You'll like cow. And who are you?"

Charles knew Maggie had to have left the bedroom during the past week, but he never saw her. She had to be sneaking out when he was asleep on the couch. There would be a pitcher of water missing from the kitchen, or a box of crackers. Sometimes he heard laughter, but not often. He was grateful for that. Other times, if he pressed his ear to the door, he heard her voice, low and rapid, but he couldn't make out her words. The relentless rhythm could be prayer, it could be nonsense, or madness: he didn't know. As the days passed he grew thirsty for contact in the buried cabin, and he hadn't named the puppies he was mothering through the hours. He tried to think of them in abstract terms but that wasn't working in the slightest as he cradled them and mixed formula and revolved about them in his isolation, so when that dappled puppy finally opened her eyes and blinked as Charles licked his stew spoon, a deep piece of his gut seemed to snap, and he was able to say, "You're Addison."

A few minutes later, one of the boy's eyes peeled open. "Welcome to the party, bud." His pewter fur gave way to a creamy face and belly. "Lot quieter than Addie. Sister's got a lot to say. What about you?" Charles set his bowl on the floor and put the puppy in his lap. "Little guy, you seem like a Fred. Wanna be Fred? Yeah, you'll be Fred." Charles picked up the boy with the steel-colored tail and head. "You're Raoul. Raoul? What kinda name is that?" Charles laughed. "You'll grow into it. And you," he said, wiggling the paw of the girl with muted gray and brown stripes across her back, "you are Lindsey. Lindsey's a pretty name. Pretty name for a pretty girl."

That left only the black runt to name. Charles grimaced to think of her as the runt, but she was: so weak compared to her brothers and sisters. Charles ached watching her shiver when she accidentally rolled away from the others. She worried him. He nursed the puppies on the rug—Raoul opened his eyes. A couple of hours later, Lindsey followed suit.

Fresh logs crackling in the hearth, Charles checked the grandfather clock: ten 'til twelve. He couldn't be certain, hidden from the sun, locked in the lantern-light, but he thought it was about to become a new year. He waited five more minutes and knocked on the bedroom door.

"Maggie? I might've lost track, but," Charles swiped at a tear rolling down his cheek, "but, it's New Year's, I think."

He closed his eyes and flattened a palm against the door. Four years ago on this night Charles and Maggie had plans to go to a New Year's "black tie" gala in the village, but the truck's engine wouldn't turn. Charles had known how silly the event was going to be—the same handful of folks from church who always put on potlucks and bingos, most likely wearing the same dresses and jackets they put on for services each Sunday and just calling it "black tie." Maybe some streamers and punch. But Charles fidgeted and fussed with the truck engine for twenty full minutes in the freezing wind, willing it to kick over, because Maggie was inside and she'd had her hair in rollers the whole day so it would lay in soft, dark curls around the shoulders of the dress she'd bought just for New Year's. It was deep emerald, a velvety material that showed her curves. Charles thought she looked so sophisticated. The one thing he'd always thanked God for was giving him such a wonderful wife, and her beauty that night made him realize the whole Bible's worth of praises couldn't capture how lucky he was.

He gave up on the truck when he looked down and saw a gash on his finger, bleeding heartily; his hands had grown so numb that he hadn't realized he'd sliced himself against part of the engine, likely against the exhaust manifold bolts, long rusted.

"I tried, baby. Truck's not going anywhere tonight."

Maggie had shut the door behind him and said, "I figured as much. Good thing we got a bottle of wine and some records right here, huh?" She handed him a glass and said, "Let's dance."

And they danced. They rarely drank: a glass of wine on Thanksgiving, a drink at New Year's, so as the bottle emptied their desires grew warmer until they stripped off the fancy clothes and touched and licked and caressed one another on the rug by the fire like a couple married for six hours as opposed to six years. They had stumbled to bed naked and talked and giggled for an hour until they fell asleep, well before midnight.

Charles rubbed his palm against the door. One of the puppies whimpered. He thought it was Raoul.

"Did you hear me? It's New Year's. We got about three minutes to midnight." Charles wanted to sob. He wanted to scream. But he spoke quietly, evenly. "Maggie, you have to talk to me. You've gotta come out. Come on out, now, and have New Year's with me."

It was muffled, but she responded.

"Wh—Mags, what was that? What'd you say?"

"When he brings darkness, it becomes night, and all the beasts of the forest prowl."

"Maggie?" Charles pounded on the door. "Open this. Right now!"

"Test the spirits."

"Right now, Maggie!"

The door opened. She had properly cleaned herself: Charles knew because she stood completely nude before him. She grinned. "Many false prophets have gone out into the world, Charles."

Trembling, Charles picked up Maggie's bathrobe and draped it over her shoulders, trying to tuck her arms into the sleeves. "It's freezing in here."

Maggie struggled out of his arms and closed her eyes. "My frame was not hidden from you when I was made in the secret place."

"Stop it."

"When I was woven together in the depths of the earth, your eyes saw my unformed body."

"*Stop it.*"

Maggie fell back on the bed and grabbed one of her breasts, slowly running a finger between her legs. "She said to herself, 'I am the one! And there is none besides me!'" The grandfather clock chimed midnight and Maggie moaned, then laughed. "What a ruin she has become, a lair for wild beasts!"

Charles yanked her hand from between her legs and pressed the bathrobe over her body.

She lashed at his face and screamed, "All who pass by her *scoff* and shake their fists!"

His lungs froze and he slapped her. He slapped her right across the face, and when the madness didn't leave her eyes, he slapped her harder.

Maggie looked up at Charles, crouched atop her, and whispered, "It's cold, Charles. It's really cold."

"Come on under the blankets." He pushed a bag of oyster crackers off the comforter, and, with a moment's hesitation, shoved Maggie's Bible to the floor as well. "There you go, snuggle in. Warmer?"

Maggie nodded, clutching at her shoulders with trembling hands. "Did you make a resolution?"

Charles shook his head. His blood was exhaustion. His skin was exhaustion. There were no words. When Maggie pulled back the corner of the blanket and patted the mattress, her eyes were wet and scared and something closer to normal. He pulled off his jeans and sweater and climbed in beside her. His eyelids felt magnetically compelled to close; he knew he'd have to be up in a few hours to check on the puppies, but the fire was strong, and he was so tired. His wife was warm, and close, and he was so tired.

Maggie kissed his cheek, murmured "Happy new year," and Charles was gone.

It was dark when Charles opened his eyes. That didn't tell him anything. It was always dark. For weeks the world had been shadow and fire and lantern-light. Maggie wasn't in bed. He kicked off the blankets and felt his skin tighten in the frosted air, pulled on his clothes and crept to the door.

The fire was almost dead, just glowing coals across the den. Charles heard scraping in the kitchen and turned the corner to find Maggie furiously working at the wall of snow blocking the back exit. She wore a puffy coat over an old pair of overalls and scraped and pawed at the snow as high as she could reach, madly diving into it with her mittened hands, pulling chunks to the floor where a puddle was spreading around her feet.

"You're gonna ruin the floor," Charles said. Maggie didn't stop to acknowledge him. Charles returned to the den to rebuild the fire and tend to the puppies, who were loud with hunger. He strapped on the nursing vest and plopped the puppies on the rug, taking care to ensure the runt got her fill, as always. Cradling the little black puppy, Charles decided to name her Dora. It was the name Maggie planned to give their first daughter, after her great-aunt Dorothy, who meant a great deal to her, but also because the name meant "gift." He heard Maggie grunt as she fought against the snow. Dora hadn't opened her eyes yet.

Charles took off the vest and left the puppies on the rug. He stood

231

behind Maggie in the kitchen. "What are you trying to do?"

Maggie pawed out a few more handfuls of snow before laughing and saying, "To *do*? What's it look like I'm trying to do, Charles?" He could see her wrists between the coat and mittens each time she reached up; the skin was red and raw.

"It looks like you're trying to escape."

"That's a good word for it."

"Suicide's a good word, too. That's all it is. You get out there, how you planning to get anywhere? You think someone's waiting for you up there? Think you're a rabbit, just gonna hop across the snow and up to town? You're just making it damp and awful for us in here, can't you hear them crying? They were starving. Didn't you hear them?"

Maggie panted, "I heard them," and kicked the snow. She sank into the icy puddle at her feet. "Hear them all the time. I *feel* them."

Charles crouched. "It's two boys, and three girls." He paused to gauge Maggie's reaction, but her face was blank. "There's Addie. Fred. There's, she's beautiful, with these stripes…she's Lindsey. Will you please come meet them? Please?"

"I always said, I always *thought*, that no bad could come our way 'cause you'd beat it off with a shovel or run it over with a tractor or something." Maggie smiled. "I believed it, I really did, that Beelzebub himself could come knocking and you, your *goodness*, would make it so he couldn't step in the door." Maggie pulled off her mittens. "But, it's been told, we can't give the devil a foothold. We can't give him that."

Charles had trouble speaking. "I don't understand."

Maggie looked him in the eye. "He warned Jerusalem. Did we miss it? Did He warn us?"

Charles pulled Maggie out of the doorway and latched the exit. "You need to get by the fire." He nodded at her overalls. "You'll catch a cold in those."

Maggie stayed crumpled on the ground. She said, "He shoots with deadly and destructive arrows of famine. He shoots to destroy." She stretched out, extending her arms, pointing her feet. "Dogs surround me. A pack of villains encircles me. They pierce my hands and my feet."

She pulled in her legs, clutching them to her chest. As Charles dragged Maggie to the bedroom to strip her, drug her, and put her to bed, she began to cry. Her words were too soft to hear, but Charles caught enough to know the verse plaguing her mind.

I will send famine and wild beasts against you, and they will leave you childless.

The grandfather clock had chimed three more days when Dora finally opened her eyes. It had chimed perhaps twelve more days, or twenty, when the puppies began to walk. They'd doubled in size, and their ears were open. The muscles grew in their legs, and in their throats: they learned to love the sounds of their voices barking in high pitches. Charles set up the playpen to give them room to romp. A detachable bracket suspended a mobile of colorful smiley faces above the playpen. Charles would wind up the mobile, and as the red and blue and yellow faces began to circle in time to the tinkling music, Raoul, Addie, Lindsey and Fred darted about, yapping at the faces and clawing at the sides of the pen. Dora stood in the middle, teetering uncertainly on her tiny legs before plopping down time and again. Again, and again, Charles wound the mobile, delighted as the puppies ran and ran and ran in dizzy puppy circles before falling into woozy naps. Smiley faces. Smiley puppies. Smiley Charles.

Charles started soaking kibbles of hard cat food in saucers of formula to transition the puppies into eating solids. He apologized each time he fed them, feeling like a failure because cat food was the best he could do.

Maggie always had a soft spot for the strays that hung out by the shed, so they'd kept a bucket of cat kibble in the house for years. He'd never cared for the cats. Mangy, whining, flea-bitten things, not that it was their fault.

But he was so proud of his puppies: only one month old, and already walking!

When the puppies tired themselves out, Charles often took the opportunity to nap. Other times, though, he lit a cigar and sat down to read about parenting. Unlike Maggie's friends, who passed along the onesies and bottles and books when they started trying for a baby, his friends had passed along a box of cigars and some old *Playboy* magazines, assuring him that once the children arrived, his wife would never put out again. Charles and Maggie had a good laugh over those skin mags; Maggie was beet red when he first showed her, but it only took some kissing and compliments to convince her to strike a few poses for him to enjoy. She didn't let him take pictures, of course, but he cherished the memory.

Now he sat reading about the unique challenges of raising multiples: feeding regimens, sleeping schedules, travel safety. Charles glanced at the plates of soggy kibble littering the floor, and the puppies drowsing in a comatose lump in the playpen. He tried to picture the world above the snow: was a smoke-belching hole, where the chimney poked through, the only indication that he existed? That they were all alive? He turned back to the book. The individualized attention bit concerned him. All of the experts recommended finding ways to spend one-on-one time with each multiple in order to develop their unique personalities, and to form a stronger parental bond. Charles had been homogenous in his fathering thus far, but he could work on that. Maybe walk Fred while the others ate, or read to Addie while her siblings napped. He would figure it out.

Cigar perched between his lips, Charles took the book into the bathroom to do his business. The plumbing had been frozen since the blizzard hit, so Charles had worked the bathroom window open, scooped out some snow, and poured hot water down the side of the cabin to melt a chute where he could dump the contents of the chamber pot, which wasn't a chamber pot at all but a regular cooking pot that he relished the thought of someday destroying. Charles squatted and read a "Helpful Hint" enclosed in a little box: "Don't be ashamed if you can't tell your multiples apart at first—this is normal! Put a small dab of nail polish on each baby's toe and create a color key so you know who's 'Aqua Blue' and who's 'Sassy Silver'!"

Charles ashed his cigar in the sink with a self-satisfied flourish; he knew how to tell all five of his apart from day one. He never had to paint them. Who paints their kids? He took his time finishing the cigar and flipping through chapters, making a mental note to revisit the selections on teething and circumcision. As Charles jimmied the window open, he heard a squeaky yip: Lindsey. A throatier bark followed: that had to be Raoul. And then nervous whining, frantic yelps, and Charles forgot about the chamber pot and raced out of the bathroom, nearly stumbling over Addie in the hallway. He quickly snatched her up and hugged her, put a finger to his lips and shut her in the laundry room. From the hallway, he saw Lindsey cowering in the kitchen, a shivering ball of soft stripes with big brown eyes, and then he was in the den.

Maggie rocked on her knees before the fire, naked, her arms submerged to the elbows in the cat kibble bucket; the kibble was strewn all about the room, lodged in the floorboards, dotting the rug. Maggie's hair ran in long, black waves down her back. Her face was pale, and her blank eyes fixed to the bottom of the bucket, to the bottom of the water lapping her forearms, lapping as she rocked and whispered frantically.

"Even from *birth* the wicked go astray, even from the *womb* they are wayward and speak *lies*, and women *will* be saved through childbearing, if we do *not* give the devil a foothold, if we watch for those evildoers and mutilators of the flesh—"

Charles leapt on Maggie, slamming her head into the brick hearth. The bucket toppled, and the water washed across the floor. Charles gently turned the bucket and reached in. The body was sodden and dense, and her legs dangled inert, paws limp. Her little square head lolled as he laid her near the flames. He rubbed her side with two fingers, and water trickled from her lips. The tiny black chest didn't rise. She was soaking, freezing, dead.

Charles looked away from Dora's drowned body to the playpen. The netting. The other puppies had been able to climb the playpen's netted sides and jump out when Maggie reached in to grab one of them, but Dora wasn't strong enough to run yet. She hadn't learned to walk.

And she hadn't known to close her eyes.

Maggie didn't scream when she woke up tied to the rocking chair, her wrists and ankles bound to the armrests and glider posts, duct tape wound thick across her stomach. Charles had expected her to scream. He'd wanted her to scream.

For the next week he let the puppies run amok. Raoul tore the heads from pastel stuffed animals. Addie loved rattles. She'd toss them in the air and whip them back and forth, *shake shake shake*, until she was too tired to move, and then she'd wake up and *shake shake shake* some more. Lindsey and Fred were wrestlers, intent to gnaw each other's napes and growl and pounce all throughout the blended days and nights. Charles lounged on the couch reading fairy tales aloud, or he sprawled on the floor and let the puppies dance across his chest and face.

He gave Maggie water and fed her potatoes. She started whimpering on the second day, when she couldn't hold her waste in anymore. Charles didn't untie her. Maggie soaked in her mess, and Charles lit more cigars to amend the den's thick odor.

On the third day, Charles pressed the puppies' paws in finger paint from Maggie's craft box and guided them across sheets of paper. He pasted the sheets into the baby memory book he found on the "MOMMY'S CORNER" shelf, and held the book close to Maggie's face so she could see each of their little paw prints.

On the fourth day, Maggie begged for the Lord to intervene. Charles duct-taped her mouth.

On the fifth day, Charles boiled gallons of water and took a long, luxurious bath.

On the sixth day, Charles removed the tape from Maggie's mouth and let her have a sip of water. He replaced the tape.

On the seventh day, he moved the puppies to the bedroom, and when the grandfather clock struck twelve, Charles cut Maggie free. He wielded the butcher knife with a light, loose touch.

"Charles—"

He pressed the broad side of the blade to Maggie's lips and shook his head.

Charles stepped into the bedroom and latched the door. He doused the lantern, and in the darkness, he tried to remember his wife in an apron scrambling eggs, knitting scarves in the passenger seat of the truck, meticulously sorting coupons from the Sunday circular, but he couldn't overcome that vision of a ghoulish woman sticky with the residues of tape and vacated bowels, her hair a den of greasy black snakes shielding a face that Charles no longer recognized.

The government didn't finalize the death count until early summer. All told, they said, the blizzard claimed eleven thousand lives. The elderly and the poor crowded in the unheated apartments of the tri-state's big cities made up a small slice. Carbon monoxide poisoning peacefully swept away some suburban families as they slept. Would-be heroes died in attempts to rescue stranded motorists. But the bulk of the corpses came from deep in the Kentucky hills, from the forgotten Appalachian villages, the inaccessible hollers. It was a winter catastrophe the likes of which the States had never seen. The cities were chaos; resources couldn't be wasted on the scattered, hidden populations of the hills.

Charles found Maggie's body in mid-March, frozen and partially submerged in the last two feet of snow. She'd made it a quarter mile from the cabin. The tunnel she dug had collapsed before Charles awoke on the day of her escape, and he had closed the back door against the crumbling white chunks and latched the deadbolt. He reported her passing as a stir-crazy accidental suicide, and the sheriff nodded, and the coroner jotted "hypothermia" on yet another death certificate before signing off to have Maggie dumped in an icy plot beside the hundreds of other corpses pouring in from the surrounding hills.

Charles felt the years, their definition and passing, evolve with the breadth of his family's sorrows and joys—the outrage when Addie became pregnant just past her second birthday, and the complete dissipation of that anger when Charles greeted his dappled grandpuppies; the unrelenting heartache of losing Raoul before he turned ten, but the wonder of watching Raoul's own grandpuppies flourish, then his great-grandpuppies, darting about the yard with drool flying from their tiny, smushed faces.

It wasn't a bad life. If he couldn't speak of it, couldn't rationalize it, then that only proved the folly of words, he reasoned.

When Charles turned ninety and the succession of years began to erode his mind's inhibitions, he told the nurses in the home about the winter the snow fell so thick that it erased the cabins in the valleys, erased the gravestones and the churches. He held a dog close to his side, the dog the staff allowed him to keep as a therapy pet, stroking her jet-black ears as he silently prayed for his memories to survive, praying the love he felt and miracles he remembered wouldn't be lost to the insurmountable whiteness just over the horizon. Charles hugged the dog, and he told the nurses of a storm so vicious that God Himself was blinded, the winter so cold that God broke the rules of His creation and sent forth His precious creatures to be born in new ways, hopeful for His children, testing the faith of the little human creatures spiraling smoke and prayers unto the heavens.

Acknowledgments

This anthology, like all of Columbus Creative Cooperative's books, was a product of many hands, and we couldn't possibly thank each and every person who contributed to this work.

Thank you to all of the writers who submitted a story for consideration for this anthology. We chose to print only eighteen stories in this book, and we regretfully had to pass on many exceptional stories.

Thank you to our editor, Brad Pauquette.

Thank you to all of the members of Columbus Creative Cooperative who attended workshops to improve each other's work, who share links and forward emails to your family and friends, and who go out of your way to support CCC through the year.

Finally, thank you dear reader. You're the reason we produce books. Without your support of our mission, and your decision to purchase a CCC book, we wouldn't be able to produce the work of Central Ohio writers.

It is with sincere gratitude and humility that we thank the contributors, the editors and the readers.

Author Biographies

David Armstrong's story collection, *Going Anywhere*, won Leapfrog Press's Fiction Contest and will be published in fall of 2014. His individual stories have won the *Mississippi Review* Prize, the *New South* Writing Contest, *Jabberwock Review*'s Prize for Fiction and *Bear Deluxe Magazine*'s Doug Fir Fiction Award, among others. His latest stories appear in *The Baltimore Review*, *The Magazine of Fantasy & Science Fiction*, *Potomac Review*, *Mississippi Review*, and elsewhere. A Ph.D candidate in fiction at UNLV, he's fiction editor of *Witness Magazine* and recipient of the Black Mountain Institute Fellowship. He lives in Las Vegas with his wife, Melinda, and their dog, Prynne. More information is available at davidarmstrongfiction.com. *Pg. 158*

Mark D. Baumgartner lives in Johnson City with his wife and son, where he is an assistant professor at East Tennessee State University. His work has been featured or is forthcoming in magazines such as *Yemassee*, *Bellingham Review*, *The Southern Review*, *Phoebe*, *Tampa Review* and *Wisconsin Review*, and he has worked as a fiction editor at *Mid-American Review*, *River Styx* and *Witness*. He earned an M.F.A. degree from Bowling Green State University in 2005, and a Ph.D from the University of Nevada-Las Vegas in 2010, where he was a Schaeffer/Black Mountain Fellow in creative writing. Excerpts of his first novel, *Mariah Black*, are currently forthcoming in *Confrontation* and *Silk Road*. *Pg. 3*

Joseph Downing was born in 1969 in Dayton, Ohio. After receiving a B.A. in English from the University of Dayton, Joseph obtained a law degree from Ohio Northern University and is currently a practicing lawyer, writer and artist. He has twice published in *Flights Literary Magazine*, is an *Impact Weekly* Fiction Contest Winner, and he writes *The Abundant Bohemian* blog. His nonfiction book, *The Abundant Bohemian: How to Live an Unconventional Life Without Starving in the Process*, will be published in 2014. Joe lives in Dayton, Ohio and can be reached at joe@abundantbohemian.com. *Pg. 30*

Kevin Duffy is a recovering lawyer. He and his lovely wife Mary Ann are enjoying retirement in Columbus, with their three wonderful children and five grandchildren living nearby. For a sample of Kevin's poetry, see Columbus Creative Cooperative's *The Ides of March: An Anthology of Ohio Poets*. *Pg. 57*

Ann Brimacombe Elliot, originally from Britain, and her geologist husband have lived in Columbus since 1967. They have three out-of-town offspring and five exemplary grandsons. After fifteen years in medical research Ann started writing and editing medical literature. Her "creative" writing netted small successes in poetry and fiction, but she is most comfortable with creative nonfiction for which she has won several regional awards, including two Nonfiction Columbus Literary Awards and an Ohio Arts Council Individual Artist Award. In 2000, Kent State published *Charming the Bones*, her biography of restoration artist, Margaret Colbert. Ann is working on another biography. Music is a passion—she plays viola—and also enjoys gardening, hiking, skiing and photography. *Pg. 168*

Scott Geisel's stories have appeared in a variety of journals and anthologies, including *Best New Writing 2008* (Hopewell Publications) and *Christmas Stories from Ohio* (Kent State University Press), from which his story was aired on WYSO. He was a finalist for the 2008 Eric Hoffer Award for fiction. Scott is the founder and editor of *Gravity Fiction* and was a founding co-editor of *MudRock: Stories & Tales* (Honorable Mention, Best American Mystery Stories 2004). He was Assisting Editor for *Flash Fiction Forward* and *New Sudden Fiction* (Norton 2006, 2007). Scott has been a presenter at the Antioch Writers' Workshop and Sinclair Writers'

Workshop, has taught workshops at the Dayton Art Institute, and founded a series of teen writing workshops and a publication for the Dayton Metro Library. *Pg. 19*

Justin Hanson was born and raised in Columbus, Ohio. He attended The Honors College of The Ohio State University and graduated with a degree in English in 2011. At Ohio State, Justin studied with authors Manuel Martinez and Lee K. Abbott. Currently, Justin is completing a Master's degree in English at the University of Illinois, Urbana-Champaign. Following this, Justin plans on working and continuing writing stories and eventually attempting a novel. *Pg. 172*

Maria Hummer is from Toledo and lives in London, England. She has a B.F.A. in Creative Writing and an M.A. in Screenwriting. Her short film *Dinner and a Movie* was officially selected for the 2013 Edinburgh Film Festival, Palm Springs Festival, London Short Film Festival and others. Currently she is in post-production of the film adaptation of her short story "He Took off his Skin for Me," published in *Devil's Lake* and finalist for the Driftless Prize in Fiction. Maria is writing her first novel. *Pg. 14*

Kelsey Lynne is an automated testing developer. She enjoys writing in her free time, typically between the hours of midnight and 1:00 a.m. When she is not coding or depriving herself of sleep to write, she enjoys painting or playing the harp. Her education consists of a computer science degree and two years of a creative writing minor, before she changed her minor to business so she could take exciting classes like Finance 101. Kelsey lives with her three cats and one dog. *Pg. 144*

Brenda Layman was born in Ashland, Kentucky, but she has lived for most of her life in Ohio. She is a member of Columbus Creative Cooperative, The Outdoor Writers of Ohio, Writers Satellite and Ohio Writers Guild and she has published many articles in *Pickerington Community Magazine*, *Ohio Valley Outdoors*, and other print and online magazines. She lives in Pickerington, Ohio with her husband, Mark. Brenda loves fishing, kayaking and traveling, and at the time this anthology was released she had recently rediscovered the joy of watercolor painting. *Pg. 37*

Alice G. Otto lived in Bethel, Ohio, a small town outside Cincinnati, until graduating from high school. She is currently pursuing her M.F.A. at the University of Arkansas, where she has received the Walton Family Fellowship in Fiction and the Carolyn F. Walton Cole Fellowship in Poetry. She holds a B.F.A. in creative writing from the University of Evansville. Alice's work has appeared in publications including *Harpur Palate*, *RiverLit* and *Yalobusha Review*. *Pg. 212*

Brad Pauquette can be found online at www.BradPauquette.com, or see the editor bio on pg. 245. *Pg. 134*

Brooks Rexroat writes and teaches in Cincinnati, Ohio. He holds an M.F.A. in creative writing from Southern Illinois University and a B.A. in print journalism from Morehead State University. His stories have been published in more than twenty journals and magazines including *Weave Magazine*, *Midwestern Gothic*, *Revolution House*, *The Montreal Review* and *The Telegraph Newspaper*'s (London) 2012 International Story Competition. Visit him online at www.brooksrexroat.com. *Pg. 202*

Lin Rice is a freelance writer and editor. A life-long Ohioan, Lin grew up in Monroe County before making his way to Columbus, by way of Athens. A recovering journalist, Lin is now trying his luck in the world of fiction—his first novel, *The Remembering Glass*, is currently in its second round of edits. He also posts the occasional rant at LinRice.com. Lin now lives in Central Ohio with his wife, their new son and a pack of half-feral cats. *Pg. 96*

Anna Scotti is a writer and teacher living in Southern California. Scotti's poetry has been awarded numerous prizes, and appears frequently in literary journals including *Comstock Review*, *Chautauqua*, *Crab Creek Review*, *Extract(s)* and *Yemassee*. Her fiction and poetry can be accessed at www.annakscotti.com. Scotti—then Anna Coates—earned a degree in psychology from Antioch College, Yellow Springs, years before that illustrious institution's closure and recent phoenix-like rebirth. She holds an M.F.A. from Antioch University, Los Angeles, and is currently working on a collection of poetry and a young adult novel, *DUCKS LIKE ME*. Before settling down and accepting her penurious destiny as poet and schoolteacher, Scotti was a nationally-known journalist and a columnist for *InStyle* and for the late, great, *Buzz: the Talk of Los Angeles*. *Pg. 123*

Heather Sinclair Shaw was born and raised in Columbus, Ohio, but now writes on her small family farm in Newark under the watchful eye of several cows, chickens, a dog and three somewhat-domesticated children. She came to the farm to raise food for people and stayed for the peace and quiet. She would like to become a saint, but writing will suffice for now. *Pg. 72*

S.E. White is a native of Bowling Green, Ohio, who earned her B.F.A. from Bowling Green State University, her M.A. from Iowa State University, and her M.F.A. from Purdue University. She has taught English at the college level since 2000. Her short fiction has been published in various venues. Her novella *A Murder of Crows* is available in paperback and Kindle. She also authors ANovelWeblog.com which often discusses growing up in Northwestern Ohio. *Pg. 80*

Sara Ross Witt, a native of Columbus, is a graduate of the New School University M.F.A. program. She authored *Pregphobic and Pregnant*, a blog about pregnancy and motherhood. Her writing has appeared in *Arch City Chronicles* and *Parent to Parent*. She lives in Chicago. *Pg. 45*

About
Brad Pauquette
Editor

Brad Pauquette is a freelance writer, editor and publication consultant in Columbus, Ohio. He lives in Woodland Park, a neighborhood on the near east side of Columbus, with his wife Melissa and two sons. In addition to serving as the developmental and production editor of this project, Brad is the founder and director of Columbus Creative Cooperative.

He is also the owner of Brad Pauquette Design (www.BradPauquetteDesign.com), a web development and media production company serving small businesses and micro-enterprises in Central Ohio.

Find his novella, *Sejal and the Walk for Water*, which raises awareness and funds for the clean water crisis in India, on Amazon.com.

You can find more information about Brad on his website, www.BradPauquette.com.

Find Brad's story "On Wilson" on page 134.

About
Columbus Creative Cooperative

Founded in 2010, Columbus Creative Cooperative is a group of writers and creative individuals who collaborate for self-improvement and collective publication.

Based in Columbus, Ohio, the group's mission is to promote the talent of local writers and artists, helping one another turn our efforts into mutually profitable enterprises.

The organization's first goal is to provide a network for honest peer feedback and collaboration for writers in the Central Ohio area. Writers of all skill levels and backgrounds are invited to attend the group's writers' workshops and other events. Writers can also find lots of resources and contructive feedback on our website.

The organization's second goal is to print the best work produced in the region.

The cooperative relies on the support and participation of readers, writers and local businesses in order to function.

Columbus Creative Cooperative is not a non-profit organization, but in many cases, it functions as one. As best as possible, the proceeds from the printed anthologies are distributed directly to the writers and artists who produce the content.

For more information about Columbus Creative Cooperative, please visit **ColumbusCoop.org**.

THE IDES OF MARCH
AN ANTHOLOGY OF OHIO POETS

Columbus Creative Cooperative books are available
from all major retailers and in popular e-book formats.

TRISKAIDEKAN
13 Stories for 2013

Find more information and order at
www.ColumbusCoop.org.

Who killed the
executioner's wife?

Capital Offense
A Serial Novel by Kurt Stevens

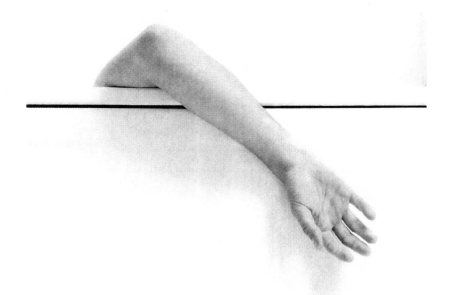

www.CapitalOffenseBook.com

Don't. Trust. Anyone.

CPSIA information can be obtained at www.ICGtesting.com
Printed in the USA
LVOW10s1014290315

432470LV00006B/749/P